T0354960

I KNOW *who* YOU ARE

Duane A. Eide

iUniverse, Inc.
Bloomington

This is a work of fiction. All of the characters, names, incidents, organizations, and dialogue in this novel are either the products of the author's imagination or are used fictitiously.

iUniverse books may be ordered through booksellers or by contacting:

iUniverse
1663 Liberty Drive
Bloomington, IN 47403
www.iuniverse.com
1-800-Authors (1-800-288-4677)

ISBN: 978-1-4502-8292-5 (sc)
ISBN: 978-1-4502-8293-2 (ebook)

Printed in the United States of America

iUniverse rev. date: 1/26/2010

Chapter 1

Faint screams came from the heavily wooded area just ahead. "Please, don't!" came the pleas in a shrill but small voice.

On his bike, Denten slowed, trying to locate the source of the cries that filtered through the trees of a small park on the edge of town. As he continued on the narrow gravel path, the cries came clearer and louder. Suddenly, he saw a large black car parked just off the path in a parking lot close to an arrangement of picnic tables. Denten slowed, then stopped. He got off his bike, wheeling it closer to this isolated car. As he approached the car, a head popped up to stare out the rear window. For a moment two large dark eyes glared at him. Black hair streaked with gray covered the head framed in the car's rear window. For just a second, Denten glimpsed a small, blonde head deeper in the back seat.

Frozen by the vicious dark eyes that bore down on him, Denten gripped the handle bars of his bike. He forced himself to look away from the scene he had just witnessed. He turned his bike, pedaling as fast as he could to escape something he knew he should not have seen.

His covers tangled around his legs, sweat dripping down his neck and under his arms, Denten abruptly sat up. He stared into the dark space of his room. He let out a long breath as his shoulders slumped. How many times had he experienced the same vision, always at night, always with the same startling results.

For more than ten years this nightmare had haunted Denten even as he attempted to erase the memory by reassuring himself that it all was now history. But it really wasn't. The memory of the horrible incident was firmly implanted in his head. In fact, he remembered it vividly.

The day had arrived warm and sunny. Denten Ballery, ten years old, decided that before he would do anything else on this beautiful Saturday morning, he would take his new bike for an extended ride. Denten lived with this two older sisters and mom and dad on a small but prosperous farm just outside Riverside, Minnesota, a small farming community clinging to the banks of the Minnesota River as it meandered its way to join the mighty Mississippi just south of the Twin Cities. The river offered many opportunities for bicycle rides or for long peaceful walks on paths following the curves of the river as it made its way passed Riverside.

Shortly after breakfast and his promise that he would complete his duties, taking out garbage, collecting eggs from the chicken coop, and cleaning his room, upon his return from his ride, Denten climbed on his bike, adjusted his helmet and headed for the main road which would enable him to connect with the path that followed the river.

Though popular at certain times of the year, the path failed to attract many users on a Saturday morning in farming country. On warm, sunny Saturday mornings on the farm other responsibilities assumed a much higher priority than a pleasure ride on a bike. Consequently, Denten encountered no one else on the path. Lost in his own little world, he pedaled slowly, just enjoying the quiet of the morning and the smells of the grass, the trees and the river.

Besides the path, the area included a park where members of the community celebrated special events, either civic or personal. This morning no celebrations were taking place. However, in the distance, Denten heard what he thought were cries for help. The cries he thought he heard brought him to a stop as he tried to listen more carefully to the sounds he heard. As he turned his head to better hear where he thought the sounds came from, he recognized a distinct cry for help and a clear, desperate, "Please don't!"

Denten got off his bike. He now just wheeled it in the direction of the cries he heard. In the distance, parked near the trail in a parking lot used for those who picnicked at the park, sat a large black car. In the back seat Denton could distinguish movement. Suddenly, a pair of eyes appeared in the rear side window. Black hair streaked with gray created a frame across the top of the dark penetrating eyes. Denten stood frozen, holding onto his bike, staring at the scene in front of him. As he did, for an instant, a small, blond head appeared behind the dark eyes and hair.

Denten knew he was seeing something he should not witness. Turning his bike around, he jumped onto the seat, stood on the pedals to pump as hard as he could to flee the scene that he realized was terribly wrong. As he rode as fast as he could toward home, the image of what he had just seen raced through his young mind. Who were those people? What were they doing? Though he did have some idea of the answer to that. Did whoever was in the backseat of the car recognize him? Should he tell his parents? Was he in a place he should not have been? Would he be accused of intruding on someone's privacy? By the time he finally arrived home, confusion compelled him to plunge into his list of things to do. He would have to think about just whom he would tell if, anyone.

Denten lay back on his bed. He gazed into the darkness of his dorm room, only a sliver of light slipping through the closed drapes. In the middle of the night darkness, he found returning to sleep futile. His mind drifted to what he faced if he was to graduate in the spring. Certainly, he needed no more distractions from that haunting memory or from anything else. Just yesterday he had received another warning from the office of the academic dean that unless his academic performance improved, he jeopardized his May graduation. Denten didn't even wish to contemplate that possibility.

He stretched, threw the covers back and sat on the edge of the bed in his small single dorm room. In this his senior year at Minnesota State College Mankato, Denten had the option of a single dorm room. He took the option without hesitation, grasping, when he could, the freedom from having to cope with a roommate with whom he may or may not share compatibility. Denten breathed heavily as he checked his bedside clock which read 4:36 a.m.

As he sat on the edge of his bed, Denten reflected on the four years he had devoted to his college education. Never a very good student, he, nonetheless, accepted the challenge of successfully completing a four year degree in business administration, a major that he selected after several semesters of vacillation from one major to another. Failing to earn that degree, now a possibility, would devastate him, to say nothing about what it would do to his parents and his sisters.

All those times during grade school and high school that his family, particularly his sisters, pleaded with him to work harder in school rushed through his mind. Margaret and Nancy, Denten's sisters, the former four years older and latter two years older, had established academic standards with which he could not compete. How many times had he heard the comment, "Your sisters were such outstanding students, I expected more of you." Not an overly confident person in the first place, comments like these only added to his feeling of inadequacy. Nonetheless, he progressed through the Riverside public schools without serious problems, gradating four years ago.

Denten stood up and made his way to the door to his room and out into the hallway. The bathroom served the needs of several students who lived on his floor. He stood before the mirror to see a young man rather handsome in an unsophisticated way. Right now his heavy dark hair gathered in messy clumps. His two day old beard gave him the look of a man much older than his twenty-one years. But his six foot frame with broad shoulders and well proportioned body ending with long masculine legs confirmed his age. Denten rinsed his face with cold water, brushed his teeth, and tried to gain some control over his ravaged hair.

Walking back to his room, he couldn't avoid thinking about his dream, one he had, repeatedly, over the last ten years. The scene etched vividly in his memory even after all the years. Again he asked himself why he hadn't told anyone about the incident? At the time, confusion clouded his ability to reach any kind of decision except to keep it all to himself. Later, after he could distance himself from what he saw, he questioned whether or not he should have used the path at that time. Did he intrude on someone's privacy? Would he have to explain what he saw to his parents or maybe even the police? All of these questions dissuaded Denten from confiding in anyone. Perhaps later he would. He never did. Even now, ten years later, he refused to share this secret with anyone.

This firm refusal reflected something about the nature of Denten Ballery. From a very early age he displayed a quiet almost shy nature. Much of his time he spent alone, his sisters not sharing in any of his interests which ranged from riding his bike to dreaming about traveling to distant places. Often he would stand outside watching the jet planes as they either headed for the Minneapolis/ St. Paul airport or had just departed from it. These planes, probably still climbing to their cruising altitude, always intrigued Denten, who wondered about the plane's destination or just from where it returned.

As a member of a farm family, Denten assumed his share of responsibilities. During the spring and fall his dad relied on him to help with the planting and the harvesting. He found this work tiring but satisfying. To please his dad pleased him as well. Oscar, his dad, did appreciate what his kids did around the farm. The girls concentrated on helping Grace, their mom. In return Mr. and Mrs. Ballery provided well for their kids and for themselves. Perhaps not considered rich, the Ballerys still lived a comfortable life thanks to the 500 acre farm they all called home.

Denten sat by his small desk reading again the recent letter concerning his academic status. One more semester would complete his degree. Under no circumstances would he squander that achievement. He simply had to rededicate himself to his studies. He had to maintain a 2.5 grade point average. Anything less than that would crush his goal of a May graduation. What Denten lacked in academic talent he could make up for with determination.

Sitting in his desk chair, he rubbed his eyes, stretched, and leaned forward, putting his head on his folded arms on top of the desk. Quickly, the image of that black car reappeared. The dark penetrating eyes peering through the rear side window of the car made that image even more disturbing. In his mind Denten could see those eyes bearing down on him as he stood paralyzed by what he saw and heard so many years ago. The question of whether or not the person whose eyes he saw recognized him lingered in his mind along with other questions, such as who cried out in agony?

A hint at the answer to the first question occurred just three years ago when he visited the Riverside Bank to withdraw money for college tuition. As he stepped to the window, Reed Howard, the bank president and a distinguished member of the Riverside community, stood ready to serve him. Denten looked up. To his shock, the eyes that peered over the top of the teller's cage had a remarkable resemblance to those same dark eyes that years before stared at him through the car's rear window. He had stood suspended for a moment in disbelief.

"Could I help you, Denten?" the deep but gentle voice of Mr. Howard propelled Denten back to reality.

For an instant longer he stared at the eyes just clearing the top of the teller's cage. "Ah, yes. I need to make a withdrawal." he remembered uttering, embarrassed by his hesitation.

Since then he had frequently thought about that moment in the bank, not really believing that one so important in the community could have committed, what Denten decided years ago was sexual assualt. This too joined the other disturbing memories of that long ago event.

Rising out of his desk chair, Denten stretched and opened the window curtain unleashing a bright morning sun that burst into his room, a hint of better days to come.

Chapter 2

Oscar Ballery squinted into the bright morning sun, the beginning of another critical day on the farm. Wet weather had delayed the corn harvest. Oscar delighted in the chance to resume that harvest and storage before serious winter weather arrived. Today he anticipated completing the storage of several bushels of corn in one of the three storage bins that lined the fringe of the farm yard. To accomplish the storage required an elevator that would auger the corn to the top of the storage bin, dropping the corn on the floor below, in reality building the accumulating corn from the bottom up.

As he moved the elevator into place, Oscar started the small engine that operated the auger that stretched to the top of the bin. That in place, he backed the truck loaded with corn into position directly in front of the elevator. Securing the truck in place, he stepped out to open the door cut into the large truck box to allow the corn to fall into the elevator. Watching the movement of the auger which channeled the corn into the elevator cups, Oscar thought of all the horror stories he heard and read about farmers losing their hands and arms in one of these elevators. Gingerly, he pushed corn from the truck box onto the wide mouth of the auger.

Oscar couldn't remember how many hours he had devoted to doing what he did now. A lifelong member of the Riverside community, he had lived his entire life on the 500 acre farm he called his home. His parents had homesteaded this piece of land or, at least, a major part of it. Oscar had added a few acres over the years. He also relinquished a few acres for windmills which now stood as noble sentries on the southern fringe of the Ballery property. For that sacrifice, the family received a small stipend. They also received a degree of satisfaction for their small contribution to the promotion of renewable energy.

Oscar had attended the same schools attended by his children. At the Riverside High School Oscar met his future wife Nancy. They dated through their senior years, delaying marriage while Oscar attended a nearby community college where he majored in agricultural science. Just three years out of high school they settled down on Oscar's family farm to continue the farming tradition as well as to look after his aging parents until their deaths several years ago.

Oscar's mind drifted over those many years as the corn fell slowly from the truck to the auger trough. Several times he caught himself day dreaming when he should have paid attention to the entire corn transferring process.

Glancing at that large trough which opened like a mouth to absorb the corn flowing from the truck, he noticed a large corn stalk which for some reason had made it through the corn picker out in the field. Not thinking, Oscar reached down to grab the stalk before it entered the elevator cups potentially to clog the machine. As quickly as he reached into the gaping mouth, one of the auger blades caught his jacket sleeve pulling his right arm into the dreaded blades sharp enough to sever a hand or an arm.

In instant alarm, Oscar pulled back on his arm. However, the auger would not let go. Panic flooded through his body as he desperately pulled to free his arm from the voracious conveyors. The pull of the auger stretched his arm, his attempts to fight off the pull to no avail. Twisting and turning his body in a valiant effort to free his arm sent sharp pains shooting through that arm and up into the shoulder. The force of the auger ripped Oscar's jacket from his arm while the edges of the blades inched closer and closer to bare skin. Suddenly, blood spurted from a deep gash just below the elbow. Realizing, now, that unless he somehow extricated that arm, he could easily lose more than just an arm. Oblivious to his arm which now hung in near shreds, he made one last violent pull to wrest it away from the auger.

The pull sent Oscar sliding to the ground where he lay dazed and bleeding. For several minutes he fought off the drift to unconsciousness. Not thinking about the serious damage to his arm, he tried to sit up. He nearly blacked out. Again he lay back, groping for control over the shock to his body. Having no idea of how long he lay there beside the elevator which continued its grinding journey to the top of the storage bin, Oscar eventually sat up seeking the strength to call out to Nancy, who worked in the house only a short distance from where he lay.

To his good fortune, Nancy had just stepped out of the house to shake small rugs. She instantly realized something terrible was wrong, her husband positioned on the ground, his arm drenched in blood. She dashed to her husband's side to discover just how mangled his arm was.

"My, God, what has happened!" she screamed.

"My arm." he whispered as his strength rapidly waned.

Grace attempted to make him as comfortable as possible, not really knowing the extent of his injury. As a farmer's wife she did know something about first aide. A tourniquet to slow the flow of blood was a part of the meager knowledge. She ripped a strip from her blouse and tied it near his shoulder.

"Can you stay here? We need an ambulance."

Oscar nodded his head then closed his eyes and lay back down.

Fully aware that he wasn't going any place, she ran to the house to make the call.

At the small Riverside hospital, the emergency room staff cleaned and inspected the damaged arm. The emergency room doctor met with Grace in the waiting room to assure her that immediate attention could possibly save the arm. That attention would best be available at the Mayo Clinic in Rochester about an hour away. Without hesitation, she agreed. In just over an hour, Oscar lay on an operating table as doctors worked to save his mangled arm. In the waiting room, Grace contacted all three kids, Margaret in California, Nancy in Montana, and Denten in Mankato. Then she slumped down in a chair staring blankly at a late autumn sun slipping below the large window of the waiting room.

"Mom, why don't you go to the cafeteria for some coffee and just relax." Denten sat next to his mother as they both watched over husband and dad.

Grace had maintained a constant vigil since their arrival at the Mayo Clinic yesterday. Following emergency surgery on Oscar's arm, she spent the entire night by his side as long tubes dripped sedatives into his left arm. Only briefly did she doze off, finally giving in to the trauma of the last twenty-four hours. Following her call to the kids, Denten drove immediately to Rochester where he met his mother in the waiting room of the Mayo Clinic. He,too, had spent a mostly sleepless night watching over his dad.

The emergency surgery served to salvage the torn portions of Oscar's right arm. The doctors believed that the arm would survive the surgery; however, its functionality lingered in question. The future usefulness of the arm would have to wait for healing and possibly further surgery. Right now Oscar rested comfortably with the help of the constant flow of sedation.

"A chance for a short walk and something to drink would be good." Denten reinforced his suggestion that his mom take a break.

"I suppose I could do that. Dad looks peaceful enough right now."

"I think I can handle things." Denten reached over to touch his mother's shoulder, his lips spreading into a smile.

Grace eased herself up from her chair, stretched briefly. "I'll be back in a short while. Remember, if you need anything, press that button at the head of the bed."

"Yes, mother. I think I can do that." Again that smile spread across his face.

Grace walked slowly toward the hospital's cafeteria. A petite lady, at 59, she was just months younger than her husband. Though at one time she had thought of a career in education, she dedicated her life to her husband and children. After graduating from high school with Oscar, she enrolled at Mankato State College with the intention of majoring in elementary education. Her deepening relationship with Oscar Ballery interrupted those plans. Instead, she got married after two years of college content to devote herself to the life of a farmer's wife.

The life of a farm family is a life of shared responsibilities. Grace insisted that her children learned at an early age the nature of those responsibilities. She gently but consistently insisted on rules governing the behavior of her kids. Even Denten's older sisters, both of whom excelled academically in school, and in Denten's mind could do nothing wrong, were not spared the rigidity of their mother's standards. Margaret, the oldest sibling, rarely crossed into that remote area of inappropriate behavior. Nonetheless, even as a senior in high school, she violated her curfew. Her mother grounded her for two weeks.

But Grace was a tender, loving mother and wife. Nothing pleased her more than to see her kids happy. Not always did she feel that Denten was happy. She made every effort to understand his moods and his frequent withdrawal from the rest of the family. Denten stood firm in his resistance to any kind of discussion about him and his feelings.

With a hot cup of coffee and a usually forbidden sweet roll, Grace found a quiet table where she could relax with a full view of the hospital parking lot.

Denten stood up and moved closer to his dad's bed. Apparently sensing some one's presence, Oscar opened his eyes.

"How you doing?" Denten moved next to the bed, careful not to touch the several wires and tubes that monitored his dad's status.

His voice weak, Oscar whispered, "Okay. Your mother?"

"She just went to get some coffee. She should be back in a bit. Can I get you anything?"

Oscar slowly shook his head, his movement restricted by the brace supporting his damaged arm.

A knock on the door produced a nurse who smiled as she entered the room. Walking directly to the bed side, she asked, "How are you doing this morning?"

With a little more strength to his voice, Oscar responded with, "Better than yesterday,"

"That's good. You really did a job on that arm. But I think you'll be back in your routine soon. Now I just want to check on your vitals. Is there anything in particular that you need right now? Your lunch will be brought here in about an hour."

"No, I guess I'm fine. Thank you."

When the nurse completed her duties, she departed as quickly as she had entered. Denten, who had stood by the window observing a grey, drab day while the nurse was in the room, now turned to his dad but said nothing.

For a moment they looked at each other without saying anything. Finally, his dad asked, "Could you raise this bed up?"

"Am I supposed to do that?" Denten asked.

"Well, I can't." His dad answered, the bit of humor a good sign, as was the increasing strength of his voice. "Just crank that handle at the end of the bed. It will raise me up some."

Denten did as he was told, putting his dad into a position much more suited to a conversation. Denten and his dad rarely engaged in a conversation. However, at this moment, facing each other in this small hospital room compelled them to say something.

"Would you pour me a glass of water?" Oscar motioned to the picture sitting on the small table next to his bed.

"Sure. Do you need the straw?" Denten asked.

"I guess so."

Oscar took a long sip of the ice cold water, smiled and said, "That tasted good."

Silence again filled the room. Denten shifted uncomfortably, moving away from the bed.

"How's school going?" His dad asked.

Thinking of that letter from the academic dean's office, Denten answered, "Okay, I guess."

"What do you mean, 'You guess'"?

Denten turned his back to the bed. "I don't know. I don't really want to talk about it."

Reaching up to wipe off his month, Oscar closed his eyes for a moment then said, "Look, son, too many times over the years we've not talked about things that we should, maybe, have talked about. I know I'm as guilty as you are. Maybe we're just too much alike. But if there is something troubling you, please let's talk about it." Oscar stopped to catch his breath, the effects of the sedative still flowing through his body.

Denten turned back to face his dad. "You know I've never been very good at school stuff. I've tried. I'm just not smart that way, the way Margaret and Nancy are. You know that for me getting through high school was tough."

"I know, son. So many times I should have offered more help or encouragement or something rather than not saying anything. Is there a problem at school?"

Denten hesitated, moved closed to bed, placing his hands on the end railing. In a calm but firm voice, Denten explained, "A couple days ago I received a notice from the academic dean that unless my grades improved I might not graduate in June."

His dad absorbed the news without any strong reaction. A moment of silence ensued. "What do you have to do?" he asked.

"Well, I suppose get better grades. But I haven't talked to the people yet. I need to do that when I get back."

"I'm sure it will work out. Just remember, son. I love you and I have confidence that you will deal with this successfully."

Never could Denten remember his dad saying he loved him, not that he didn't. He just never said it. "Thank you, Dad. I love you, too. I think it will work out. I have over a semester to correct what needs correcting."

Silence again returned. As it did, so did Grace. Upon entering the room, she encountered the silence. Looking first at Denten and then at her husband, she said, "Am I interrupting something?"

Oscar looked over at his son, smiled and replied, "No. We just were having a short conversation."

"About what?" his wife asked.

"Just man talk. Important but man talk."

Denten spent the rest of the day with his parents, the subject of his academic problems not discussed any further. The conversation with his father delighted and surprised him. For just a moment he thought about bringing up his reoccurring dream but didn't. Perhaps another time.

Confident that his dad rested in good hands, Denten drove back to Mankato, the late afternoon sun brushing the tree tops as he headed west out of Rochester.

Chapter 3

Casey's arm reached around Cayla's shoulder, his hand gently resting on her breast. Cayla's body tensed, near panic racing through her body. Yet, she made no attempt to remove the hand. She sat transfixed, staring out the window of Casey's car. Casey inched closer, his hand pressing gently against her breast. He could feel the rigidity of her body against his.

"What's the matter?" he asked releasing his hand from her breast.

Cayla slumped down against the front seat. She covered her face with her hands as tears traced the contours of her cheeks. "I'm sorry." She sobbed. "I just can't."

"You can't what?" Casey's voice revealed his irritation. "I don't intend to commit some kind of assault. Just a bit of tenderness."

The tears continued to flow. Cayla reached into her pocket for a tissue. Through her sobs she repeated, "I'm sorry. I can't explain it. Please, can we go back now?"

Clearly annoyed by her refusal even to explain her reluctance to engage in innocent love making, Casey asked, "Don't you think I deserve some kind of explanation? How many dates have we had now?"

Following a deep breath, Cayla reached for Casey's hand. "I've really enjoyed our time together. You're a great guy. I just can't explain what happens. Please accept that."

"Is there anything I can do to help? I mean is there something bothering you?" Casey leaned back against the driver's side door.

Of course, there was something bothering her. She just hadn't talked about it with anyone for nearly ten years. Someday she would do that but not now. "No, I don't think so. Let's, for now, forget about it."

"Cayla, I really enjoy being with you. You are a wonderful lady. I just can't forget about it." Casey pleaded.

Tears again made their way down her cheeks. Dabbing them with her tissue, Cayla responded, "Please, can you trust me on this? Let's leave it for now."

Cayla sat on the edge of her bed in a dorm room she shared with Andrea Palmer, like her, a junior at St. Mary's College in Winona, Minnesota. On this early spring Saturday night, Cayla occupied the room all by herself. Andrea had gone home for the weekend.

Cayla regretted another damaged male relationship. She lay back on her bed, staring blankly in the soft light of the room. How many times had this happened over the years. In high school she dated occasionally. Many of those relationships lasting only briefly. Others lasting longer until confronted with her date's natural inclination to make love. Each time that happened she suffered the same feelings of dread and fear that produced near panic, her body suddenly rigid, clearly rejecting any advances from her date. Because of this reaction she gradually avoided dating unless she felt compelled to, such as for her senior prom.

At St. Mary's she wished to engage in the social life of the college. However, she also wished to avoid that horrible feeling of panic over which she had little control. Consequently, she dated infrequently, refusing to date any one boy more than once or twice. After that she realized that her date could expect more from her than a simple kiss on the cheek.

Unable to sleep, Cayla's mind drifted back to that fateful Saturday morning when she had recently turned eight years old. Only three years before, she and her parents, Harvey and Alice Finch, had moved to Riverside from rural Wisconsin. Her father, Harvey, a sales representative for a large farm machinery company, had the chance to increase his territory by moving to this southern

Minnesota farming community. The family quietly and quickly settled in to life in Riverside.

An only child, Cayla received exclusive attention from her adoring parents. Though she didn't necessarily demand it, she just accepted it as the natural thing for parents to do, pay close attention to their kids. A beautiful child with thick auburn hair, a ready smile that exposed perfect white teeth, and the flawless skin of a child not yet confronting adolescence. Cayla attracted the attention of both other kids and adults. For religious reasons or maybe for unabashed over protection, Cayla's parents decided to send her to a small parochial school near Riverside. There, a vivacious personality quickly made her a favorite among teachers and students.

On most Saturday mornings, Cayla would join others her age for choir practice at the local Baptist church to which she and her parents belonged. On this particular Saturday morning in late spring, Cayla insisted that she walk the few blocks from her home to the church. After all, the weather was perfect, and she loved being outside. After choir practice Cayla prepared to walk home. She had walked only a mere half a block when a huge black car pulled up next to the curb. Even now as Cayla reflected on the details of that horrific day, her body tensed, perspiration causing a chill.

The passenger side door opened. A big man with abundant black hair streaked with gray and huge dark eyes leaned over to ask, "Can I give you a ride?"

That big man, Reed Howard, enjoyed a position of importance in Riverside. President of the Riverside State Bank as well as president of the local Chamber of Commerce, nearly everyone either knew Mr. Howard personally or knew about him. Since her father banked at the Riverside State Bank and Cayla had frequently accompanied her dad to the bank, she knew Mr. Howard. On this particular Saturday morning, Reed had attended a special council meeting at the same Baptist church where Cayla sang in the youth choir. The meeting ended about the same time as Cayla's choir practice.

Not quite sure what to say, Cayla stood on the sidewalk looking into the car. She immediately recognized Mr. Howard. Also she immediately recalled what her parents had always told her, "Don't take a ride with a stranger." But, she thought, Mr. Howard was no stranger, and even though she preferred to walk home, she didn't wish to refuse his offer. In her mind that would not show the proper respect for such an outstanding citizen of the community.

"I guess so." Cayla answered in her soft voice.

As she stepped into the car to sit in the passenger seat, Reed reached across her body to close the passenger door. When he did, his face came very close to hers. For an instant, time stopped as Reed peered into Cayla's marvelous blue eyes.

"Here, let me help you with the seat belt." Reed announced, leaning closer to grab the belt.

"I can do it." Cayla quickly replied, embarrassed by Mr. Howard's closeness.

Putting the car in gear, Reed pulled out onto the street. "How have you been?"

"Fine." is all Cayla could think of to say.

"I've seen you many times at the bank with your dad, a fine man." Reed repeatedly looked over at Cayla, who moved as close to the passenger door as the seat belt allowed.

Silence filled the car.

"I live just down the next street." Cayla advised

"I think I know where you live." Reed paused briefly as if seriously measuring what to say next. "It's a beautiful day. How about a short ride through the park?"

Cayla looked straight ahead as the car passed her street. "I suppose." She answered in a voice now more strained than usual.

Again silence filled the car.

Reed looked over at Cayla as she sat rigid in her seat. "You know, you are a very pretty young lady."

Cayla blushed. "Thank you."

Lying on her dorm bed, Cayla glanced at her alarm clock, 3:30 a.m. Reluctantly, her mind reached back to the details of what happened once she and Reed arrived at the park. The struggle he had in wrestling her to the back seat, the futility of her efforts to fight off his attempts to pull down her shorts, the shock when he pulled down his pants all now gripped her in revulsion, making her shutter with just the thought of those dreadful moments in the back seat of the car.

Cayla vaguely remembered Reed's sudden reaction to something outside the car. Whatever distracted him apparently restored his rational sense. For he got out of the car, secured his pants, climbed in the driver's side, and drove out of the park. Nearly to her street, Reed fixed his eyes on Cayla cowering in the back seat.

" Remember, young woman, if you know what's good for you, you say nothing. You understand?"

Cayla nodded.

Just blocks from her home Reed simply pointed to the rear door. In a blur, she got out of the car to make that short walk home, a short walk that seemed an eternity.

Cayla sat up on the edge of her bed, the memory of those backseat moments too overwhelming even now, ten years later. Also still vivid in her memory was the thought of just what she would tell her parents, if anything. What would she say? She should not have gotten into the car in the first place, a violation of what her parents had told so many times. Ultimately, she said nothing. She escaped to her room stating simply that she didn't feel very good. With the passage of all those years, Cayla still had never told anyone about that devastating Saturday morning.

Cayla got up from her bed, walked to bathroom just down the hall. There she paused in front of the mirror which revealed a young lady, with dark circles under tear stained eyes, and hair messed from hands too often filtering through it, all evidence of another stressful evening.

Chapter 4

Reed Howard leaned back in his office chair, rubbed his eyes, took a deep breath and slumped deeper into the chair's rich leather. His day had evolved into one of stress. Why can't people make their payments on time? He despised having to deal with delinquent accounts. On his massive desk, always meticulously organized, lay a small pile of delinquent accounts. He edged closer to his desk, reaching for the pile, arranged alphabetically. Paging through the documents he stopped at "Deluca." For decades the Delucas had used the services of the Riverside State Bank. Now for some reason they were three months delinquent in their mortgage payment secured for remodeling of their restaurant. Reed deplored having to deal this way with long time customers, but bank profits came first.

Tipping back again in his chair, he concluded he needed some relaxing. He dialed his secretary to inform her that he wanted no interruptions for the next half hour. Turning to his personal lap top computer, he scrolled through his personal files until he reached "relaxing."

A click brought forth a picture of a very young girl, naked. She stood innocently looking directly into the camera which recorded her picture. Reed clicked the file again. Another picture appeared, another young girl, this one smiling as she, too, stood completely naked. As he watched a parade of naked young girls filling his computer screen, a smile spread across his face. He eased farther into his chair, a twinge racing through his body.

An obsession with young girls had accompanied Reed Howard his entire life. Even as a young boy young girls intrigued him.

Escaping to the privacy of his own room, he would fantasize about these young girls he met on the street, in the neighborhood or even in church. He yearned to stand next to them, to look at them, to touch them. Only a couple times did his obsession create problems. One of those times involved a young second grade neighbor girl. At the time in middle school, Reed lured this cute little second grader into his room where he persuaded her to undress, explaining it in terms of a game. The little girl told her mother about the incident. A heated encounter with Reed's parents ensued; however, not much else happened. After all, "boys will be boys" served as the only explanation.

That Reed was a member of a prominent Riverside family helped to shield him from discovery or even suspicion. His grandfather had started the Riverside State Bank decades ago. Reed's father assumed the office of president of the bank upon the grandfather's retirement. Upon his father's retirement, Reed claimed the role of president.

The position of president of the only bank in town carried with it considerable influence and respect. Reed acquired a reputation for honesty tinged with compassion, dealing with a variety of financial concerns in the small rural community that was Riverside. Recent increase in delinquent payments deeply troubled Reed.

However, throughout his formative years he had little reason to be troubled about anything. His father provided very well for Reed and his older sister who had left the security of small town Minnesota for the big city of Chicago. Unlike so many kids his age, Reed didn't have to worry about a new bike, or toys he wanted or the latest in teenage fashion. Dad generally gave him what he desired. Reed even acquired a car of his own on his seventeenth birthday. No other classmate could make that claim. Neither did any other classmate that he knew of share his obsession with nude, juvenile girls.

Throughout high school and college, Reed pursued his consuming interest in child pornography, accumulating an extensive collection of tantalizing material. The arrival of the computer age brought a whole new world of pornographic potential. In his spacious home on the edge of Riverside, Reed maintained a private den, off limits to his wife and his two kids when they still lived at home, where he would float in ecstasy as young girls stood before him on his computer screen in all their naked glory.

The appearance of Reed's life offered a dramatic contrast to the reality of Reed's life. His position as president of the bank gave him respectability reinforced by his position as president of the Riverside Chamber of Commerce and member of the council of the local Baptist church. He discretely shielded his private addiction. On only a couple occasions did that addiction threaten to destroy everything that proclaimed him a success. One of those occasions occurred about ten years ago when he could no longer resist the temptation of a Cayla Finch. That moment in the park when a young boy on a bike interrupted his moment of glory with Cayla stood clear in his memory, a constant reminder of the danger of carelessness. Since that time he satisfied his urges in the fantasy land provided by his private den. However, the years had not erased the threat posed by that boy on the bike whose identity Reed had never definitely confirmed.

Chapter 5

"No, son, I will not let you sacrifice your education to hang around here to help me."

"Dad, I'm not going to sacrifice my education." Denten leaned onto the kitchen table to emphasize his determination to skip spring semester to help his dad on the farm.

"I really don't need your help much during the winter." Oscar folded his good arm across his chest in a gesture of determination to ensure Denten's spring graduation.

"Dad," Denten rose out of his chair. "Who's going to finish the corn storage? Who's going to finish picking the corn on that piece north of here? Who's going to help you plow? Who's going to help seed in the spring?"

Oscar looked away, concentrating on nothing in particular. "Neighbors can help. I've certainly helped others in the past."

"Yes, dad, I know our neighbors have shown generosity in the past. But you can't expect them to take over what you have to do."

"I don't expect them to take over. I'm not an invalid."

Both of them glanced at Oscar's right arm resting in a sling. Two weeks had passed since the accident which nearly destroyed his right arm. In that time doctor's had concluded that more surgery would not alter the status of the arm's functionality. In that time, too, the arm had healed quickly; however, the healing did not include the return of former function. Just how useful the arm would be nobody would know until all healing had taken place and a schedule of therapy established. Doctors advised Oscar not to expect much from the arm which had sustained major damage to muscles, tendons as well as bone. Only minor damage had occurred to the shoulder area. Regardless of speculation about future usage of the arm, all agreed that the accident would force a life style change for particularly Oscar and his wife.

Eventually Denten, with the help of his mom, convinced his dad that his suspending college for a semester to spend time helping him was the right thing to do. Denten would complete the fall semester, coming home weekends to help with the fall harvest, the storage of corn and the preparation of the land for spring planting.

Actually, Denten needed time away from the academic world. He needed time to assess just what he wanted to do with his college degree, an assessment he should have made months ago. In discussion with an academic counselor, Denten learned that delaying his graduation for a semester would matter little. More important, he needed to improve his academic performance to satisfy the requirements for graduation.

The first weekend Denten came home to help his dad, he had to face the reality of using the elevator that nearly severed his father's arm. Always he had used caution when working around the farm machinery. Now, just looking at the elevator made him tentative and nervous. Nonetheless, he had to complete the job. That job would require most of the weekend since several loads of corn stood ready for storage.

"Are you sure you want to do this?" his father asked.

Denten looked at his father then at the elevator. "Somebody's got to do it. Why don't you guide me as I back the truck up to the auger bin."

Oscar stood off to the side as he motioned Denten to back slowly. The truck in place, Denten started the engine on the elevator. His dad stepped back, his eyes locked on that auger. Carefully, Denten opened the small door on the back of the truck box allowing corn to pour out into the auger bin. Father and son stood next to each other. Denten gently placed his arm around his dad's shoulder.

"See how easy it is." Denten joked.

His dad smiled. "Just be careful. Things can happen so fast."

As the fall progressed, Denten did spend most weekends at home. Much of that time he worked plowing the corn fields in preparation for spring planting. During long hours of riding the tractor, he reflected on his decision to suspend pursuit of a college degree. In a month the fall semester would end. Thinking about that end gave Denten a sense of relief. The problems had multiplied during the semester for reasons he knew were his fault. He found difficult dedicating himself to his studies, a problem that had burdened him through most of his formal education.

Driving the tractor required little thought. It did require paying attention to what he was doing. And what he was doing gave him an immediate sense of satisfaction as the plow his tractor pulled turned over the dirt leaving a smooth black expanse of ground. The drone of the tractor created a sort of creative monotony during which Denten's thoughts ventured back to times as a young boy when much of life proved mysterious. He smiled as those thoughts turned to his early fascination with traveling to other parts of the world. He remembered standing in the farm yard watching those huge commercial jets streaking over head as they flew to and from the Minneapolis/ St. Paul airport.

During those moments he wandered what flying in one of those jets was really like. He wondered where the people in them lived and where they had traveled. Someday, maybe he, too, would take a trip in a jet, flying someplace exciting and different. He still retained that hope that maybe someday it would happen. He had all kinds of years to satisfy his desire to travel.

The solitude he experienced in the field also, on occasion, brought back memories of that incident in the park so many years ago. Sneaking out of his memory during the day made it less traumatic than during those moments at night when it rushed upon him as he slept. Whenever it happened it never ceased to torment him. Though now he understood what brought them to the park, he still did not know for sure who was in that car. Who belonged to the lighter hair briefly glimpsed before those dark eyes peered through the back door window? Would he ever find out the truth? How many times over the years had he asked himself that question?

The fall drifted into early winter, those weekend trips home less frequent as the fall work gradually ended. Denten prepared for semester finals scheduled for the week before Christmas break. For Denten that break would extend until at least next year's fall semester.

Studying never qualified as one of Denten's strengths. His sisters never let him forget it either. His tenuous academic standing at the college and his decision to give up the spring semester demanded, he believed, the best performance he could deliver for the current semester. This would give him something to build on when he did return to the campus next fall. Therefore, the final days before semester's end found Denten spending most of his time doing what he knew he did not do well, study.

"Merry Christmas!" Margaret and her husband Peter Munson stepped through the front door clinging to suitcases and a shopping bag of gifts. "It's so good to see you." Margaret set her luggage down and rushed to embrace, carefully, her dad whom she had not seen since the accident. She released her hold around his neck, leaned back to look her dad in the eye. "How have you been?"

Oscar had returned the hug only with his left arm, his right he could not raise much above his waist. "Wonderful. It's so good that you could come. How was the flight?"

"Everything went well. We even arrived in Minneapolis ahead of schedule. Our car rental was also waiting for us." Margaret stepped back to permit her husband to move closer to her dad.

"Good to see you, Peter. I hear the software business goes well." Oscar reached out his left hand to shake Peter's right.

"Good to see you looking so well. You've had quite a fall. Sorry we could not have visited earlier. Things get a bit hectic at home."

"We certainly didn't expect you to come running for a stupid thing I did." Oscar reassured Peter. "We're just glad you could make it now."

Grace waited for her turn for a greeting. "Mother, you certainly have had your share of misery as well." Margaret also treated her mother to a big hug.

"Maybe for a bit. Really, your dad is the one who faced the misery. But, look at him. He's better than ever." Grace touched her husband's shoulder and smiled.

Denten stood off to the side during these moments of reunion of his parents and his oldest sister. Detecting a pause in the greeting, Denten stepped forward to welcome his sister and her husband, whom she had met in college and whom Denten liked for his good humor, his engaging personality and his humility, qualities that would work well in a marriage to his relatively aggressive and persistent sister. Still, those qualities had served her well all through high school and college. Even now she enjoyed impressive success as a fashion marketing agent for a large department store chain in California. Peter, a computer software representative, also had achieved remarkable success. So far success did not include children.

The group moved into the living room where they talked about all that had transpired over the many months since the family had gotten together.

"When do Nancy and Collier arrive with their little Timothy Oscar?" Margaret asked as she settled into the sofa.

"Sometime later today, I guess. You know they are driving from Montana, an eight to ten hour drive and with a little one year old." Grace entered the room with a tray of Christmas cookies and coffee.

"I talked with her just a few days ago. Apparently Timothy is growing fast." Margaret rose from the sofa. "Here, mom, let me help you with that."

"Yes, she's real excited about coming here to show off their wonderful son."

Denten's other sister Nancy, married a young man, Collier Foster, whom she met a few years ago during summer employment at the main lodge in Yellowstone Park. Collier grew up on a large Montana ranch where he now lived with his wife and young son.

Nancy's college degree in secondary education, she asserted in jest, prepared her well for her role as mother and house wife on a large Montana ranch. She insisted that someday she would like to try the classroom as a high school chemistry teacher. First, though, were her husband and her son.

That evening Nancy, her husband and son did arrive to reenact the greetings occurring earlier upon the arrival of Margaret and Peter. Of course, Timothy captured the attention of everyone, particularly of Grandpa Oscar from whom Timothy acquired his middle name. With great caution Grandpa held his grandson, careful to avoid using his right arm.

The next day, Christmas Eve, would find the family together again for the first time in over three years. Complications in travel had prevented getting together since Thanksgiving now over three years ago. Christmas Day would also find them together.

Denten generally had enjoyed a good relationship with his sisters even though they pressured him too often about his scholastic negligence. All through high school they, especially Margaret, had pleaded with him to work harder, not recognizing that he did try to work harder. For him working harder was not always the answer. He frequently reminded them that maybe he just wasn't as smart they were.

As they now sat in the kitchen reminiscing about their lives on the farm, Margaret asked Denten, "How's school in Mankato?"

Looking down at the floor, Denten answered, "Okay. But I'm not returning for the spring semester."

"You're not!" His sisters responded in unison.

"Why not?" Nancy asked.

'It's a long story. I supposed it's a familiar one. I do need to boost my GPA to graduate. But helping dad and mom here is a more important reason."

"You will go back to finish your degree." Margaret expressed this more as a command than a comment.

"Yes, next fall. If all goes right, I will graduate at the end of the fall semester."

"That's great. Both Margaret and I admire what you've done for Dad and for Mom for that matter. But please return to finish your degree."

"I will."

Christmas Eve and Christmas Day included much great food and abundant conversation. However, Denten looked forward to a return to a more normal routine. With no college classes, no final tests, or no course papers to worry about, he could relax in the knowledge that he was helping his parents. He definitely would have ample time to consider his options for the future, a future that he hoped would offer answers to questions that had haunted him for years.

Chapter 6

"Cayla, you need to stop by the bank to sign for that loan," Harvey Finch sat with his daughter at the breakfast table. In her junior year at St. Mary's College in Winona, she had never previously signed for her college loans. Her dad had always done that for her. Even a mention of the Riverside State Bank sent tension racing through her body. Of course, her father knew nothing about the reason for her aversion to visiting the bank. Today, he simply lacked time to stop by the bank himself. Problems with one of his accounts in a near by community required his immediate attention. As a district manager for a large farm machinery company, he assumed considerable responsibility for dealing with unhappy customers. As a result, Cayla had to sign for the loan herself.

All morning she agonized over stepping into the bank and coming face to face with Reed Howard. The fear she had experienced as a young girl had gradually transformed into an intense bitterness, resentment, and hatred toward the man responsible for the anguish she had suffered all those years. Someday, maybe, he would have to answer for what he had done to her and her life. Today, though, she would attempt to complete quickly the signing of the loan without having to confront Reed Howard.

As Cayla walked from her car to the front entrance to the bank, her mind replayed again those horrible moments ten years ago in the park. Pushing open the entrance doors, Cayla couldn't control the slight trembling that sent a chill through her body. Upon entering the bank, she quickly surveyed the lobby, one she had not seen for a number of years, but one that had changed little since she was a young girl. She saw no sign of Mr. Howard.

She located the loan officer's small office in the rear corner of the lobby. Briskly, she walked back to the office. She stood in the door way waiting for the officer, a middle aged woman, to acknowledge her presence. In a moment she did.

A brief explanation by the woman and the signing the papers required just minutes. Cayla thanked the lady, turned and stood face to face with Reed Howard.

For the longest couple minutes she had suffered in years, Cayla stood speechless, unable to look directly at him.

"Hello, Cayla. I haven't seen you for a long time. How are you?"

Hardly finding the strength to answer, Cayla mumbled, "Fine. Excuse me. I'm late."

She rushed right passed Reed. He moved to the side as she made her way to the front entrance. Reaching the front sidewalk, she paused, took a deep breath, trying to relax her tense muscles. Adding to the accumulated resentment she felt was now the audacity displayed by Reed Howard, confident in his capacity to do whatever he pleased with impunity. When she returned to her car, she got in, slamming the door shut. Placing her hands on the steering wheel, she rested her head agains her hands until her breathing slowed, and she gained control.

Not one given to visiting bars in the middle of the afternoon or generally any time, Cayla decided that she needed a drink to help settle her nerves. One of the more popular bars in Riverside was the River's End, a well established part of the local culture. When she entered, she paused to adjust to the rapid change in light. Her vision adjusted, she noticed only one other couple in the bar sitting by one of the small tables. A bit guilty about being there in the first place, she rejected the idea of sitting at a table. Instead, she walked up to the bar where she ordered a simple rum and coke, the only drink she could think of.

The drink did accomplish what she wanted. It relaxed her. The bartender attempted to engage her in conversation. However, her obvious reticence convinced him to give it up. She just wanted to savor the moment.

Half way through her drink, the door of the bar opened for a young man who did what she did when she entered, pausing for a moment as his eyes adjusted to the dim light. He glanced around the bar noting the couple sitting at the table as well as the young lady standing at the bar. The young man approached the bar to order a beer. He took a long swallow before turning to face the young lady standing only a few feet away.

"The pause that refreshes, I guess." Denten was not a man of creative expressions.

"Yes, I'll go along with that." Cayla turned to face Denten but moved no closer.

Looking at her near empty glass, Denten asked, "May I buy you a drink?"

Cayla looked at her glass and up at Denten. "Yes, thank you."

Denten stepped closer, "My name is Denten Ballery."

"Hi, Denten. I'm Cayla Finch. Pleased to meet you."

"Thank you. Pleased to meet you, too" Denten reached out to shake her hand. "Do you live around here?"

"Practically all my life." Cayla answered with conviction.

"So have I." Denten affirmed with a smile.

Their conversation continued as each found the other very easy to talk with. That she had attended a parochial school explained why they had not met previously. They talked about their respective families, the recent holidays, and their current situations. Denten explained his suspending his spring semester, feeling comfortable in discussing with her his academic problems. Cayla listened intently to the description of his father's recent accident. He listened to her talking about life at St. Mary's.

They engaged in conversation for well over an hour, not really paying attention to the passage of time. Denten had spent most of the day hauling corn to the local elevator, the price for corn now allowing for a respectable profit. She mentioned the demand for money dragged her to the bank.

With no commitment to establish future contact, Cayla and Denten walked out of the River's End Bar having enjoyed a conversation with a new friend.

"Nice to have met you." Cayla commented as they parted to walk their separate ways.

"Nice to have met you, too. Maybe we'll bump into each other again sometime." Denten headed for his truck thinking, "That was the best beer I've had in a long time." He turned to have one last look. Cayla did the same. They waved.

Chapter 7

"Denten, are you coming with us for dinner tonight?" His mom asked as she walked through the living room with her "dust wizard," her ever present weapon against the accumulation of dust anyplace in the house.

"What time?" Denten looked up from concentration on the second football game of the day.

"Probably about 7:00. We're just going to Deluca's"

Alda and Gilberto Deluca had operated their restaurant in Riverside for decades. Perhaps the most popular restaurant in town, it gave up nothing to more recent fast food stops. From Italy, Alda and Gilberto had immigrated to America in their early 20's. Though they did not know one another at the time, they eventually met in Chicago where both their families had settled. After two short years in Chicago, Alda and Gilberto married and headed west to Minneapolis/St. Paul where they heard one could realize the American dream. Of course, realizing that dream was not easy. They both worked in a variety of jobs, most of them in the food industry.

By accident one Sunday, they read an article in the local paper lauding the beauty of the Minnesota River Valley and small rural towns that clung to its shores on its way to meet the Mississippi near Minneapolis. They both had dreamed of opening a restaurant where they could serve tantalizing Italian cuisine. They possessed a marvelous collection of recipes for food they believed no one could resist. Consequently, in the early spring of 1953, Alda and Gilberto

Deluca made the two hour journey that took them to Riverside, Minnesota, in the heart of corn and wheat country.

Their small restaurant failed to attract immediate attention. The Delucas over estimated the appeal of Italian cuisine in rural Minnesota. In just months, however, word spread about the great food at that Deluca place on the Riverside's main street. Since that time few people in and around Riverside had not eaten at Deluca's. For years the Ballerys had eaten there by themselves and with their children. Denten knew the Delucas very well.

On a Saturday night a few days after Christmas, Denten and his parents entered the restaurant to the effusive greetings of Gilberto himself. While Alda managed the kitchen, Gilberto managed the customers, a job for which he possessed a marvelous talent. A small man in his early 80's, Gilberto maintained a much more youthful appearance. Only his vivid, white hair suggested his actual age. Under that hair, his bright dark eyes sparkled as his lips spread into one of his engaging smiles. Gregarious and animated, Gilberto invariably made an appearance at each table, checking on the service, the food, the weather, and about any number of topics he considered worthy of comment.

"Good evening, my friends." Gilberto approach Denten and his parents shortly after they entered the restaurant. "Did you have a good holiday?" His speech revealed not a hint of his native language.

"Thank you. Yes, we did." Oscar extended his hand.

"Good to see you again Mrs. Ballery." Gilberto touched her arm gently.

"Good see you, too."

Alberto turned his attention to Denten. "It's been a long time. How's school going?"

"Fine. But I'm taking a little time off to help Dad." Denten answered.

"You're such a loyal son." Gilberto padded Denten on the back.

During their meal, Gilberto paid a few more visits to their table, pausing only to ensure that everything was okay. Having completed their meal, the Ballerys paid the bill and stood ready to leave when Gilberto asked if they had a few minutes. Of course, they did.

Gilberto directed them to an empty table in the corner of the restaurant. Shortly after they sat down, Alda joined them.

"As usual, the dinner was great." Grace complimented Alda.

Gilberto moved his chair closer to the table. "Forgive me for intruding on your evening, but I have a favor to ask. As you know, Alda and I have run this restaurant for more years than we wish to admit. You also know that we did come here from Italy also more years ago than we want to admit."

Denten and his parents sat quietly listening to Gilberto as he prefaced his favor.

"Both Alda and I are now in our 80's. We want to return to our first homeland when we still can." He paused, looking at each person sitting around the table.

Oscar smiled, "Why that's great. When will you go?"

"Well," Gilberto ran his hand through his thick white hair. "We had planned on going earlier this year. But we ran into a bit of a problem with the restaurant."

"What kind of problem?" Oscar asked, concern evident in the sound of his voice.

"A minor financial one with the local bank." Again Gilberto paused, hesitant to discuss a privatematter but still striving for honesty. "As you know, recently we did a little remodeling here in the restaurant."

"Yes, I remember. It looks good." Oscar quickly surveyed the main dining room.

Gilberto continued. "I think it does too. Sadly, business dropped off at a bad time. We missed a couple mortgage payments which have not made Mr. Howard at the bank very happy. I tell you this so you understand why our trip was delayed and why we want to go ahead with it before something else happens."

Oscar nodded his head. "We understand completely."

Denten and his mother had said nothing since they sat down. Now they joined Oscar in simply nodding their heads.

"Right now," Gilberto resumed, "our trip is scheduled for the last week in February and the first week of March, a two week stay with family there."

"That sounds great." This time Denten responded.

"Now, I suppose, you must be wondering why I'm telling you this." Gilberto folded his hands on the table in front of him then looked at his wife. "Well, Alda and I would like someone to join us on our trip. We don't feel comfortable traveling all that way by ourselves. We want someone to come with us to help us with all that goes into traveling. For one thing we'll need to rent a car when we get to Rome. I'm not good at that stuff." Gilberto stopped, glancing down at his folded hands.

Looking up again, he pointed out to Denten. "Son, would you be willing to join us on our trip since you will not attend college this winter?"

Denten sat up straight in his chair, evincing some shock over the request.

"Of course, we would pay your flight. When we get there, we will stay at my cousins, free of charge." Laughter circled the table.

Denten started to respond then stopped. "I'm not sure what to say. It sounds like a great opportunity. But the added expense."

"Don't worry. We can take care of it." Gilberto spoke with conviction.

Oscar looked at his son. "Of course, whether he goes or not is his decision. But you will not pay his way. That is out of the question."

"It is the least we can do for someone to guide a couple old cronies on a pilgrimage back to where they came from. Look, why don't you think about it. We have time. Do you have a passport, Denten?"

"No."

"Getting one takes a little time. We still have plenty."

For the next few days Denten and his parents did think about the proposal. Oscar assured his son that his absence would not drastically hinder work on the farm. During the winter not much happened. Denten thought about all those times when he dreamed about traveling to far off places or all those times he watched with envy those commercial jets, so tiny in the sky, filled with travelers venturing off to places they dreamed of.

Three days later Denten walked into Deluca's restaurant, approached Gilberto standing near the checkout counter and asked, "When do we go again?"

"We are ready." Gilberto exclaimed from the back seat of Oscar's SUV.

Since the day that Denten walked into the restaurant to accept the Deluca invitation, he had thought of little else than the thrill at last of flying to a foreign destination. Despite his interest in travel or, at least, the thought of travel, he really had done very little. Nor had the family. He had not previously thought about the fact that his family never did take a family vacation. Oscar and Grace had not even visited Margaret's home in California. Why travel had lacked importance in the Ballery family, Denten didn't know. He hadn't really thought about it.

Now he and the Delucas stood at the threshold of a great journey for all of them. Gilberto and Alda behaved almost like little kids as they had prepared for this trip, so excited about returning to the place they were born. Denten, too, experienced more excitement in his preparation than he could remember. Probably, he had't felt this excited since those days prior to his high school graduation.

The two hour drive to the Minneapolis/St. Paul airport brought them there in plenty time for check in and security clearance. Their itinerary called for a mid afternoon departure from Minneapolis to Chicago where they would board the direct flight to Fiumicino, Italy, a suburb of Rome and the location of Rome's international airport.

With growing anticipation, Denten waited for their departure, seeing in his mind those tiny commercial jets crossing the sky above their farm. Already he had served his role as an assistant for Gilberto and Alda, who found walking long distances painful, her life long commitment to both making and eating Italian food resulting in her distinct weight problem. Without difficulty, Denten guided the Delucas to their international departure gate.

Denten couldn't believe he actually sat in one of those commercial jets that he watched with such longing so many years ago. He could hardly believe that a plane as big as a 747 could actually get off the ground. But get off the ground it did, creating for Denten a sensation both thrilling and inspiring. While the giant aircraft reached for its cruising altitude, he sat back in his seat, closed his eyes, smiled, and thought, "My God, I'm flying!"

The three hour lay over in Chicago gave Denten another chance to guide Gilberto and Alda. The vastness of the O'Hare Airport perplexed them as Denten attempted to display confidence even though he obviously had never been there before. But again they found their gate in the international terminal to wait patiently for their all night flight to Rome, a nine hour journey.

Sleep proved elusive during the nine hours from Chicago to Rome. Perhaps Denten did doze for a short time. Most of the time he sat staring at the map displayed on the compartment wall depicting the flight's progress. He envied Gilberto and Alda, who, at least, appeared to have found enough comfort for sleep.

A glimmer of light alerted Denten to the rising sun, a specular sight viewed from over 36,000 feet. It also alerted him to the imminent ending to the nine hour flight. The ending occurred shortly after 7:30 a.m. Rome time. Waiting to walk off the plane, Denten ensured that the Delucas did not leave any personal items at their seats or in the overhead bin. A renewed sense of anxiety gripped him as he contemplated steps yet to be taken before they would head north out of Rome for their destination, Montecatini, Italy, a small city about 200 miles north of Rome and the home of Gilberto's cousin, where they would stay for most of their two week Italian adventure.

"I don't know how we could have gotten here without you, Denten." Alda commented from the backseat of their small rented car.

"You are a natural at this travel business." Gilberto affirmed. "You haven't traveled much, you said."

"No, I haven't. But thank you. Maybe you won't feel the same after I mess up on this long drive."

"I doubt that." Alda offered.

Collecting luggage and securing the rental car had produced no complications. Denten had acquired directions out of Rome and onto the major highway leading to Montecatini. Winding their way through the snarl of traffic around the airport and on toward the freeway, Denten had hardly the chance to realize exactly where he was. The roadway and buildings looked much like any city he had visited at home. Passing the Colosseum made no significant impact on Denten and his passengers, more attention devoted to where they were headed than the sights they passed. However, they did take special note of the Vatican as their route took them directly passed the massive center of the Catholic church.

The drive north to Montecatini impressed Denten and his passengers, the beauty of the country side, inspiring Gilberto to carry on an almost constant narrative about his early days in the rich wine country of Tuscany. Denten noted that freeway travel in Italy was little different from that he had experienced at home. Trucks dominated in Italy too.

By late afternoon the travelers entered the narrow road that would bring them to the home of Gilberto's cousins, Antero and Belina Costa. About a half hour out of Montecatini, the farm owned by Antero and Belina specialized in the production of wine and olive oil, products that had made the Tuscany area of Italy internationally famous. It was here that Denten and the Delucas would call home for the next two weeks.

Not unlike Gilberto, Antero was gregarious and animated, welcoming his guests with an effusive hospitality Denten found refreshing. Gilberto had informed him on the way that his cousin spoke perfect English, a relief for Denten, who knew for sure four Italian words: benvenudo, ciao, arrivederci, and vino. Belina, abiding by traditional Italian hospitality, had prepared a tantalizing lunch for the hungry travelers. Following the lunch, Belina directed them to two small bedrooms they could call home during their stay.

When Denten emerged from his bedroom, he returned to the kitchen where they had eaten lunch. Seated at the table talking with Gilberto and Alda was without question the most beautiful girl he was sure he had ever seen. Caught by surprise by her presence, he stood staring at her for longer than he knew was acceptable. But her magnetism was irresistible. Quickly, Antero came to his rescue.

"Denten, this is my niece, Anna Moretti. She's here helping around the farm for a few weeks. Anna, this is Denten here to learn something about life in Italy."

Anna rose from her chair only to confirm what Denten already had concluded. She was simply gorgeous with her black hair pulled back in a pony tail, full dark eye brows over eyes that sparkled in the reflected light of the kitchen. A radiant smile revealed gleaming white teeth framed by full lips. Denten caught his breath as she approached him with open arms. Denten discovered early that hugging was an essential greeting for Italians. Never had a hug stirred so much tingling sensation.

Antero explained that Anna had recently graduated from high school in Florence, the historic city only miles from their farm. Rather than plunge into college, she decided to spend some time with her uncle and aunt helping them with their wine and olive oil production. As Denten listened, he thought he would dearly love being a grape or olive in her hands.

"How about I take everyone on a little tour of the farm." Anna invited. "Since I do most of the work, I'm the best one to explain what it's all about." Anna's laughter involved her entire body, trim with a figure perfectly designed to capture attention, certainly Denten's attention.

As they walked outside to the buildings housing the production equipment, Anna explained that the Costa farm had been in the family for decades providing a comfortable living for the current owners. Featuring the production of both olive oil and wine, she noted that the farm prospered even though it encompassed a mere 30 acres, tiny by America's standards. Denten found the tour intriguing, never having visited a winery before. Even more intriguing was watching Anna. Vivacious and playful even when explaining the process for squeezing oil from an olive, she laughed often, gestured always and made touching a vital part of her communication. She simply overwhelmed Denten.

The next few days saw constant activity with tours led by Anna to Florence, according to her, the commercial and cultural center of the 13th Century. Gilberto and Alda did well in walking the narrow streets of historic Florence. Also included in their tours was Siena, the walled city and the impressive, medieval center of art and architecture. Anna performed brilliantly as their tour guide, Denten enjoying every minute of listening to and watching her explain the various historic sites they visited. Names like Dante, Donatello, Michelangelo, and Leonardo da Vinci came up frequently. Anna possessed a startling depth of understanding of her country's history. Finally, they had to visit Pisa with its leaning tower. Actually, the leaning tower was the only attraction in Pisa, a very small village also only miles from the farm.

The highlight of the trip for Gilberto and Alda, probably the main reason they made it, occurred at near the end of their stay. Antero and Belina hosted a party for a collection of the Deluca's relatives, friends and former neighbors. Never had Denten witnessed such exuberance, so much laughter, and so much wine. Throughout the two weeks, Denten had spent considerable time with Anna as she conducted Gilberto, Alda and him so expertly around the historic cities only miles from the farm. During those tours, they had spoken about their respective lives, noting the commonalities in their academic experiences. He found standing next to her, smelling her fragrance, the scent of her hair captivating. On a couple occasions as they walked around the historic cities, she had reached for his hand, grasping it firmly, looking into his eyes, her magnetic smile drawing him into a world of near fantasy. But beyond that nothing transpired between them. That changed on the night of the big party celebrating the return to Italy of Gilberto and Alda.

The final days of their stay troubled Denten. He had acquired a powerful feeling for Anna, not just a physical one but a deeper affection he had never before experienced in his relationship with girls. He wished to build on that feeling. However, he really didn't know if Anna shared his feelings. She had offered subtle hints during their time together. Still, he did not know if he had misinterpreted her response or if she truly wished to pursue a relationship with him.

The party had consumed most of the afternoon and stretched into the evening. Surrounded by people he didn't know, Denten stayed off to the side of the activity in the farm house, definitely large enough to accommodate more than twenty people.

As darkness settled over the farm, Anna approached Denten, took him by the hand and asked, "Do you want to go for a walk?"

Denten turned to look directly into those sparkling eyes, "Absolutely."

Hand in hand they walked out into the farm yard, the evening cool but the sky clear. They stopped next to a large bench encircling one of the few trees on the property that did not produce either olives or grapes.

Anna faced Denten, grasping both his hands. "I really have had a great time getting to know you. I take back all those thoughts I had about guys from America." Even in the dark her white teeth shined through her lips as her face lighted in a smile.

"Anna," Denten paused, not accustomed to talking seriously to a girl and not quite certain what to say. "Anna," he started again. "I've never met anyone quite like you." He shifted self-consciously from one foot to another. "I doubt I'm the first guy to tell you this, but you're beautiful."

Anna stepped toward Denten, reached up with both hands, pulling his face down to hers. She kissed him long and tenderly on the lips. He took her in his arms, pulling her tightly against his body. They kissed again, the contours of her marvelous body melting into his. Breathing heavily, they allowed the passion to grow, Denten's hands searching for access through her shirt. She made no attempt to stop him. Soon his hand gently caressed her breast. Their bodies pressed tightly together. Carefully, he guided her down on the bench where she leaned back inviting him to lie on top of her. Their bodies moved in unison. Denten reached down to release his belt and attempt to unsnap her jeans.

Suddenly her movement ceased. "Maybe we should stop." Anna whispered.

Denten relaxed. Looking down at Anna, he replied, "I suppose you're right."

He sat up reaching to fasten his belt. Anna moved next to him. With her arm around his neck, she reached up to kiss him on the cheek then on the lips. "I think I've found someone to love." She spoke softly but convincingly. "I don't know what will happen next. I just know that I'll always remember this moment."

"There's got to be a way. I love you too. I don't want to lose this thing we've started." Denten held her closely in his arms, her head resting on his chest.

"In two days we leave for home. Really tough to think that you will be here and I will be way over there across the ocean." Denten released his embrace.

"Denten, love is a powerful emotion. It can move mountains. Maybe it can keep us together."

"You must be right. You certainly were right about history stuff."

Rising from the bench, they both straightened their clothes and arm and arm, slowly walked back to the house where music and laughter filled the air.

Denten slept hardly at all his last night in Italy. The powerful emotion he experienced with Anna combined with the regret over leaving rendered sleep almost impossible. A morning knock on his bedroom door announced a delay in his departure. Gilberto had suffered a seizure during the night.

Chapter 8

Silence hung heavy in the car. Cayla stared straight ahead slouched in the passenger seat. Her mother drove on their way back to Winona and St. Mary's College. Neither had spoken for several minutes.

"Don't you feel good?" Alice Finch looked over at her daughter.

"I'm okay," Cayla replied in a voice barely audible.

"You just haven't seemed yourself lately." Her mom persisted.

Sitting up straighter, Cayla apologized, "I'm sorry. I guess it's just going back to school and facing that grind for the next four months."

"But you're doing so well." Her mom reassured.

Actually, Cayla's grades had fallen the previous semester. Normally, a near straight A student, she had faced increased distractions last semester, the agonizing memory of that fateful Saturday morning the major cause. Still she had told no one in all these years. Hardly a day passed when she didn't think about it. It wasn't getting any better.

"Christmas is an emotional time of the year," Cayla turned philosophical. "So much anticipation and finally so much regret as the season ends."

"Yes, I suppose you are right about that." Alice agreed. "But we have to move on. It's a new year with new challenges and opportunities." She also sounded a bit philosophical.

Silence again returned, only the sound of the wind rushing over the car breaking the silence. Cayla stretched out her seat belt in order to reposition herself. Turning toward her mother, she asked, "How did you and Dad meet?"

Her mom jerked her head to look over at her daughter. With a puzzled look on her face, she asked, "What on earth brought that up?"

Cayla smiled, "I don't know. I was just curious. You and Dad seem to have such a good relationship."

"Well, thank you. I guess we do most of the time. Two people don't live in perfect harmony, of course." Alice kept her eyes on the road as she explained.

"You read about so many problems people have trying to get along." A hint of sadness sounded in Cayla's voice. She thought about her own situation with boys earlier in her life and now men. In fact, she had dated little over the years, her latest date with Casey like so many others had apparently ended that relationship, too. She had not heard from him since that night.

"So much goes into a relationship, compromise, commitment, honesty, faithfulness, love. That's a lot to ask of two people. But it's worth the effort. At least it has been for us." Her mother affirmed.

"How did you meet?" Cayla persisted.

"Do you really want to know?" Alice asked.

"Yes, I do."

"It was at one of those Wisconsin county fairs. When we were young, they were a big deal."

"Why didn't we ever go to one?" Cayla asked.

"They're not the same any more." Alice paused before continuing. "Well, anyway, a bunch of us girls were standing near one of those game tents. You know, the ones where you throw a ball at a doll or something. You can win a big teddy bear." Though she refused to admit it, Alice savored those moments so many years ago.

"Two or three of us tried but failed to knock even one doll over. These guys stood off to the side watching, grinning. Suddenly, one walked up to ask if he could try for us. He'd even pay for it."

Cayla listened with an awakened interest, smiling as her mom seemed to relish telling the story.

"Well, what happened?" Cayla asked.

"The one who made the offer, eventually became your dad. He did win a big teddy bear. He gave it to me. The rest is history, as the saying goes." Alice looked over at Cayla. Mother and daughter shared a moment of understanding.

Cayla sat alone in her dorm room. She reflected upon her rather unusual conversation with her mom on the short drive from Riverside to Winona. She envied the relationship that developed from that time at the county fair when her mom met the man she would eventually marry. Cayla wondered if she would ever meet someone she could trust. She wondered if she could ever feel comfortable in intimacy with a man.

Her thoughts were interrupted by the arrival of her room mate, Andrea Palmer. Cayla and Andrea had fashioned a relationship of mutual respect during the two years they shared a dorm room. Friendly and considerate, Andrea made the perfect room mate in Cayla's mind. Always concerned about her room mate, Andrea, at the same time, didn't pry into Cayla's private life even though, at times, Cayla's mood tempted her to do so. This was one of those times.

"Did you have a good Christmas?" Andrea gave Cayla a big hug. Andrea was big on hugs.

"It was okay." Cayla answered quietly.

Andrea stepped back to look intently at Cayla. "Maybe, it's none of my business, but is something bothering you?"

Cayla glanced done at the floor before looking up at Andrea. Earlier in the day her mother had asked her basically the same thing. It really must show, she thought. "No, I don't think so." Cayla spoke without conviction. "Why do you ask?"

"Do you want to sit down?" Andrea motioned to the one lounge chair they shared in their small room. She moved back to sit in the desk chair.

"I don't know." Andrea continued. "I just feel sometimes there's something behind those sad eyes and the silence. You have such a beautiful smile. You need to do it more often."

With that comment, Cayla smiled. "Thank you for the compliment. And thank you for the concern." Cayla folded her hands in her lap, her eyes looking off into the corner of the room.

Recently, the memory of the horrible Saturday had surfaced more often. Visiting the bank and meeting face to face with Reed Howard hadn't helped much. For years the horror of that moment almost daily clawed at her emotions adversely affecting so much of her life. Would telling someone about the nightmare help? Cayla had asked herself that question hundreds of times over the years. Yet, she had told no one, not even her mom with whom she shared an admirable relationship. Of course, as a child, fear played a major role in her decision to tell no one. However, now she did not feel fear as much as a sense of guilt. As this recent Christmas break dragged on, she again entertained thoughts of just what she would do. She had to do something. The secret was making more of a difference in her life.

Cayla looked again at Andrea. She said nothing. Her body relaxed. She drew in a big breath. Slowly, she started. "A long time ago something terrible happened."

Andrea sat up attentively, leaning closer to her room mate. "To you?" Andrea asked, her voice rising in pitch.

"Yes, to me." Cayla answered with resolve.

Now she sat back in the lounge chair, closed her eyes momentarily and began, "It was on a beautiful Saturday morning. I was at church for choir practice. I was eight years old." Cayla described in raw detail the horror of what had happened to her following choir practice in the back seat of that car.

Through out Cayla's narrative she spoke firmly, almost defiantly, as if she was thrusting out all the agony she had tolerated for more than ten years. Andrea listened intently, her mouth dropping open in astonishment with Cayla's description.

As she finished telling her story, Cayla slumped in the chair, dropped her head into hands, and broke into sobs. Andrea immediately jumped up to comfort her friend. Folding her arms around the trembling Cayla, she whispered, "Let it come out, all of it."

For several minutes they embraced each other, Cayla clinging to her friend. Gradually, Cayla regained control of herself. A marvelous feeling of relief swept through her body. That she had actually told her secret amazed her. Andrea sat back on her knees.

"Do you know where this guy is now?" Andrea asked.

"Oh, yes, I do. He's still at the bank. Over the break I had to sign for a college loan. I met him face to face." Cayla wiped her eyes with a tissue.

"He's gotten away with this all these years." Andrea commented, shaking her head.

"He had the audacity to ask how I was doing." Cayla's voice dripped with contempt.

"Are you going to do anything about this guy?"

Cayla stood up from the lounge chair, walked over to the small frig on the floor in the closet. "Do you want a soda?" She asked.

"Sure."

Bringing back two sodas, Cayla handed one to Andrea. "What can I do after all this time? It's my word against his."

"To let this creep get away with what he did to you is not right, Cayla." Andrea now displayed some of the defiance displayed earlier by Cayla.

"Maybe someday some justice will be served. Right now will you promise me not to repeat what I've told you?" Cayla asked.

Andrea stood and moved to meet Cayla in the middle of the room. She gave Cayla another big hug. "Of course, I promise. Now, would you promise me something?"

Cayla stepped back. "What?"

Andrea fixed her eyes on Cayla. "Promise me that someday you will seek some justice."

Cayla again breathed deeply. With a voice calm but determined, she answered, "I promise."

Chapter 9

Italians possess no shortage of emotions nor means of expressing them. Gilberto's seizure created an avalanche of emotion, Belina frantic with concern that Gilberto would surely die within the hour. The commotion in the house aroused Denten from a restless sleep anticipating the long day of driving and an even longer night of travel. Getting up, he quickly dressed, fully expecting to complete packing in preparation for the drive back to Rome. Instead, he encountered two frantic ladies as they debated just what to do about Gilberto.

Antero responded with a bit more composure, calling the hospital in Montecatini, just a few minutes away. Gilberto sat in a kitchen chair, looking pale and tired but otherwise alert. The seizure had occurred earlier in the morning shortly after he arose from bed. He attempted to minimize his condition, insisting that he had simply gotten up too fast. His slipping back onto the bed where his body quivered uncontrollably shocked Alda, who ran into the kitchen yelling that Gilberto was having a heart attack.

With Denten's help, Antero managed to guide Gilberto to the car for the short ride to the Montecatini hospital. Small, but efficient with a reputation for professional treatment, the hospital admitted Gilberto immediately. Just over an hour later, a doctor came to the waiting room to explain that Gilberto suffered nothing serious, his problem perhaps related to too much wine, food and celebration. Nonetheless, the examination of a potential heart attack, which he did not suffer, revealed a partial arterial blockage. The doctor explained that correcting the blockage was essential but could wait until Gilberto's return home. He also suggested that he not travel for two-three days. He needed a chance to relax and regain his strength.

Having to delay their departure thrilled Denten. Two more days with Anna would suit him perfectly. However, the process of changing their flight required several agonizing steps including a verification from the doctor confirming that Gilberto should not travel. To Denten even all that could not alter the delight he felt in having two more days with Anna.

The night before, Denten and Anna had quietly escaped the tumult of the typical Italian celebration by sitting together on the porch which extended from the front of the Costa home. There they would avoid most of the activity taking place in the living room well within the interior of the house. The emotions that had dominated the evening for Denten and Anna now subsided as they contemplated the next day and the departure of Denten, Alda and Gilberto. The future for them stood as a question. However, they would always remember this night for the brief moments of splendor it offered.

When the three men returned from the hospital, of course, the ladies stood anxiously awaiting the prognosis. With audible sighs of relief they listened to the doctor's report as repeated by Antero. Anna stood silently in the background, a smile spreading across her face. For she, too, realized that the entire incident gave Denten and her a few more hours together.

The doctor had advised that Gilberto spend his time resting prior to his long anticipated journey home. What Anna and Denten would do or where they would do it mattered little. Doing it together did make all the difference. Together they traveled back to Florence to meet Anna's parents, Joseph and Emma Moretti. Anna had lived in Florence nearly all her life, her father a manager of a relatively large men's clothing store. Though Anna had taken Denten and the Delucas on a tour of Florence, her parents at the time had left town for a brief buying trip that had taken them to Rome.

Joseph and Emma greeted Denten graciously welcoming him into their home and into their daughter's life. Middle aged, Anna's parents retained trim bodies, much like many Italians Denten had seen during his two week stay and despite what he observed as an obsession for food. Joseph asked of Denten's life in America, his plans after college and his parents. Denten learned that Anna had enjoyed a wonderful high school career, graduating at the top of her class while excelling on the girls' soccer team, achievements she had failed to discuss with him. Possessing the best physical qualities of both, Anna obviously occupied a place of high esteem in the eyes of her parents. Playfully, she protested her father's praising her talents. Still, she, too, took pride in what she had accomplished in her young life. When Denten and Anna left after a light lunch, her parents wished Denten a safe trip and good luck to Gilberto, whose condition had assumed a part of the conversation.

Montecatini did not have the marvelous history of Florence or Siena or any number of other famous Italian, historical cities. It did have what people believed was medicinal water that could treat kidney and bladder ailments. For generations people from the immediate area as well as those from around the country came to Montecatini to drink the precious water. The next morning Anna led Denten to the famous water fountain contained within a huge building where people could savor the famous water in the comfort of spacious sitting rooms. With moderate anticipation Denten placed the drinking cup to his lips to sip the water. He held it in his mouth for a few seconds, then swallowed. Anna watched him with curiosity, knowing that nothing significant would happen, the benefits of the water, to her, likely all in the minds of those who believed it would help them.

Denten turned to look at Anna expecting some comment.

Her only comment was, "Well?"

"Well, what?" Denten responded.

"What do you think? Did it do anything?"

"I'm not thirsty anymore. I don't think I have any kidney problems." Denten reached for her hand.

"I'm just kidding. I don't know of anyone whose bladder problems this water has cured. But it sells."

These final hours together made possible precious moments of tender intimacy, moments that etched permanently indelible memories, such as a special smile, a light touch, a gentle embrace, or light kiss on the cheek. By the time Denten at last had to leave, he and Anna promised to stay in touch through email and cell phones. Standing before the rental car, Anna and Denten embraced one last time.

"Anna, I've had great time. Thank you." Denten squeezed her a bit tighter.

"Thank you for coming into my life. I know we met only days ago. But I love you, Denten. I don't want to lose what we've started."

Denten kissed her lightly on the mouth. "I love you, too. I never believed in love at first sight, at least until now." He stepped back with both hands grasping Anna's shoulders. Looking directly into those enchanting dark eyes, he said, "If we really want what we've started to last, we will find a way."

With that Denten climbed into the car, turned to look first at Gilberto and then at Alda sitting in the back seat, "Are we ready gang? Next stop Rome."

Anna stood on the driveway watching the car gradually vanish in the distance. Behind her Antero and Belina placed their hands on her shoulders. Anna turned to fall into Belina's arms, resting her head on her aunt's generous bosom. Tears trickled down the cheeks that helped make her face one of the most beautiful Denten had ever seen.

Chapter 10

March, in the Upper Midwest, serves as a month of transition from the harsh winter to the renewal that comes with spring. When Denten and his travel companions touched down at the Minneapolis/St. Paul International Airport, a bright sunshine with a temperature in the low 50's greeted them. The last leg of their flight from Chicago, of course, required less than an hour. Still all three of the travelers waited anxiously for the long descent and final touch down, bringing them home following their extended seventeen day stay in Italy.

Gilberto tolerated well the ten hour flight from Rome to Chicago. He likely suffered a bit more on the relatively short, by comparison, drive from Montecatini to Rome. Confined by his seat belt to a narrow car seat made him uncomfortable and restless. He had suffered no ill effects from his one seizure. The prospect of by-pass surgery bothered him, however. He had not faced any serious health problems during his more than eighty years. His unfamiliarity with medical procedures increased his apprehension about the surgery and his stay in the hospital.

Denten's mom and dad, as planned, met them at the airport, excited to hear about the trip and concerned about Gilberto's condition. The drive from Minneapolis to Riverside offered time to hear about the trip and learn of Gilberto's experience. Denten's parents brought them up to date with life in Riverside. Not much had happened in their absence except an increased anticipation for spring cultivation and planting.

One of the first priorities upon their return to Riverside was scheduling the by pass surgery at the Mayo Clinic in Rochester.

Gilberto found Denten's assistance indispensable in making the arrangements. Just three days following their return, Denten drove Gilberto and Alda to the Mayo Clinic where Gilberto underwent successful by-pass surgery. Following a two day stay in the hospital for observation, Gilberto returned home, again courtesy of Denten.

Their time together during and after the trip had established a close bond between Gilberto and Denten. Despite their vast age difference, they tended to agree on most issues. They did spend time together discussing a wide range of social and political issues. Upon his return to Riverside following his surgery, doctor's orders compelled Gilberto to a life of quiet relaxation, at least for a few weeks while his body adjusted to his new "pipes." Denten's occasional company made the prolonged periods of inactivity much more tolerable.

On top of preparations for the approaching spring planting season and his devotion to Gilberto, Denten frequently thought of Anna. Quiet moments when he sat watching TV or just prior to going to sleep, he could almost feel her warm, tender skin, smell her minty breath or her sweet fragrance. Anna had plunged into his life with far greater impact than any other girl he'd ever met. He tried to analyze exactly what made her so different from other girls he knew and had dated. The answer eluded him. But that didn't alter the rich memories he savored of this wonderful young lady who lived so far away. Just what they would do about that remained a question.

Perhaps his busy schedule, his increased responsibility around the farm, his protective sense for his father, or the new people in his life distracted him. Whatever the reason, that disturbing dream occurred less frequently. Still it did occur. When it did, Denten addressed more seriously the question of sharing this traumatic experience with someone. At one time fear prevented his doing so. Now, he didn't really feel fear anymore. It was almost as if the event demanded secrecy, his private torment.

Since meeting her, Denten had thought, what if the other person in the back seat that Saturday morning so many years ago had been Anna? That image generated, not fear, but an intense anger considering how the sinister person with the dark eyes had affected his life to say nothing of the life of the other person in the back seat.

And just what if Anna had been that person? He shuddered at such thoughts and fought to suppress them. Would the shocking memory of that day ever fade? Denten had no answer. However, recent events did tend to dull that memory. Maybe talking about it with someone would help.

A phone call from Montana informed Denten and his parents that Nancy had slipped on ice, wrenching her back and leaving her in some pain. Though Nancy did not even suggest it, her mom decided that they would drive to Montana to give her daughter a bit of assistance and a little moral support. Oscar's arm prevented him from driving long distances. Consequently, Denten again assumed a new responsibility. He would drive his parents to Montana even though he knew about the unpredictability of March weather. Besides, neither Denten nor his parents had visited either one of his sisters. His parents simply had not traveled much. Now both of them, particularly Grace, decided that they must make the trip regardless of the vagaries of March weather.

Denten consulted an atlas to determine just which route they should take. Nancy had suggested a route. Denten wished to confirm it. That route would take them north on I-29 to Fargo/Moorhead, then west all the way to Miles City on I-94, a drive of approximately ten hours. Nancy lived on a ranch east of Miles City.

The family quickly prepared for the long drive, Denten listening attentively to weather predictions along their selected route. A hint of potential bad weather failed to deter their departure early on an usually mild March morning.

"Dad, do you want to drive for a while?" Denten realized his dad quietly rebelled against the restrictions imposed by his handicap.

"No, I don't think so. Maybe later. We've got a long way to go."

With Grace secure in the back seat of their SUV and Oscar in front with Denten, the family embarked on the day long journey to Montana. On the way they talked about a wide range of topics, the scenery along their route an expanse of decaying snow with occasional patches of black as the late winter sun struggled to melt the accumulated snow cover. Anna's name came up. Of course,

Denten had told his parents about his new Italian friend, his mom pressing him for details which he willingly provided. Now, though, the conversation centered on his intentions in the relationship.

"What are you going to do about her?" His mom asked.

Denten paused, that familiar image of Anna emerging in his mind. "I don't know. We do exchange emails a lot."

Oscar had not displayed much interest in joining the conversation. However, he looked over at his son. "Is she going to college?" he asked.

"Yes, she is. I guess the University of Florence. She doesn't live far from the campus." Denten remembered the day when they visited Anna's parents and the walk they took to the campus.

A mother's deep concern colored Grace's voice. "Can a relationship survive the distance?"

"I don't know, mom. I hope so. She has hinted at coming to Minnesota this summer. She is a distant relative of Gilberto. She could stay with them." The thought of her visiting in the summer gave Denten's voice a discernible lift.

"We'll be eager to meet her." His parents spoke in unison.

They reached Fargo/Moorhead without incident. Clear markings made access to I-94 West easy. A sign outside Fargo read "Bismarck 198." Silence settled over the car as miles and miles of flat white land spread out before them. In the distance Denten could see clouds gathering on the horizon. He switched on the radio to secure any late weather news. Nothing suggested any thing major, just a remote possibility of a few snow showers around the Bismarck area. Toward that North Dakota city they headed, driving on a flat, straight, and dry freeway.

A few miles east of Bismarck, they encountered a fine mist. In just a few miles it turned to light, then heavy snow. Driving around Bismarck brought them to portions of the freeway turned slippery from the initial mist, followed by drizzle, then snow. Denten slowed to under forty miles per hour. Others on the sparsely traveled freeway did the same. No more than twenty-five miles west of Bismarck, a car headed east on the freeway swerved then plunged through the median, heading dangerously in the direction of Ballery's car.

Denten tensed, closely watching the car plunge out of control into the median. As the car plowed through the median, Denten feared it would travel right through the median and unto their west bound lanes. Both his parents stared in disbelief as the car bounced over and through the snow filled median.

Not sure where the car would end up, Denten applied his brakes, only to discover the treachery of the snow packed freeway surface. The Ballery car began skidding sideways, Denten frantically struggling to gain control. Suddenly, their car careened off the road and into the right side ditch. The car that had started the moment of crisis had thankfully stopped before reaching the west bound lanes.

Denten sat stunned, the car buried in three-four feet of snow. Gaining control of his senses, he immediately turned to check on his parents.

"Everybody okay?" he asked in a voice barely audible.

"I'm fine." Answered his mom.

"Me, too." His dad echoed.

They all looked around to determine how many other cars were involved. They saw just the one that had started the whole sequence.

Denten attempted to step out of the car. The deep snow made difficult opening the door. Finally he did succeed in opening his door. Getting out, he quickly sunk into snow up to his knees.

"You two stay in the car." He advised. "Mom, give me your cell phone."

From a brief examination of their predicament, Denten knew he could never drive the car out of the shallow ditch without help. He dialed 911, knowing of no other number to call at the moment. A dispatcher assured him that a tow truck would reach him from the small town of Hebron about fifteen miles away. Next he called his sister to inform her of their delay. He would call her again when the car once again stood on the pavement rather than buried in snow up to the fenders.

In about one half hour, a tow truck did arrive to extricate their car from the ditch. A brief inspection by the tow truck driver determined that the car had suffered no damage. With wide smiles and abundant relief, the Ballerys thanked the tow truck driver. Weather conditions had improved, the report, nonetheless, still calling for snow flurries.

After nearly fourteen hours on the road, and a few off the road, Denten and his parents arrived at the home of their sister and daughter thankful for the end to their long journey and thankful nothing serious happened on the freeway near Hebron, North Dakota.

In the warmth of Nancy and her husband's ranch home, Denten and his mom and dad relaxed, telling about their lucky escape from a potentially serious accident. Actually, Nancy's back had improved, thanks to therapy and medication. Two year old grandson, Timothy Oscar, delighted in sitting on grandpa's lap with intense interest in grandpa's funny arm.

Over the next three days, Collier, Nancy's husband, showed Denten and Oscar his large operation including a huge herd of beef cattle and acres of land under cultivation, ready for spring seeding. Both Oscar and Denten could appreciate the challenge that those acres posed as they talked of their own acreage at home.

Witnessing their daughter's obvious happiness made Oscar and Grace pleased that they had made the trip. However, the four days passed very quickly and soon found Denten and his parents preparing for another long ride home, a ride they hoped would not bring them so close to tragedy. Holding Timothy, Collier and Nancy stood outside in the brisk morning air to bid goodbye to their guests, promising that they would all get together again probably sometime in the summer. After all, only a ten hour drive, virtually all on freeways, separated them.

Chapter 11

In the quiet of his small bedroom, Denten studied the computer screen, savoring each word of the email from Anna. Since his return from Italy, these email messages served to enliven Denten's life, reminding him of the precious moments in Anna's arms. Almost daily he received emails from Anna that gave him assurance that she felt about him the way he felt about her. Still pursuing a relationship separated by thousands of miles posed a challenge for both of them. So far the emails had satisfied their need for contact. How long they would offer that satisfaction Denten had not even contemplated.

His return home at the conclusion of the first semester had seen Denten busily engaged in a variety of activities and responsibilities. Taking care of his dad, and by extension his mom, consumed much of Denten's time. His dad's arm had healed well; however, it afforded him only minimal use. For someone who needed to drive farm machinery this posed a serious handicap. As spring approached bringing planting season, Oscar's anxiety increased, the urge to get back to work making him restless and mildly irritable. Denten and his mom reminded his dad that he would not work the fields as he had in the past. What he could do and what he couldn't do only time could tell. They would all have to confront the reality of his handicap. Oscar, for the time being, accepted that. Nonetheless, it didn't reduce his restless movements around the house.

Of course, the trip to Italy and the near disastrous drive to Montana accounted for time filled with excitement. Both trips were rewarding in various ways. Meeting Anna Moretti surpassed, in sheer delight, most other events in Denten's life. He found the thoughts of her endlessly fascinating, the memory of those tender moments in Italy nearly tangible. The only distraction to those thoughts occurred when Denten considered how long their distant relationship could survive. He dismissed those thoughts quickly.

Denten benefitted from the trips in another way. They fueled his persistent interest in travel even though until recently he had done very little of it. Even now, years later, he could see those commercial airlines flying high above Riverside often leaving a white contrail in their wake. Especially, the trip to Italy intensified his fascination with travel, particularly travel by air.

His relationship with Gilbert and Alda had grown into a true friendship. In addition to the trip to Italy, Denten's role in Gilberto's surgery and subsequent recovery increased their contact and fostered their friendship. At least on a weekly basis, Denten would stop by the restaurant to check up on Gilberto, making sure he abided by the precautions imposed by his doctor. His by pass surgery had gone well. He just needed to recognize that it did impose restrictions. Gilberto's life did not include much physical strain; therefore, abiding by a more limited life style did not prove a burden to either him or Alda.

On a recent visit to the restaurant, Denten found Gilberto unusually glum, not characteristic of this normally jovial man. Seated across the table from Denten, Gilberto gazed down as he stirred his cup of coffee.

"Something bothering you today?" Denten asked concerned about this friend.

Looking up at Denten, Gilberto apologized, "I'm sorry. It's not your problem."

"What's not my problem?" Denten leaned in closer to the table.

Gilberto hesitated. "Look, son, I don't want to bother you. You've done so much for us already."

Denten sat up straighter. "Come on, what's happening. You've got my attention. Let's hear it."

Again Gilberto paused, took a sip of coffee, and set the cup back on the table. "Remember that night last winter when we sat here and talked about traveling to Italy?"

"Of course, I do." Denten replied.

"I told your dad that we had delayed our trip to Italy because of a conflict with the bank."

"The bank here in Riverside?" Denten tensed whenever that subject came up.

"Yes. I doubt you remember the conversation. But the problem results from a decision Alda and I made months ago to do a little remodeling in this place. We went to the bank and talked to Reed Howard about a loan." Gilberto explained in a quiet monotone.

The mere mention of Reed Howard alarmed Denten, who even in the absence of concrete evidence strongly suspected that he was in the back seat of that car. The image of those dark eyes under dark eye brows was firmly etched in his memory. As he listened to Gilberto's explanation, Denten's mind drifted to that Saturday. If the eyes he saw in that back door window belonged to Reed Howard, did he recognize Denten? Did he know to this day that the boy on the bike was Denten? Would he still maybe do something about it? Denten seriously doubted he would, but the mystery of the whole horrible incident lay like a rock in the background of his memory. Though the nighttime replays of the scene in the park had declined, they still happened. And how long would they continue to happen? What did Denten have to do to wash this from his memory?

Gilberto told of the sessions with Reed Howard after Gilberto and Alda had missed two mortgage payments. The late fall and winter had seen, for some reason, a drop in patronage of the restaurant, adversely affecting cash flow. Always good, reliable customers of the bank, the Delucas simply assumed that missing a couple payments wouldn't cause any problem. Well, according to Reed Howard, they were delinquent, and he insisted on payment or he would initiate foreclosure proceedings.

The whole story shocked Denten, who though he so far in his life had not secured a mortgage of any kind, certainly his dad had. For Denten, disbelieve followed the shock. Just how could this guy treat good people like the Delucas with such harsh disregard?

"Since the surgery we have caught up on the missed payments," Gilberto announced with a smile. "But just yesterday Reed informed us that we still owed him $300.00 in late fees. I don't understand that guy." Gilberto sat back in his chair and crossed his arms over his chest.

Denten shook his head. "Boy, I don't either. It just doesn't make any sense. What are friends for?"

"He's not much of a friend. Gilberto acknowledged. "We'll pay the $300.00. It's just that I don't do business that way. We won't do business with him again either."

"I don't blame you. I guess when it comes to that time for me, I think I'll look for another bank." Denten affirmed, fully aware that for other more drastic reasons he would never do business at that bank.

Gilberto stood up. "I think I've wasted enough of your time for one day. But thank you for listening."

"That's what friends are for. By the way how is that new, what do you call it, pipe?"

Gilberto chuckled like only he could. "It's fine. Thank you again for all you did during that kind of scary time." Gilberto stepped toward Denten giving him a gentle pat on the back.

Denten smiled, "I enjoyed it."

As Gilberto accompanied Denten to the door, he put his arm around his shoulder. In a nearly conspiratorial voice, he asked, "Say how are things with Anna?"

With an even bigger smile, Denten replied, "Just wonderful. We are in touch often by email."

"That's good. She's a sweet young lady."

"I'll go along with that." Denten agreed as their hand shake said goodbye.

Denten squinted into the afternoon sun. Already it had climbed much higher in the sky than just a few weeks ago. On this day the warmth of the sun, the water flowing in the small streams along the road to Mankato and the hint of green over the trees gave evidence of the arrival of spring. It also signaled the hours of work Denten and his father faced. The preparation for planting and the planting of nearly four hundred acres represented a daunting task. Considering the hours and days of hard work ahead, Denten thought that maybe going to college wasn't all that bad.

On this day he drove to Mankato to prepare for his return at the beginning of the fall semester. Meeting with his academic advisor would acquaint him with what he had to do to ensure graduating the next spring. Contact with the college had set a meeting with an advisor on this warm spring afternoon.

The meeting with the advisor told Denten nothing that he didn't already suspect. He simply had to improve his grades to a minimum 2.5 average out of a 4.0 system, not a complicated expectation. The complication, perhaps, was in Denten's dubious commitment to studying harder. He really didn't have a choice if he wished to graduate. While there, Denten completed the registration for the fall semester ensuring that he enrolled in courses fulfilling requirements for a degree in business administration. Thanking the advisor for his time and his assistance, Denten stood up, shook the advisor's hand and left the office, content with his meeting and eager to return to the academic world.

Stepping out of the advisor's office, Denten faced a large bulletin board covered with a wide variety of announcements and advertising. Located in one corner of the board a flyer caught Denten's eye. Large print across the top read, "Do you like to travel? We can use you." Denten paused to read the flyer representing a travel company in Mankato called Travel Incorporated. Attached to the bottom of the flyer a pad of business cards made easy remembering the name and number of the company. Denten took one of the cards. Maybe this offered something for him. He'd certainly keep the card for future reference. The drive home found Denten more optimistic regarding his future than in recent months.

Serious work on the farm began just days after Denten's drive to Mankato. Tilling the soil before seeding required endless hours of monotony riding a huge tractor pulling an even bigger cultivator which awakened the dark soil from its long winter rest. Like plowing in the fall, this spring cultivation allowed for hours of day dreaming warped around times of serious attention to the work of the cultivator and the operation of the tractor. During those times when he needed simply to steer the tractor in a straight line, Denten could think of only two subjects, his impending return to college and, of course, his future with Anna Moretti.

During one of his brief reveries, Denten was yanked back to reality by a strange grinding sound from the cultivator the tractor lugged. A quick inspection revealed that he needed to drive to the farm machinery dealer in town for a wheel bearing, a small part but an essential one for the operation of the cultivator.

Checking on his dad, who found that he could handle the smaller tractor, to let him know of his mission, Denten drove to the machinery dealership on the edge of Riverside. Entering the expansive show room and parts department, he walked to the counter where two clerks waited to secure what he needed. Without hesitation they acknowledged having the bearing Denten needed and quickly found it among the rows of shelving housing the hundreds of parts required to keep the farm machinery running.

Turning around to leave, Denten nearly bumped into Cayla Finch. They both stopped abruptly. Denten apologized for not watching more closely. At first he did not recognize her until she said, "Hi, Denten."

With a look of surprise on his face, Denten responded, "Cayla Finch, right?"

"That's right." A smile spread across Cayla's face revealing a perfect set of shiny white teeth.

"What are you doing here?" Denten asked, obviously perplexed by her presence in a machinery dealership.

"My dad sells this stuff. He needed someone to help with paper work. I got the nod." Cayla stood facing Denten.

"I guess I timed this pretty well. It's good to see you again." Denten found looking at Cayla a pleasure. Her light brown hair hanging to her shoulders, her bright smile and her eye brows which bounced to add charm when she spoke combined to add to her appeal. He really hadn't noticed her that closely when they first met in the Riverside Bar.

"Yes, it's good to see you. Have you returned to school?" she asked.

"No. But I will in this fall. How about you?" Denten stood facing Cayla noting just how pretty she was.

"Yes, I'm back, home right now just for a couple days. In fact I'm going to summer school with the hope of finishing next spring. I'm thinking of going on to law school if I get accepted someplace." Cayla, too, found Denten much more appealing than she remembered from their earlier meeting.

"That's great. A lawyer. Maybe we can celebrate our graduation. I intend to finish next spring too," Denten expressed with a hint of pride.

"Hey, you have a date," Cayla laughed. "Should we meet here or in the bar?"

"If all works out, we probably could find something better." Denten offered.

"It's good to see you again." Cayla expressed with conviction.

"For sure. Handle that paperwork. I need to fix a wheel bearing. Maybe we can get together sometime before graduation." Denten smiled, walking toward the exit. As he looked back before reaching for the door, Cayla raised her arm in a delicate wave goodbye.

Chapter 12

Reed Howard leaned back in his plush executive chair. At last he could relax at home in his own private refuge. The Christmas season, the demands of customers, mostly farmers seeking loans for the approaching planting season, and his urgent need for escape into his own world of sexual delight combined to make these moments of quiet solitude so imperative. The bodies of young girls remained Reed's passion even after all these years. More often than he cared to contemplate, his mind produced the image of a squirming Cayla Finch as she struggled to protect herself. But what a marvelous image of a beautiful young girl, a young girl who had developed into a gorgeous young lady. Reed admired young women but they failed to excite him as did young innocent girls.

Since that Saturday morning so many years ago, Reed had exercised great restraint in controlling his sexual urges. So far he had suffered no personal or professional repercussions from that moment of recklessness. After all, living in a small town, where news traveled very fast, imposed restrictions on behavior. News in a small town. His various positions of importance in the community, in addition to his presidency of the bank, made him a bold target for scandal. As a result he fed his desires primarily through his extensive collection of child pornography.

At home he could enjoy his collection in his special den-his refuge-one to which no one received admission except under very close supervision. Over the years Reed's family had respected his desire for privacy in this private room. Nonetheless, he took special precautions to store his prized collection. A few years ago he even limited his moments of "relaxation" at the bank. Stroking his passion at the bank carried with it too much risk. As a result, the chance to venture into his private world at home assumed even more significance.

This past winter and early spring had produced a rush of customers seeking financing for one project or another. Many of Reed's customers worked the huge farms that surrounded Riverside. The impending planting season brought many of them into the bank for loans to purchase seed and fertilizer. Last fall's abundant harvest had reduced the requests for financing. Still, the line of "beggars," the epithet Reed reserved for his own private musing to describe his farm customers, stretched from one week to the next. Dealing with his customers was his job. Without customers Reed would have no bank. Still, at times when paper work threatened to cover his desk, he contemplated why with all the money most farmers earned, they persisted in requesting help from the bank.

Reed possessed little sympathy for customers delinquent in making their payments. With the increase in loans came the increase in potential delinquency. Diligence had always guided Reed in the conduct of his finances.

He expected nothing less from his customers. After all, he did them an enormous favor in smoothing their finances from one season to the next.

Reed turned in his chair and shook his head as if to cleanse his mind of thoughts about his customers. Turning back to face his desk, he turned on his lap top. His pulse quickened as the images appeared on the small screen. How many times had he viewed pictures of delicious young bodies? Whenever he did gave him a sexual high with which nothing else could compare. On occasion he had questioned why these young things were so irresistible to him. However, he could never find the answer. Furthermore, to explain why mattered little. Satisfying the thirst mattered enormously.

As he studied the screen in front of him, his mind traveled back all those years to the wonderful little Cayla Finch. Of all the young girls who had paraded through his imagination she aroused him most. The rich memory of that time drew Reed's attention away from the computer. He leaned back on his chair, staring blankly at the shelves above his desk. For the past several weeks seeing Cayla and Denten Ballery together deeply disturbed him.

On that afternoon, the same one which brought Cayla into the bank, Reed later saw Cayla and Denten emerge from the Riverside Bar. The sight of them together ignited another image from that Saturday morning in the Riverside park. The boy on the bike. Reed saw the boy on the bike. Always, he questioned whether the boy saw him. Over the years Reed heard nothing from anyone about that moment when he definitely let down his guard. Though he saw the boy on the bike, Reed never learned, definitely, the boy's identity. Suspicion swirled around his mind whenever he saw or heard about Denten Ballery. Not often did this happen, but it did happen on occasion. Only infrequent customers of the bank, Reed did not know the Ballery family very well. He did know about them. He'd heard about the accident last fall. He knew that Denten sacrificed his college education to help his dad. But whether Denten was the young boy on the bike deeply puzzled Reed. The few times he saw Denten, Reed thought he could detect a similarity between the face he saw that Saturday morning and face he now saw.

Observing Cayla and Denten together only increased his suspicion. If they had established a relationship, might they not talk about what had happened over ten years ago? Would the two of them have the courage to expose him. The thought of that exposure frightened and incensed him. Apparently, Cayla had accepted his threat made years ago. He'd faced no repercussions. He just did not know about Denten.

Reed pondered what he should do, if anything. Perhaps he should leave things alone. His life and professional career found him a respected member of the community. He could not sacrifice that. Nor could anyone else sacrifice it for him. A resolve stirred in his mind. The more he thought about the consequences he could suffer, the more that resolve expanded into a call to action. He again reminded himself that after more than ten years nothing had happened to jeopardize his standing in the community. Why, he wondered, did he now feel this compulsion to act? Seeing Denten and Cayla together offered part of the answer.

Reed reached into his desk drawer for a plain sheet of paper, nothing that would identify him. Taking up his pen, he sat for several minutes contemplating what he should write, something that would prevent Denten's disclosure. If Denten was not the boy on the bike, what difference would an anonymous threat make? Releasing a long breath, Reed bent in toward the desk to print in large letters, "I know who you are."

Reed sat back considering what he had just written. He picked up the paper, studying it again. He lay the paper back on the desk, folded it neatly, and placed it in an envelope. Staring at the blank envelope, Reed debated about the address. He didn't know the Ballery address, but he could find out. However, he thought, perhaps, placing the note in the mail was not a good idea.

Time had passed swiftly during this session in Reed's private world. Already darkness sheltered those who had nefarious errands to run. Reed announced to his wife that he had to make a quick stop at the bank. She had grown accustomed to Reed sequestered in his den. To her, Reed did his most productive thinking by himself in that private room. Never had she questioned exactly what else he did in that room.

Guilt tinged with apprehension accompanied him as he drove out of town toward the Ballery farm. Never had he ventured out in the dark in search of a rural mail box. He knew only generally where the Ballerys lived. However, his many years in the Riverside area made him confident that when he saw the farm, he would recognize it. While he drove the narrow country roads, his mission dominated his attention, dismissing all concerns for the logistics of the mission. Stuffing terse, threatening notes in rural mailboxes was not something Reed Howard usually did.

Reed slowed the car as he recognized the Ballery farm yard with its high storage bins. The mail box he spotted across the road and a few yards beyond the driveway. Looking to see if he could detect lights in the Ballery home, Reed slowed to a stop by the mail box. Without another thought about what his mission would accomplish, he leaned across the front seat, reached out to open the mail box, and dropped the note inside. Sliding back behind the wheel, he glanced again at the Ballery house. Nothing had changed. Reed drove home, the guilt and the apprehension clinging like a bad dream.

Chapter 13

In the bright, late afternoon sun, Anna trudged toward the house. Her day began at just after sunrise. Her job for today: tending the two huge wine vats from which would eventually emerge that delicious wine produced by her uncles's winery, located just miles from Montecatini, Italy.

For nearly a year Anna had stayed with Antero and Belina Costa, her uncle and aunt, helping with the production of the two products for which her uncle's farm was noted: fine wine and virgin olive oil. Graduation from one of Florence, Italy's, high schools over a year ago found Anna undecided about her future. A better than average student, graduating near the top of her high school class, she was reluctant to plunge into college without some idea of just what she wished to do with her life.

Money did not pose a problem for Anna. Her father occupied an important position in one of Florence's major clothing stores. Still, a practical strain Anna inherited from her mother prevented her from making rash decisions, particularly those that had anything to do with money. Eventually, she would enroll in college, likely the University of Florence, which carried a heavy price tag. Consequently, rather than seek a part time job in or around Florence, she accepted the invitation from her aunt and uncle to spend time with them helping around their olive and wine operation which was about a two hour drive from her home in Florence.

What at first Anna found fascinating about life on the farm, gradually became tiring and stressful. Especially during the harvest, days stretched endlessly as grapes and olives demanded picking when they were ready. They waited for no one. Anna's role in the entire operation included a variety of jobs, all under the close supervision of Antero, who found her help indispensable.

Now Anna looked with some anticipation at a conclusion to her escape to the farm. In weeks she would embark on her college career, her application accepted for admission to the University of Florence. She looked forward to the change in her life from that of physical labor to one of mental challenge. In just days she would return to Florence where she would have the chance to register for fall semester classes.

During her months on her uncle's farm, Anna met with several new experiences, most of them having to do with production of wine and olive oil. However, the one experience that surpassed all others happened in late February with the arrival from America of Alda and Gilberto Deluca and their young companion, Denten Ballery. The few precious days she and Denten spent together occupied a prominent place in her memory. Each day little things that she did around the farm reminded her of the days when she showed Denten just what happened in a winery or in the production of olive oil. In the weeks since Denten's departure, she had maintained mostly email contact with him. On occasion they communicated by cell phone. However, again her innate frugality dictated an infrequent use of her cell phone for international calls.

The immediate intensity of their relationship time had tempered just a little. Nonetheless, never had Anna felt about a guy the way she felt about Denten. His kindness, his unassuming behavior, his casual handsomeness, his smiling sense of humor all remained vivid in her mind. Amazing to her was the fact that they knew so little about each other yet found such a profound mutual attraction. Of course, they had spent hours talking about their respective lives when he visited so many weeks ago. Those conversations had only touched on the more obvious aspects of their lives. Since then their almost daily emails had probed a little deeper into hopes and dreams for the future with reminders of their love.

The ease with which they talked about love, at times, bothered Anna. Both young adults, she nineteen and Denten twenty-one, neither had previously experienced this thing called love, at least not the depth of love they professed. Anna, at times, questioned the strength of love that had emerged so quickly. However, she could not deny the feeling that she had for Denten when she last saw him, a feeling that had changed little over the months since his return to America.

This would be Anna's last long day on the farm, at least for a few days. In the morning she would return to Florence to register for fall term classes at the University of Florence. After that she intended to spend some time with her parents, whom she had not seen very much during her time making wine and olive oil.

Dressed in white shorts and a pale blue T type top that accentuated her trim figure and richly tanned skin, Anna stepped out of the long line in an attempt to judge just how far she was from the desk where she could discuss class registration with a college counselor. An early morning drive to Florence gave Anna time to greet her parents and to prepare for the registration process, a process she previously had not confronted. Not knowing what to expect in terms of time, she had arrived early for the 11:00 a.m. registration only to find out that so had dozens of other prospective students. Already, for half an hour she had stood in line growing a little more impatient with the sluggish movement.

In addition, she more than once felt eyes looking at her. Considering her arresting appearance, Anna was accustomed to eyes following her. This time those eyes belonged to a man standing off to one side of the auditorium where the registration process took place. Each of her quick glances found him looking at her. His persistent stare produced a tiny chill down her back. Maybe it was his appearance that troubled her. His rumpled suit, his large horned rimmed glasses, his comb over hair, his round shape all added to the suspicion generated by his incessant eye contact.

Making an effort to ignore his stares, Anna studied the folder containing the course descriptions of her choices. Though she had studied the descriptions in great detail, she had to do something to distract her attention from this man's glaring eyes. As the line inched closer to the registration counter, the man simply stood off to the side, hands clasped behind his back, occasionally shifting from one foot to the other. His presence Anna failed to understand. Why would the college permit someone with possible ulterior intentions into this auditorium filled with young college students? Thinking that the college certainly would not endanger the security of any of its students calmed Anna's concern as she, at last, approached the registration table.

After a wait in line for nearly an hour, Anna completed the course registration in minutes. She thought of inquiring about that man off to the side but decided she didn't wish to display paranoia on her first encounter with school officials. Anna gathered her papers outlining her class schedule and turned to seek the quickest way out of the auditorium. As she headed to the closest exit, the man stepped toward her. She walked faster in an attempt to avoid contact with him.

"Excuse me, miss. Can I have a word with you?"

Anna paused, looking around for anyone who could help her if she needed help. The man approached her. Anna stopped, stiffened, and waited to hear what this guy had to say. With people milling around in the auditorium she felt nothing serious could happen.

Standing now directly in front of her, the man smiled revealing prominent teeth gray from neglect. "Pardon me. My name is Nino Conti. I'm sorry to intrude but could I talk with you for a moment?"

Anna stood silent, not knowing what to make of this intrusion, and he was right. It was an intrusion. Looking at him standing close, she felt a revulsion that prevented her from uttering a sound.

Nino detected Anna's obvious reaction to his presence. "Please, let me explain. Could I?"

Anna just nodded her head. As long as they stood in the auditorium, she felt safe. She just wanted to get this over.

Reaching into his suit coat pocket, Nino secured a business card which he handed to Anna. "I represent the Alpha Modeling Agency with offices here in Florence and in Los Angeles."

Anna backed away, obviously suspicious of his intentions.

Sensing her resistance to his proximity, Nino echoed his apology. "Forgive me if I offend you. The college does give us permission to talk with prospective candidates for our agency."

Anna's shoulders slumped as the brief explanation reduced some of the tension.

Picking up on this hint of receptivity, Nino continued. "You appear to have great potential. We would like to talk to you about that potential."

Anna looked away, considering what Nino had just told her. She had heard of modeling contracts offered by illegitimate agencies which exploited young women. Without saying anything, Anna simply shook her head and turned to walk away.

"Please, miss. Take the card. Check us out. If you don't approve, fine. But give it a chance. You are a beautiful woman."

Anna paused again, thinking that if the college had given this guy permission to do what he did, maybe it was legitimate. Maybe she should, at least, try it. Why not take advantage of her talent, even if it was only physical.

With some hesitation, she reached out her hand to accept the business card. She still said nothing. Stuffing the card into her pocket, she turned toward the exit, leaving Mr. Conti standing alone, smiling as he watched her walk away.

"How in the world do these guys get permission to prey on young college students?"

"Come on, Dad, give me a break. I'm old enough to take care of myself." Anna sat across the dinner table from her dad as they discussed Anna's encounter with the model agency rep.

"I know you can, honey, but does the college approve of this?" Joseph Morretti moved his chair back from the table folding his arms across his chest.

"That's what the guy said. Besides, college staff saw him standing there. They didn't say anything to him." Anna looked directly at her dad, doubt and skepticism evident in the tone of her voice.

"What if the guy is legitimate?" Joseph spoke softly but firmly. "Have you really considered the life of a model?"

"No."

"Do you really think you would like that kind of life?"

"Dad, I've never really thought about it. Some models make big bucks, I guess." Anna leaned back in her chair, folding her hands in her lap.

"I suppose some do. But what about the hundreds who don't?" Joseph asked without really expecting an answer. "What about your education?"

Anna sat up straighter. "Dad, I'm not going to sacrifice my education. You know me better than that."

"Yea, I know. You wouldn't do that. It's just that sometimes these offers look very tempting to young people."

Silence drifted over the table as Anna's mother, Emma, entered the dining room.

"Why so quiet? She asked. "Were you talking about me again?" Emma sat at the end of the table, her comment eliciting a smile from all.

"No, we're just talking about this business card from the modeling agency." Joseph shoved the card closer to his wife.

"What have you decided?" Emma had previously expressed concern over the invitation offered by Mr. Conti. However, she respected her daughter's judgement, a bit more confident in that judgement than her husband.

Anna, looking directly at her mom, admitted that they had reached no conclusion.

"Do we really know what kind of agency this ah, what it is called?" Emma reached for the business card. "This Alpha Modeling Agency is?"

Anna looked at her father, who only stared back at his daughter.

"Well, do you know anything about it?" Emma persisted.

Anna slumped in her chair. "I guess not."

"Then why don't you find out." Her mom urged. Again she grabbed the business card. "Here, the phone number is right here. Call them."

Emma sat looking at first her husband and then her daughter both of whom said nothing. Finally, Joseph shrugged his shoulders and got up from his chair.

He moved closer to his wife. Placing his hand on her shoulder, he announced, "Good idea."

Anna stood before the door containing in large letters the words, "Alpha Modeling Agency." Squeezed between a gift shop and a small restaurant, the agency would attract little attention unless you were actually looking for it. Anna was, indeed, looking for it.

Following the discussion with her parents, her dad had taken her mother's advice, had called the agency and had discovered that it did exist. Furthermore, in his capacity as manager of a local clothing store, Joseph had access to information about the legitimacy of other local businesses. From those resources, he discovered that the agency had existed for several years, establishing a good reputation in the Florence business community.

Anna and her parents gathered again to discuss what Joseph had discovered. As before, they discussed what she wanted to do. They agreed that visiting the agency to discover what it had to offer would not interfere in Anna's college plans. Consequently, a call to the agency produced an appointment to meet with Mr. Conti to discuss in more detail where Anna could fit into the world of modeling.

Anna, aware of her tendency to attract attention, wore loose clothing that concealed the attractive contours of her body. She took a deep breath as she pushed open the narrow door to enter a world that eventually would play an important role in her life.

Chapter 14

Denten jumped down from the tractor, stretched, then reached up to grab his jacket from under the tractor seat. A day that began just after sunrise was now ending just before sunset. Turning to face the vast field on which he worked all day, Denten felt a sense of satisfaction on having achieved something very tangible, a smooth expanse of rich black soil extending for almost a half mile. Under that black dirt the machine attached to the tractor had deposited corn seeds that in just weeks would emerge from the ground and grow into tall stalks of corn. Denten thought to himself, "What a miracle of nature."

With the tractor and planter parked in the shade of a small grove of trees, Denten walked to the truck which stood next to the road. Climbing into the truck, he let out a sigh, a reaction to his long hours sitting on that tractor seat. With a slight turn of the ignition key, the truck instantly sprang to life. Quickly, Denten drove to the small crossing which gave him access to the road.

Approaching the farm proper, he drove by the rural mail box, not really thinking about picking up the mail. His parents usually did that. However, when he passed it, he noticed that the box still contained mail. At least he could see papers sticking out of the small door. Backing the truck, he stopped, got out, and reached into the box to grab a collection of mail and advertising. A single sheet of paper folder but with no visible writing lay with three or four advertising brochures. Denten paid little attention to any of that, concentrating instead on a letter addressed to him from the college in Mankato.

Back in the truck, Denten placed the advertising along with the single sheet of paper on the seat next to him. Holding up the letter from the college, Denten whispered, "What the hell did I do now?"

He ripped open the letter to read that his program leading to graduation had received approval from the academic dean's office. The letter stated that the office welcomed Denten back to campus in the fall. He smiled, placing the letter on the seat next to the pile of "junk mail." Considering the long days he had put in recently, returning to college would be a definite improvement even though that return would demand more serious study than in the past.

Denten pulled into the farm yard, parking the truck near the large storage bins, the very ones that last fall were the scene of his father's serious accident. As he stepped out of the truck, he reached back to grasp the mail. When he did, a single sheet of paper drifted to the ground, landing open. Reaching down to pick up the single sheet, Denten noticed the words spread across the page, "**I know who you are.**"

Nothing registered right away. He stared at the words, his forehead furrowed in deep concentration. Perplexed, Denten shook his head, and asked, "What the hell is this?"

He dropped his arms to his side, and stared off into the early evening sky, seeing nothing. Suddenly, he inhaled audibly and leaned back against the truck. The image of the dark eyes in the car's rear side window flashed through his mind. Could this have something to do with the awful Saturday morning at the park, the incident that he had carried with him for more than ten years? Denten slumped against the door of the truck.

"What else could it be?" He asked himself.

With his breathing much slower, his heart rate calmed, he was thankful that he had picked up the mail. What would his parents have thought of this mysterious paper with no postage and no name? Maybe it's just a prank. Denten speculated. He could think of no other explanation, though, than the paper's connection to that horrible moment years ago.

How many times had he considered telling his parents or even telling anyone about what he had seen? Perhaps, he considered, now would offer a good time to tell them. Maybe sharing the experience with his parents would weaken its effect on him. Though the frequency of the dreams had decreased, they still occurred too often.

Walking toward the house, Denten decided that he would have to think more about telling his parents and about the source of this mysterious note. From that Saturday, who belonged to those dark eyes remained a mystery. The image of Reed Howard peering over the teller cage that day at the bank flashed through Denten's mind. He possessed his suspicions, but he had no way of confirming them. At least he had no way right now. Telling his parents because of this stupid note wouldn't help the confirmation.

Stuffing the paper into his rear pocket, he stepped into the kitchen to the smell of roast beef and to the greetings of his parents.

Chapter 15

The afternoon sun beat down on Denten's back and hatless head. He simply did not like caps of any kind even though his mom constantly reminded him of the dangers of too much exposure to the sun. Farm labor demanded spending time in the sun. It didn't demand wearing a cap.

Summer days found more freedom from farm labor than did those late spring, early summer days during the seeding time when the vagaries of Minnesota weather made completing the planting urgent when weather cooperated. Once done with seeding, mostly corn for Denten and his father, they waited for the corn to emerge from the ground. When that happened, they then had to cultivate to keep weeds from damaging the young corn stalks.

On this hot day Denten cultivated a large field of emerging corn. The advanced design and automation of tractors and cultivators made the job relatively easy, just prevent the sharp cultivator blades from severing the young corn stalks. Still, the job allowed for moments of reflection while following the corn rows in rounds of over a mile. Denten studied the rows in front of him as he thought back a few days to that strange, disturbing letter stating, "I Know Who You Are." Since that evening Denten had been preoccupied with the note and the whole dreadful incident to which, he believed, it alluded.

The note had two immediate effects. It reinforced Denten's decision to refrain from telling his parents about his secret, residual fear a factor in that decision. It also thrust the incident back into frequent focus, not that he had succeeded in suppressing the memory. However, he had succeeded in reducing the times the memory of that Saturday morning interrupted his sleep. The mysterious note ruined all that. He confessed to himself that he should have shared his story years ago with his parents. Now with each passing year, telling them seemed irrelevant. Besides, the note provided a tangible threat, otherwise why would whoever was responsible take the time to prepare and deliver it. Who was responsible always deeply troubled Denten, who held to the notion that those dark eyes peering through the car's rear side window belonged to the influential Reed Howard. Who would ever believe a young boy's memory over the word of an important figure in the community?

The end of the long row brought Denten back to the reality of his cultivating. Since his father's accident the previous fall, much of the work on the farm fell to Denten. Nonetheless, his father could assume several of many tasks associated with running a farm. Again the advanced design of modern farm machines enabled Denten's dad to spend some time in the field. Much of the work, though, Denten assumed. He frequently thought about this fall's harvest when he was back at school determined to walk across that graduation stage in the spring. Somehow it would all work out. Neighbors always could be counted on to help.

As the sun slowly made its way toward the horizon, Denten decided to quit early. He had not done any socializing for weeks. Too often he sat before his computer reading emails from Italy, rarely driving into Riverside to meet friends for a beer or for a light dinner. Those few days with Anna remained fresh in his memory even though the vividness of the memory may have dimmed just a little. In his mind he saw her sparkling eyes, her inviting smile and her fabulous figure. If only she wasn't hundreds of miles away. Still thoughts of Anna tended to shield him from those of that ugly Saturday morning. They had talked of getting together soon. But Denten's responsibilities on the farm besides college for both of them took priority. Someday, perhaps, if it were meant to be, they would find a way to reunite.

Denten rushed into the house determined to enjoy a Saturday night in places other than his own room.

His mom busied herself in the kitchen preparing the evening meal. "Why such a hurry?" she asked as Denten headed for his room.

"I'm going out for a while. Dad back yet?"

"Yes, he's taking a shower before dinner."

"Did he have any problems today?" Denten asked. He could not dismiss the reality of his dad struggling with his severely damaged right arm.

"He didn't say anything. He can take care of himself." Grace smiled as she stood before the kitchen stove.

"Yea, I know." The image of his dad's mangled arm flashed in his mind.

"You going to eat with us?" His mom asked.

"I don't think so. Just clean up and have something downtown."

"It's about time you get out of this house." Grace spoke to Denten's back as he mounted the steps leading to his room on the second floor.

Denten parked in the lot next to the Riverside Bar. Though he spent little time in downtown Riverside, when he did, he spent it at the Riverside Bar or at Deluca's restaurant. Tonight he would try the Riverside Bar.

Stepping through the front entrance, Denten paused as his eyes adjusted to the dim light. Several patrons stood around the bar while others crowded the small tables scattered around the room. He approached the bar, finding a space unoccupied. He ordered a light beer. The cool zest of the beer tasted wonderful after a long day in the hot sun riding on a tractor. On the TV the Twins battled the White Sox from the Metrodome in Minneapolis. Content to take his time, Denten pulled up a stool, resting his elbows on the bar.

Enjoying this time of relaxing, Denten didn't notice the young woman who walked up behind him. He felt a light tap on his shoulder. Turning, he looked into the smiling face of Cayla Finch. Dressed in a Twins' T shirt and jeans, Cayla looked better than he remembered.

They greeted each other with a brief hug initiated by her. Denten willingly participated.

"Good to see you." Cayla stepped back placing her hand on Denten's arm.

"Good to see you, too. Last time was at the machinery dealer, I think." Denten looked into her dark brown eyes accentuated by perfectly contoured eyebrows. He also noticed charming dimples that accompanied her captivating smile.

Since that conversation with Andrea Palmer, her college roommate, Cayla gained some relief from the haunting memory of the sexual assault. It was after Christmas break and a particularly depressing time for Cayla. Andrea, finally persuaded her to talk about what bothered her. And so she did. In addition, demands of summer school had diverted Cayla's attention. Her goal of graduation in just over three years required taking a full class load, a challenge even for a capable student like Cayla.

Taking a weekend break from the rigors of her college schedule, she arranged to meet her roommate for a Saturday night on the town in Riverside.

"Haven't spent much time there since. My dad had to get someone else to help him." Cayla's laughter produced charming dimples in each cheek.

"In summer school, aren't you?" Denten set his beer glass back on the bar.

"Am I ever." Cayla shook her head to give emphasis to demands of her academic life.

"You here alone?"

"No, with my college roommate. We're sitting right over there under that big beer sign. Want to join us?"

"Sure." Denten grabbed his beer bottle and followed Cayla to her table.

After introductions, Denten assisted Cayla with her chair before settling into his.

Andrea, a petite blonde with dark rimmed glasses which gave her an executive look, sat across from Denten clutching her glass of wine.

A brief pause confirmed a little self-consciousness among three people who didn't know each other that well. Aware of the slight uneasiness around the table, Andrea looked at Denten, smiled, and asked.

"You from here?"

"Yes, all my life." Denten answered with a hint of regret.

"Is that bad?" Andrea smiled, her white teeth a contrast to her summer tan.

Another girl with impressive white teeth. Denten sometimes wondered just what they did to make their teeth so white. Someday he would garner the courage to ask.

"No, it's been a good place to grow up I guess. What do you think?" Denten turned to Cayla.

Cayla suddenly looked very serious, as if he had said something wrong. She glanced quickly at Andrea and looked down at her glass. In a moment that seemed longer than it was, She looked up at Denten.

"I guess, ah, I didn't have much choice." Quickly changing the subject, Cayla asked, "How is life on the farm?"

The evening continued on with good conversation, mostly about summer school, about farming and about Andrea's job at a small restaurant in Winona. During the conversation Denten and Cayla discovered just how much they had in common. They shared an interest in the Twins. For Cayla, her T shirt established that. They both would graduate in the spring provided all progressed as planned. They both, Denten discovered, liked light beer. Finally, their evening in the bar established the lure travel had for both of them.

Driving home later that evening, by himself, Denten made a decision. He would see more of Cayla Finch.

Chapter 16

Cayla eased the car out onto the street from the cramped parking lot next to the Riverside Bar. Andrea sat beside her. Silence dominated the car while Cayla merged into the late evening traffic slowly moving up and down Riverside's main street, the only one in town.

"How long have you known Denten?" Andrea moved to attach her seat belt.

"Not very." Cayla turned toward Andrea, a smile spreading across her face. "Maybe a few months. We met in that bar, purely by accident."

"Seems like a nice guy." Andrea stated. "Did you ever date?" Cayla shifted uncomfortably. Again looking over at Andrea. "I've hardly dated anyone. I guess you know why"

"I'm sorry. Of course I do."

"You're right, though. He is a friendly guy, very easy to talk to. Under different circumstances." Cayla's voice trailed off into silence.

"Stop me if you feel I'm invading your privacy, but what's gonna happen with that?" Andrea asked hesitantly.

"No, that's fine. Talking about it smooths some of the sharpness of the memory. I just don't know what to do, if anything after all these years." Cayla answered with a firm voice.

"To think that this pervert can get by with what he did to you is beyond belief." Andrea stared straight ahead shaking her head remembering the emotion of that time months ago when Cayla confided in her about her treacherous secret.

"I know. Don't think I haven't thought about that a thousand times."

"You've never told your parents?" Andrea asked even though she believed she knew the answer.

Cayla slumped behind the wheel. Shaking her head, she choked out, "No."

Andrea saw the profound effect this conversation had on Cayla even after all the years. She reached over touching her on the arm. "I'm sorry." She quickly changed the topic. "When do you return to school?"

"Tomorrow morning. You don't have to be sorry, Andrea. I should have told them years ago. I guess I question what good it would do now. They don't need that burden at this stage in their lives."

"Maybe someday."

Pulling into the Finch driveway, Cayla stopped the car just short of the garage where her much older car stood ready for her drive back to Winona and St. Mary's college.

She turned to Andrea. "Thank you for understanding my poor judgement. I can't bring myself to deal with the situation probably as I should. You're, right. Maybe someday."

In the house Cayla's parents sat watching TV.

"Welcome back." Cayla's dad voiced as the two girls entered the living room. "Did you have a great time on Riverside's strip?" He laughed as he turned down the TV volume.

"Yes, we did." Cayla offered.

"What'd you do?" Cayla's mom asked.

"Sat in the Riverside Bar talking to a nice young man." Cayla announced, her dimples accentuating her smile.

Her mom sat up straight hearing her daughter mention an amiable young man. Over the years, Cayla's parents frequently encouraged their daughter to date. She did but not very often. This perplexed her parents. They believed their daughter very attractive, intelligent, and engaging. Yet rarely did she date and never very long with the same boy. On numerous occasions they attempted to discuss their concerns with her. Invariably she resisted pursuing the topic, telling her mom and dad that she just didn't find boys in Riverside very appealing. Besides she had attended a private school which limited the contact she had with the boys who attended Riverside's public school.

During these discussions Cayla a few times threatened to tell her parents her horrible secret. One such time occurred when her dad implied that she might be a lesbian. Cayla was very tolerant of differences, cultural, sexual, or ethnic. However, she adamantly denied a preference for same sex relationships. Her dad dropped the subject, never to bring it up again. Cayla never completely dismissed that discussion. Whether her parents accepted her denial she did not know. They just never mentioned it again.

"What's his name?" Cayla's mom asked.

"Denten Ballery." Cayla offered.

"A local boy?" Her mom persisted.

"I think he has lived here most of his life. On a farm." Cayla explained.

"Farm boys are good." Her dad said with a chuckle.

"Did you say his name was Gallery?" Alice Finch persisted in her inquiry of Denten.

"Ballery," Cayla corrected.

Harvey Finch suddenly looked deep in thought. "That isn't the guy who lost an arm last fall in an accident?"

"No, that was his father." Cayla spoke tentatively fearful of the direction the conversation was taking.

"What does Denten do? How old is he?" Cayla's mom fired quick questions.

"He's in college." Cayla straightened up, tension evident in her face.

Alice turned her attention to Andrea, who sat next to Cayla on the living room sofa.

"What did you think of this Denten?"

"He's fine. I enjoyed meeting him." Andrea answered, sensitive to what Cayla obviously feared.

"Do you have a boyfriend?" Alice persisted, looking directly at Andrea.

"No."

"Do you date very often?"

"Mother," Cayla interrupted. "I don't think Andrea wants to talk about her dating."

"I don't know what's the matter with girls now days. They don't want to talk about boys anymore." Alice lamented. "Cayla hardly ever talks about boys."

Cayla's body stiffened in response to her mother's reference to her erratic dating. "Mom, that's enough. Let's not talk about dating. It's kind of personal."

Alice sat back, noticeably offended by the rebuff from her daughter. For years variations of this conversation had played out in the Finch household. Cayla's mother could never accept the reality of a beautiful daughter with so few dates and with such a disinterest in boys. Like Cayla's dad, her mom had also intimated that Cayla might have an attraction for other girls. Also like her dad, her mom never pursued that suspicion, at least not in Cayla's presence.

Cayla rose from her place on the sofa. "Mom and dad, we have an early morning. I think we'll get to bed."

Andrea followed Cayla's lead. "Thank you so much for every thing. I've had a good time."

"Oh, you're welcome." Cayla's parents answered in unison.

"You're welcome here any time. We always appreciated your looking after our daughter." Alice spoke with a smile, displaying a playfulness not apparent during the earlier conversation.

While they prepared for bed, Andrea asked if Cayla and her parents often engaged in a conversation about dating. The only person besides herself who knew about the tragic incident which had such an impact on Cayla's life, Andrea possessed a deeper appreciation for Cayla's aversion to dating than others.

They had discussed earlier in the evening Cayla telling her parents. Nonetheless, aware of the obvious conflict the subject engendered, Andrea brought the subject up again.

"I'm sorry, but I think you should tell your parents. The truth could, maybe, remove some of the tension of the subject."

"Yes, I suppose I should. As I said before, I just don't know how it would affect mom. I mean, she probably would call the police immediately. Then what?"

Andrea leaned against the door contemplating Cayla's comment. "I guess you're right. Listening to your mother tonight, it could be a problem."

"Thank you for understanding." Cayla paused. "We'd better get to bed. Morning comes early."

Andrea turned to leave for the guest bedroom across the hall. As she did, she stopped. "Remember, Cayla, whatever happens, I will never tell anyone unless you want me to."

Cayla stepped to Andrea and gave her a hug. In a soft, halting voice she said, "Thank you."

Reed Howard spent very little time driving the streets of Riverside on any evening let alone a Saturday evening. However, a promise to complete another farm loan took him back to the bank on this Saturday night. Thinking about the promise distracted from his relaxing evening. To erase the distraction he decided to return to the bank to complete the paper work.

On the way home he drove slowly down Riverside's main street, amazed at the traffic, thinking to himself just where did all these people come from. Passing the Riverside Bar, he noticed with a sudden shock two very familiar people emerging from the bar. Denten Ballery and Cayla Finch walked together along with a girl Reed did not know toward the parking lot.

Violently, Reed struck the steering wheel while visions of Denten and Cayla planning revenge rushed through his mind. The second time he had seen the two together suggested that they certainly must have shared their secret, his secret too. That threat had compelled him to warn Denten with the recent mail box note. What effect that note had, Reed, perhaps, would never know. That in itself would indicate that it had the desired effect.

As the years had passed since that fateful Saturday morning, Reed's sexual appetite had changed little. What had changed was a growing paranoia about disclosure. The satisfaction of his, what he described to himself as special sexual needs, generally was gained through his extended collection of adolescent pornography, a collection he treasured as his world of delicate darlings. The incident with Cayla Finch was the only time Reed fell victim to his strong sexual urges. The chances of exposure from that kind of behavior were much too great. Seeing Denten and Cayla together not once but twice hinted at exposure which would destroy Reed's status in the community along with a life style that he and his family had enjoyed for years. He would not permit one indiscretion to destroy what he had worked so hard to achieve.

Standing in the driveway of the Finch home, Cayla and Andrea gave each other a brief, good bye hug, Andrea off to the Mall of America for a little summer shopping, Cayla off to St. Mary's and a return to summer school. Cayla waved one last time as Andrea backed her car out onto the street. The topic of dating and boy friends had not come up again while the two friends prepared to leave. Neither preferred a full breakfast, both content with juice and a bite of toast which Cayla's mother happily prepared.

A final hug for her parents and Cayla stepped into her car for the short drive back to Winona. As she backed out of the driveway, she waved again to her parents, the sting of last night's conversation nearly forgotten. Still, as Cayla drove away from her home, her mind wrestled with several thoughts. Of course, the dating issue was one of them. The tragic moment so many years ago always lay in the back of her mind like a festering blister. As she had hundreds of time over the years, she briefly thought about what she would do to heal that blister.

More pleasant was the thought of Denten Ballery. She smiled thinking about the three times they had met, each time by accident. She enjoyed talking with Denten, who possessed an unassuming personality that made him easy to get to know. Besides he was handsome in a modest way. The brief meeting between them had established how much they had in common. With those thoughts, she smiled.

As she headed for the highway to Winona, other thoughts swirled through her mind, thoughts about her future and her goal of attending law school. Just a few months stood between her and graduation from St. Mary's. Before that, she would have to begin that process of applying to law schools, a process that made her nervous. She knew of the excessive demand for admission to major law schools. At times she feared that she was simply not qualified for admittance, for example, to the University of Minnesota Law School where she dreamed of attaining her law degree. Generally, she suppressed these concerns with the reality of her impressive academic record.

Occupied with these divergent thoughts, Cayla paid little attention to a car that followed her at a reasonable distance and had followed since shortly after she left her home. In that car sat Reed Howard. No note in the mailbox this time. He would confront Cayla with the danger she faced if she decided to get careless about disclosing their encounter.

Cayla reached the intersection with Highway 52 which would take her to Rochester and on to Winona. She accelerated, concentrating on her driving and on the next day‘s class schedule.

A glanse in the rearview mirror revealed the car behind her. The driver apparently had no intention of passing as he maintained a constant distance. The four lane road ahead was clear. Yet, the car made no move to pass. Cayla watched the car in her rearview mirror, curious about the driver's intentions. After a few miles of following, the car suddenly pulled out in an apparent move to pass. However, it didn't pass. Instead, the car pulled up even with Cayla's. The horn sounded. The driver motioned for Cayla to pull over.

That the car finally would pass gave Cayla a reason to relax. Its persistent following had given her reason for concern. The sound of the horn, however, shocked her. As she looked over into the face of Reed Howard, she froze. Her hands gripped the wheel, her body rigid. For a moment she couldn't catch her breath. Those piercing eyes wakened the horror of years ago.

The horn blared again. Reed more adamantly pointed to the side of the road. Cayla looked to the shoulder but having gained some control of her emotions decided she would not succumb to Reed's demands. She never again would permit this man to cause such grief in her life. Determined, she looked straight ahead, trying desperately to ignore the vehement gestures of an agitated Reed Howard. Suddenly, Reed accelerated, pulling in front of Cayla dangerously close to clipping her front bumper. She slowed down for fear that he would hit her. He also slowed. Cayla pulled into the passing lane in an attempt to get around him. He moved into the passing lane in front of her. He refused to let her pass.

Realizing the danger in this crazy maneuvering, Cayla pulled over to the shoulder. She soothed her fear with the thought of what could happen out on the highway in full view of the world? She stopped the car, locked the doors, and sat waiting to see what Reed would do. He got out of his car, walked back to Cayla's car where he stood outside her driver's window with a sickening smile on his face.

"Open the window." He commanded, that sneering smile printed on his face. Acknowledging that she had little choice, she lowered the window just enough to allow her to hear what he had to say.

"How you doing?" He asked in a voice soft and artificial.

Gaining more control over herself, Cayla blurted out, "What do you want?

Reed leaned against her car placing his hands on the edge of the roof. "How are you and that Denten Ballery getting along?"

Cayla said nothing, curious what Denten had to do with anything.

The smile had vanished from Reed's face, replaced by a snarl. "Don't go shooting your mouth off if you know what's good for you." His voice echoed through her car.

Cayla sat motionless behind the wheel. She refused even to look Reed in the face. She said nothing, for what could she say that would make any difference to him?

"Did you hear what I said?" He shouted. "I can make things difficult for your parents. Don't think I can't!"

Cayla fought the urge to speed off leaving him standing on the road. However, good judgement prevailed. Still, she said nothing.

Her silence only urged Reed on to offer more threats. The good intentions of a passing motorist who stopped to offer assistance cooled Reed's anger. Finally, he stepped back from Cayla's car, tapped his finger on the window, and warned one last time, "Remember, young lady, I know a lot about what goes on in this town. Don't think you can get away with shooting your mouth off. You're not going to ruin what I have. Do you understand?"

Cayla nodded her head as Reed stepped back from her car. Shaking, she put the car in gear. Her foot trembling on the accelerator, she moved out onto the highway away from this sinister man. For miles she struggled to calm herself, reluctant to stop for fear that Reed still followed miles back. Gaining some control over her emotions, she thought again of Denten and why he would have anything to do with what happened years ago.

When she finally arrived at the St. Mary's campus, she parked near the dormitory, rested her head against the steering wheel and breathed a long sigh. At that moment, she remembered the conversation with Andrea when they had talked about justice. They had agreed that someday it would happen. Sitting in her car in that parking lot, she vowed that someday she would make sure it happened.

Chapter 17

"I'm coming to America!" Denten sat back in his chair and looked away from the computer screen. A slight tremble spread through his body. In his mind he relived briefly the thrill he felt when he first saw her at her uncle's farm. He envisioned the tender moments months ago when he said goodby to Anna. He could almost feel her soft lips against his as they parted. He could almost sense the fragrance that always surrounded her. Now she was coming to America. In just days she would be there.

Over the weeks and months since Denten last saw her in Italy, they had maintained regular contact, mostly emails. On occasion they spoke on their cell phones; however, cost discouraged their use. Regardless of the means of contact, the distance between them and the passage of time did tend to weaken the intensity of their mutual feeling. Even remembering Anna's parting assurance, all those months ago, that if they really loved each other, their relationship would thrive had lost some of its power to give Denten comfort that their relationship would endure. Now, though, they would renew their relationship.

For Denten harvest had started. Classes would begin in just four weeks. Anna's visit would, for a few days, divert attention away from these two very important responsibilities. Denten needed diversion. Except for the chance to meet Cayla Finch, he had done very little else all summer except work. Though harvest would impose serious demands on his time, finding time for Anna would prove a delight.

The email only hinted at the other reason for her visit, something about a meeting in LA. Anna had avoided saying anything about modeling, unsure of what would become of the invitation to discuss a career in modeling with the Alpha Agency. For Denten, whatever the reason for her trip, he was thrilled she would spend a week in Riverside, staying with her relatives, Alda and Gilberto Deluca.

During the weeks and months since she last saw Denten, Anna faced many decisions, some about college but most about her prospects for modeling. Of course, that day standing in line for registration for her fall semester classes stood out in her memory as an important moment in her life. The attention she received from Mr. Conti and the small staff at the modeling agency made her feel good about herself. The frequent mention of her attractiveness, of her poise, of her charming personality added to her confidence and her self esteem. Besides it was simply fascinating to have people attending to your every need, something Anna had not experienced before.

When the agency started to talk seriously to Anna about her future in modeling, she spent several sessions with her parents discussing what pursuing a career in modeling would mean for her. They talked about the uncertainty of success. They discussed exploitation they had heard of, modeling agents who took advantage of unsuspecting young girls. They considered Anna's college education. In recent years college had been one of her most important goals. She was a good student. Her parents believed she had something to offer the world perhaps more important than parading down a ramp with an exaggerated walk. They also discussed keeping in perspective one's importance in the world. Modeling had the potential to distort that perspective.

Anna understood the importance of what her parents discussed. She also believed that she could blend the worlds of college and modeling. She had not convinced herself that a career in modeling was what she wanted. Still, if she could earn money modeling while still keeping up with her college classes, she felt it would prove advantageous for her and for her father, who earned a comfortable living but certainly would not reject Anna's earning extra money for college expenses. Just how modeling and college attendance would blend, she did not know exactly. However, she believed that if both options represented something important to her, she could accomplish both.

The opportunity to travel to America concluded a series of interviews, photo shoots, and sessions with makeup professionals. Anna's natural beauty made their work relatively easy. However, their work did highlight the sparkle in her dark eyes, the shine in her rich black hair, and the curve of her lips. In a span of no more than four weeks, Anna had advanced from an attractive college freshman standing in line to register for college classes to a prospective model potentially gracing the covers of leading magazines. At least Nino Conti believed that was in Anna's future. However, first she had to sit down with the officials at the headquarters of the Alpha Modeling Agency located in Los Angeles, California. There she would sit for further photo shoots and discuss a contract.

Though Anna and her parents had traveled extensively in Europe and Asia, they had never traveled to the United States. The opportunity had just never arisen. Now it did. The thought of America gave Anna chills. The thought of perhaps having the chance to visit Denten in Minnesota added to her excitement. She simply had to work out the details with the agency since it naturally would pay for the trip to LA. Who would pay for the extension to Minnesota she wasn't sure. Nonetheless, she would make it to Riverside, Minnesota, one way or another.

By mid August the agency had completed all details. Those details included her trip to LA, from LA to Minneapolis and, of course, her return flight from Minneapolis to Rome. Learning of the details, Anna sent Denten the email which produced in him a level of excitement similar to hers.

According to her, she would arrive in LA, spend six days doing what she needed to do there. She then would fly to Minneapolis, arriving on Saturday, just one and one half weeks away. Denten, of course, would pick her up at the Minneapolis/St. Paul airport. She would stay with the Delucas while in Riverside. Nonetheless, they both knew that during her short stay in Minnesota, she would spend most of her time with Denten.

Anna's flight was scheduled to arrive in Minneapolis on Saturday afternoon at 1:30. As the time approached for Denten to drive to Minneapolis, his excitement grew, thinking about seeing Anna for the first time in months. In cell phone calls from LA, Denten learned that she had concluded very successful contract talks with the people in the Alpha Modeling headquarters. Though only a teenager, Anna possessed a mature understanding of the real world and along with coaching at a distance from her father, she arrived at a contract that enabled her to model part time while attending college classes in Florence. Now Denten drove anxiously to Minneapolis, the two and one-half hour drive seeming to take longer than usual as he anticipated seeing Anna again.

Denten stood waiting in baggage claim, watching the crowd of travelers arriving from places around the country. With him others crowded around the restricted exit from which the arriving passengers would emerge.

Suddenly, Anna stood at the top of the escalator, her vibrance and charm setting her apart from those crowded around her. She stood straight and proud, a sharp contrast to the others gathered at the top of the escalator. As she moved closer, she spotted Denten. She waved vigorously. A gleaming smile spread across her beautiful face. At the bottom of the escalator she rushed into Denten's waiting arms. For a few marvelous moments they relived the thrill of each other's touch.

"Welcome to Minnesota." Denten whispered through the fragrance of her hair swept just over her ear.

"Thank you." Came her soft reply.

Denten released her and stepped back to look at this girl who for months he saw only in his memory. Her natural beauty had not changed. Makeup now accentuated that natural beauty. Her enchanting, dark eyes sparkled with even more vitality. Her lips outlined more distinctly. Her hair darker with a greater shine. She was simply more stunning now than when he last saw her.

With little hesitation they walked arm and arm to the baggage carrousel where Anna's two bags moved slowly on the conveyor. In just minutes they were in Denten's car headed south and west out of the Twin Cities toward Riverside. During the drive, they had so much to talk about. Anna explained her plunge into modeling and her experience in LA. Denten confessed that the months since their brief time together had not included much excitement. He explained that she had arrived during harvest, a time she could relate to since her work on her uncle's farm. Generally, an atmosphere of excitement pervaded the car as they attempted to squeeze months of absence into a couple hours.

Anna would stay with the Delucas. The first stop, though, was at the Ballery's farm where Anna met Denten's parents. The brief meeting included answering a number of questions Anna asked about farming in Minnesota. Her sensitivity to the interests of others reflected her maturity. Her questions thoroughly engaged Denten's dad, who delighted in talking about his farm and its operation. Of course, the accident came up during the discussion, Oscar freely talking about the effect that had on his life and lives of both Denten and Grace. Anna's long day's journey ended a short time later when Denten delivered her to the door of Alda and Gilberto's restaurant where Anna received a warm and animated reception.

Anna's stay would last only five days after which she would return to Italy to start her freshman year in college and blend that with her modeling. Consequently, Denten and Anna plunged into doing things together. They didn't particularly care what they did. They just wished to do it together. Much of their time involved driving around the countryside. Anna marveled at how it resembled the area around her uncle's farm in Italy. The big difference replaced wheat and corn with grapes and olives. On two different evenings they shared dinner with Denten's parents and then with the Delucas at their restaurant.

The few days Anna and Denten had to spend together made each minute of that time very precious. On the last afternoon before Anna's departure, she and Denten drove aimlessly around Riverside and the surrounding area. They simply wished to spend the last few hours together. Driving out of Riverside they passed the community park where so many years ago Denten came upon a scene that had haunted him ever since.

"Do lot of people use that park?" Anna asked as they drove slowly by the entrance.

Denten paused before he answered. "Some times in the summer." The tone of his voice hinted at a reluctance to talk about that park.

"Can we go in?" Anna persisted

Denten looked straight ahead, a frown on his face. "I guess so."

Rarely over the years had Denten returned to this park. However, he remembered the lay out perfectly. Driving to the same parking area where years ago he saw the big car, he stopped.

"Is that a walking path up ahead?" Anna asked. "Let's go for a walk."

He definitely did not want to be in this park. He did not wish to walk that path. However, Anna wanted to. He relented. As they walked, Anna rested her head on Denten shoulder. She sensed something bothered him. For a short time, she enjoyed the quiet that surrounded them. Nearby the river rippled in its journey south to meet the mighty Mississippi. An occasional bird sang in the trees. Denten and Anna walked in silence.

In his mind he could see that big black car. He could see those large eyes peering at him. Anna sensed his mood. She stopped, turned to face him, and reached to hold both his hands.

"Is something wrong? Have I said something?" She looked directly into his eyes, a tear glistening in the corners of each of hers.

A look of profound sadness and confusion crossed Denten's face. He stood in deep concentration. In all the years he had never told anyone about his experience or about his reoccurring dreams. Now he faced the girl whom he said he loved and who said she loved him. Was this the time? Would it make any difference if he, at last, shared his nagging secret? Saying nothing, Denten put his arm around Anna's shoulders and guided her to a wooden bench along the path. There they sat down. He turned to face her. In the next few minutes more than ten years of harboring his secret vanished as he revealed to Anna the details of that terrible Saturday morning.

Chapter 18

The small boy rode his bike on the path. A large black car was parked ahead. He heard the cries, "Help me!" Huge, penetrating eyes glared at him.

Denten sat up, his body damp with perspiration, his heart racing. He pushed the blanket to the end of the bed. He glanced at the clock which read, 2:38. A bright, early spring moon shined through the thin dormitory drapes. He rubbed his eyes and ran his hands through his hair messed from a restless sleep.

"Damn, damn, damn," he said out loud. "Will this shit ever stop?"

At one time early after the incident so many years ago, these night time episodes created a sense of foreboding and fear. He would cower under the covers shivering as the images rushed through his young mind. Now this fear was replaced with anger. This reoccurring dream interrupted his sleep. It offered a frequent reminder of an experience Denten would rather forget. But, of course, he couldn't.

Denten got out of bed and stood by the one window in his single dorm room. He pulled back the curtain. The full moon revealed the huge oak tree that graced the area just outside his dormitory. He stood mesmerized by the moonlight dancing on the new leaves only recently emerged. His mind wandered. He reflected on that afternoon months ago sitting with Anna in the same park, where it all happened, describing the scene so indelibly burned into his mind. At last sharing his secret with someone offered him some temporary escape from the horrible memory. He could still see the anguished expression on Anna's face as he told her of his experience. They had held each other close as he described the countless nights of the reoccurring dream.

Anna had asked why he hadn't told his parents. A question he had asked himself numerous times over the years. She had asked about the man in the car with the dark piercing eyes. Did Denten know who he was? Denten had shared with her his suspicion but confirmed that it was only that, suspicion. She also asked about the other person in the back seat, the one with the light hair. Denten confessed that he had no idea who that could have been except that it was a young girl by the sound the voice. Anna was shocked that anyone could get away with such brutal behavior. She had only heard about such heinous things. She had asked if Denten ever intended to pursue his suspicion? That question occurred to Denten more often as time had passed. He believed without question that eventually justice should be served. But how to go about it? He felt a profound inadequacy. However, he had grown weary of these night time visits, of the disruption they caused to his sleep and to his life.

Denten let the curtain fall back over the window and turned to looked at his rumpled bed. He needed his sleep. The academic world imposed demands on him that required all his intellectual talents. This, his last year of college, was going very well. He had rescued his grade point average, bringing it up to the required minimum for graduation. He had returned to the campus last fall ready to do what he had to do to ensure a spring graduation. Today would give him some relief from the usual class schedule. Instead of his regular classes he, as a business major, would attend a conference on campus dealing with matters related to small business. A portion of that conference included a session on banking.

Still, Denten needed his sleep. Already another hour had slipped by as he struggled with his private nightmare. He walked down the hall of the dormitory to the bathroom he shared with others on his floor. He attempted to wash the night's memory away with cool water splashed on his face. Returning to his room, he crawled back into bed determined to salvage something out of the night, if only a couple hours.

At 8:30 Denten sat in the large lecture hall of the main academic building on the Mankato campus. Gathered in the hall were at least two hundred business majors from freshmen to those seeking a master's degree. On the large stage sat several representatives from various businesses in Mankato as well as from the surrounding area. The representatives were identified by a name card placed directly in front of them. From where Denten sat in the large lecture hall he couldn't read the names clearly. However, when the representatives began to take their respective places, he needed no name card to recognized one of them, Reed Howard. Seeing Reed position himself behind the long table sent a chill running through Denten's body. He had read the information about the conference. He even knew that a part of it would concentrate on banking. He just never imagined that Reed Howard would represent the banking business.

Sitting, staring at Reed Howard, Denten replayed in his mind the events, past and present, that had connected him to this outstanding business man and community leader. Nearly convinced that Reed was the man in the back seat of that car, Denten found looking at him nearly intolerable, to say nothing of listening to him talk about banking. Nonetheless, he was committed to sit through the conference since eventually he would be required to prepare a report on what transpired and what conclusions he could draw.

Denten used all his powers of concentration listening to the various speakers. Time passed slowly. The different speakers possessed a wide range of skill in public speaking. As a result, frequently, his concentration drifted. He thought of his meeting tonight with Cayla Finch. A silly game they played had resulted in Cayla driving from Winona to Mankato for dinner on Denten. Exactly who had won and who had lost made little difference. Yes, Cayla had to make the one hour drive, but Denten had to foot the bill for the dinner.

Cayla and Denten had seen very little of each other during the previous summer. The couple times they did meet had fostered a mutual attraction. However, during the summer, Anna had captured much of Denten's attention.

Christmas break offered another spontaneous occasion for Denten and Cayla to meet, this time at the local grocery store in Riverside. Both were happily approaching graduation which gave them something else they had in common. Always when they did meet, they found conversing so easy and so natural, as if they had been friends for years. During their brief meeting in the grocery story, they decided to exchange email addresses, just to keep in touch about progress toward graduation they said. Over the ensuing weeks they kept in touch about more than just graduation. The meeting that evening, not quite a date, was one result of that contact.

Denten waited patiently at a small table in a popular restaurant near the campus. They had agreed that they would meet at the restaurant rather than at his dorm. While he waited, he thought about the relationship that had developed between Cayla and him. Almost by accident their relationship had started. He remembered with a smile that time in the Riverside Bar when they each had stopped for a quick drink. At the same time he couldn't avoid seeing Reed Howard at the conference talking commandingly about the world of banking. As suddenly as the image appeared to Denten, as suddenly he succeeded in erasing it from his mind. Tonight he would not let Reed Howard intrude in any way on his time with Cayla.

He looked again at his watch. She was late. He took another sip of wine, not his usual drink but tonight he would join Cayla in a glass of wine or so. He leaned back in his chair; he focused on the glass of wine. The taste of wine reminded him of Anna. She had kept in contact over the previous months, her emails replete with details about her modeling, more details than Denten thought necessary. From the emails he concluded that modeling now must be more important than college. She said very little about college. In recent emails Anna had included pictures of herself that captured her stunning beauty, pictures that she suggested would likely appear on the cover of a popular magazine for teens. He hated the thought but these recent emails gave Denten the feeling that Anna was gradually slipping away from him. For a moment he stared into his glass of wine, remembering tender moments in Italy and again last summer with Anna.

"I'm sorry."

Denten looked up. A radiant Cayla Finch stood next to the table apologizing for her late arrival. Immediately, he stood up to greet her with a brief hug. They had adopted this greeting over the past few months.

"You wouldn't believe the traffic between here and Winona." Cayla confessed. "I don't think any body stayed at home tonight."

Denten smiled. "You look great. You deal well with adversity." He assisted her in getting seated, taking delight in being close to her.

"Thank you." Cayla settled into her chair.

For a moment they looked at each other across the small table. Cayla smiled. Brilliant white teeth and charming dimples captured Denten's focus. She simply was a very beautiful woman. Sometimes Denten questioned just why they hadn't capitalized on an obvious mutual attraction. For him Anna had something to do with that. For her, he had no idea.

"How was your conference?" Cayla asked.

"Long and not very exciting." Denten shrugged his shoulders dismissively.

Their conversation covered a range of subjects, mostly related to their respective schedules. Cayla's was particularly rigorous since she expected to graduate in just three years. Following a glass of wine, they ordered, their conversation continuing without hesitation. They found so much to talk about. Nearly finished with their meal, Denten watched as Cayla's body grew rigid, her hand moved up to her mouth. She stared in disbelief at the entrance to the restaurant. Denten turned in his seat. He sat up straight. His breath quickened. Reed Howard stood by the entrance talking to the hostess. Denten's body stiffened. A chill filtered through his body. Cayla sat transfixed, her eyes unblinking. A look of fear spread across that beautiful face. Denten immediately noticed Cayla's dramatic reaction.

"Do you know who that is?" Denten asked, reaching across the table to place his hand on Cayla's.

Cayla didn't answer right away. She continued to stare at Reed. Looking directly at Denten, she quietly said, "Yes. My dad banks there."

Denten squeezed her hand. "So does mine."

Appearing more relaxed, Cayla asked, "What is he doing here?"

"He was at this conference I attended today." Denten answered with disgust.

"Why was he here?"

"He talked about banking. I didn't listen." Denten admitted.

To their mutual relief, Reed did not see them or at least if he did, he made no attempt to talk with them. As they waited for the check, Denten mentioned briefly the importance with which people in the community viewed Reed Howard. While they talked, Cayla retained a distance Denten found perplexing. However, they quickly moved away from their table and out onto the sidewalk. Cayla thanked Denten for the dinner. They embraced briefly each with a quick kiss on the cheek. They agreed to keep in touch. Denten walked Cayla to her car. As she stood before the open door, he placed his hands on her shoulders.

"Thank you for coming." He then leaned toward her, kissing her gently on the lips.

Instantly, her body resisted then she relaxed, letting her body move closer to his. "Thank you for the dinner." She whispered in his ear. She then looked into his eyes, smiled, and returned the kiss. Releasing him, she said, " I think I had better get going. I have a ways to go."

Denten helped her into her car, closed the door, and stepped back as she backed out of the parking space. He watched her drive away, eager to understand their relationship and their mutual aversion to Reed Howard.

Denten walked slowly to his car. The evening relatively young, he had no immediate need to return to his confining dorm room. He drove aimlessly, thinking about Anna, about Cayla, and about Reed Howard. Would he ever escape the damage that man had done to him. What about the one in the car with him? These thoughts he carried with him as he pulled into the dormitory parking lot. He stopped in his usual place, turned off the engine and shut off the lights. As he walked toward the dorm entrance, another car pulled into the parking lot. Denten paid little attention since students came in at all hours.

The car drove right up to Denten. The car stopped. The window rolled down. Seated behind the wheel was Reed Howard. Denten stood stunned by his sudden appearance. He could think of nothing to say.

In his casual, condescending manner, Reed said, "Good evening Denten. How are you?"

"Fine." Denten answered, his voice strained.

"Saw you at the restaurant with Cayla. You two have quiet a thing going."

Denten regained some composure after the initial shock of seeing Reed in the dorm parking lot. "We're friends. Is it any business of yours?" Denten made no attempt to conceal his irritation.

"Don't take offense." Reed made a feeble apology. "I just want to thank you for being good customers at the bank. Also I admire young relationships. I wouldn't want anything to ruin them. Good night."

Reed glared at Denten as he put his car in gear and raced out of the parking lot. Denten stood locked in disbelief.

Chapter 19

Denten leaned back in his desk chair. His shoulders slumped. His lips spread in a grin. On his computer a young woman of stunning beauty filled the screen. Anna Moretti's smile captivated him even from a distance. Her natural beauty enhanced by the makeup department, accentuated her marvelous dark eyes and her sumptuous lips which not long ago his had touched. He unconsciously licked his lips, in his mind tasting their sweet flavor. The picture showed Anna in an advertisement for some Italian hair products. She had attached it to her latest email.

The radiant beauty of the picture was pleasing to the eye. Still, it did not represent the girl Denten had for a time fallen in love with. The marketing of her beauty had done something to the natural grace and charm he found so enchanting during those precious few hours they had spent together in Italy and again last summer in Riverside. Anna had obviously found an outlet in modeling. She talked of little else in emails they shared less frequently. Rarely, did she mention their relationship or her college experience so far. Denten regretted having to admit that the intensity of their relationship had faded over the past few months. For him completing his degree as well as contact with Cayla offered an attractive alternative to the diminishing contact with Anna. Anna's world now revolved around modeling. At least that's the impression Denten got from the content of the few recent emails he had received.

Denten reached for the letter which arrived in the mail just yesterday, an invitation to Cayla's graduation party. Scheduled for her home in Riverside, the party would celebrate not only her graduation from St. Mary's but also her acceptance at the Northwestern University School of Law in Chicago. When she had informed Denten of her acceptance, he joined in her excitement. What a marvelous opportunity to gain acceptance to one of the nation's outstanding law schools. Cayla would enter Northwestern University as perhaps one of its youngest candidates for a degree in law.

Denten looked back at the computer screen and the perfection of Anna's picture. He then held up the invitation written in long hand on simple white paper. His raised his head, looking thoughtfully at a space just above the computer screen. The simple written invitation and the email stood as metaphors for the contrast in his relationship with these two women as well as the contrast in personal communication currently popular around the world. He shook his head and smiled, impressed with his profound insight.

He looked again at the invitation he held in his hand. Of course, Denten would attend Cayla's party. He had already informed her he would. For his own graduation occurring just days before hers, he would have no special party. Instead, he would join his parents in a quiet celebration over dinner at a place yet to be determined. Much more important to Denten and his parents was the fact that he would finally receive his degree in business. The process had stretched beyond what they had envisioned. The injury to Denten's dad along with the academic problems Denten faced at Minnesota State University Mankato accounted for a part of that extension. Now, however, he stood ready to walk across the stage to receive a bachelor's degree in business.

Events of the past few months remained vivid in Denten's mind. The strange note in the mail box and the appearance of Reed Howard in the dormitory parking lot only a few weeks ago were tucked away in Denten's memory within easy access. He thought about these events often, concluding that most certainly Reed Howard was the man in the backseat of that big car he saw in the park so many years ago.

Denten suddenly rose from his chair, aware that he had spent too much time thinking about the past. With a deep sigh, he stood for a moment considering one more question. What would he do about what he considered conclusive evidence implicating Reed Howard? He just didn't know. Again he reminded himself that perhaps this was not the time to contemplate what he would do. He still had two finals to take as well as preparations to make for graduation in a few days. Shutting off the computer, he placed the written invitation carefully on his desk, grabbed his back pack, and headed for his 10:00 a.m. class.

Though Denten rarely discussed at length with anyone his career plans, as graduation neared, he had broached the subject with his parents. Growing up on a farm, he had experienced the life of a farmer. Especially, this past year, he had learned of the endless responsibilities that came with farming. Before his father's accident, Denten had not assumed responsibility for much except for what his father told him to do. That changed when his father no longer could take charge of the demands imposed by the harvest, the seeding, and the cultivation. Through all this Denten never seriously discussed his future as a farmer. If his parents just assumed he would continue on in his father's footsteps or if they simply left that decision up to Denten never came up for serious discussion. Perhaps, his dad's accident and his academic problems in college dominated the family's thinking.

Recently, however, they had sat down to discuss Denten's future. With the degree now assured, they all viewed this discussion as far overdue. Except as a young boy dreaming of growing up a cowboy, he never expressed any preference for what he would do when he grew up. One thing, however, had always intrigued him: traveling. Buried deep in his memory were those many times he watched as the jets cut contrails across the blue, Minnesota, summer sky as they flew to and from the Minneapolis/St. Paul airport or the Air Force base in Rapid City, South Dakota.

Now, just days before graduation, the family no longer needed to discuss Denten's career choice. He had made it. Upon graduation he would assume his role as an assistant account executive for Travel

Incorporated with offices located in Mankato. In contemplating his future, Denten never forgot about the flyer he saw posted in Mankato's admission office. The flyer advertised a company named Travel Incorporated. He had returned to the campus to discuss his schedule for the fall semester. With the approach of graduation, Denten had contacted a Mr. Ted Bennett, the president of the company. He discovered that the company was more than a travel agency. It served as a corporate planner, assisting companies in planning and implementing both meeting and incentive programs. Denten emerged from his meeting with Mr. Bennett impressed with the possibilities for travel and advancement the company offered. Within a few days he had completed an official application for employment. After a comprehensive interview, Mr. Bennett offered Denten a contract. He accepted.

With hundreds of excited, proud parents, friends and relatives crowded in the State University Mankato's Myers Field House, an atmosphere of anticipation hung in the air. Among that crowd sat Oscar and Grace Ballery. No body with the possible exception of Denten himself savored this moment more than his parents. His sisters and their families sent warm congratulations. His sisters both playfully commented that their academic example had finally paid off. However, the distance and demands of family and jobs made their attending impossible. Cayla also had wished to attend the graduation. A conflict in her schedule prevented it.

At one time, Denten's poor academic history made a college education questionable. Today, though, it would happen. He would walk across the stage along with slightly over six hundred other graduates to receive their diplomas, for most their passport to the future.

At the conclusion of the prolonged ceremony, Denten's parents waited for him outside the field house. Denten had refused any big celebration. Instead, they made reservation at a popular Mankato restaurant, the Applewood Restaurant and Banquet Center.

There they enjoyed a quiet conclusion to a day of excitement and satisfaction. In just two weeks Denten would return to Mankato, not as a student but as an assistant account executive with Travel Incorporated. Before that, however, he would attend the graduation party for Cayla Finch at her home in Riverside.

Denten parked on a side street a good two blocks from Cayla's home. Obviously, Cayla's party attracted an impressive crowd. It was a perfect early summer, Sunday afternoon, a bright sun pushing the temperature into the low 80's. He entered the house hesitantly aware that he likely would know few of the people there. Cayla surrounded by well wishers spotted Denten as he gingerly stepped into the living room.

She excused herself and walked quickly to meet him. "Thank you for coming. I wondered if you would make it." She gave him a brief hug.

"Never a doubt." Denten smiled, noting the radiance she exuded on this most important day. Her enchanting smile produced those charming dimples. "By the way, congratulations, again."

Each had joined the other in acknowledgement of the rush of good news for both of them. Her admission to the Northwestern School of Law, his acceptance of a position with Travel Incorporated, and, of course, their graduations provided abundant reason for celebration. Though mostly by way of cell phone, those expressions of congratulations still carried with them considerable importance. Now in person they could again share their mutual excitement.

Taking Denten by the hand, Cayla ushered him around introducing him to several of her relatives. Also, he finally saw someone else he knew, Andrea Palmer, Cayla's college roommate and someone he met at the Riverside Bar several months ago. They talked briefly of that time at the bar and of the one more year Andrea faced before her graduation from St. Mary's.

"You don't know how much I envy you two." Andrea confessed.

"Your time is coming." Cayla reminded her.

"What will I do without you as a roommate?" A sadness crossed Andrea's face.

Cayla gave her a big hug. "You'll do just fine without me taking up your time."

Their eyes met. Both knew what she referred to.

For the next hour, Denten stayed close to Cayla, feeling some discomfort among mostly strangers. He stayed for lunch and for casual conversation with a few of the relatives who expressed an interest in his new career and his relationship with Cayla. Before he left, he and Cayla agreed that he would return in the evening giving them a chance to spend some time alone together.

"What a gorgeous evening." Cayla lightly grasped Denten's hand as they walked away from her home.

"A great time for a walk." Denten agreed. "How'd the party go?"

"Fine. So many people. And all there for me? Kinda scary."

"What do you mean? You deserve every minute of it." Denten reached his arm around Cayla's shoulder. She moved closer resting her head on his shoulder.

"I don't know." Cayla paused, not quite sure what to say next. "I didn't do any thing you didn't do."

"But you did it in three years. Besides you're beautiful." Denten stopped to face Cayla. He smiled into her bright eyes. She smiled back.

"I'm not sure about that, but thank you."

They walked for a few blocks then turned back to Cayla's house.

"Where do we go from here?" She asked.

The question took Denten by surprise. "Ah, how about the back yard?"

Cayla laughed. "I mean us. What happens to us?"

"I hope nothing."

"You here and me in Chicago?" Cayla asked.

They reached her house. They walked around the back yard, now dark and quiet. She guided him to a small patio in the far corner of the yard. Here they sat on a bench her father had built around a fire pit where Cayla had entertained many friends over the years. They sat down facing each other. Denten reached for both her hands. He gently squeezed them.

"Look, Cayla, you're not only beautiful but talented. You think I'd let that get away?"

Even in the growing darkness Cayla's smile revealed her perfect teeth.

"I'm serious, Denten." Cayla looked intently into Denten's eyes.

"I know you are. I am too." Denten reassured her. "If we are serious," Denten continued, "things will take care of themselves." For a moment he remembered a similar conversation months ago in Italy. "Look, let's enjoy this time. So much to be proud of."

Denten stood up offering his hand to Cayla. She stood up directly in front of him. He stepped forward, placing his hands around her shoulders pulling her closer. Instantly, her body stiffened. He could feel its sudden rigidity. He leaned forward prepared to place his lips on hers. Before he could, she stepped back away from him. She said nothing.

Denten dropped his arms to his sides. With his hand he lifted her chin. "Cayla, is something wrong? Did I do something wrong?"

She stood erect, unmoving, staring off into the distance. "Something happened." She spoke in barely a whisper.

"To you?" Denten sensed her tension and anxiety.

She nodded her head.

"When?"

He could hear her sobs. Her shoulders trembled. "Long ago."

"What happened?" He asked, his heart pumping a little faster.

Cayla stared off in the distance almost as if she was reading a script. With force, she confessed, "I was sexually assaulted."

Shock ran through Denten's body. He couldn't find words to respond. He reached for the sobbing Cayla attempting to draw her into his embrace. She resisted.

"It was a warm Saturday in the summer." Cayla continued in a voice barely audible but a voice filled with anger and resentment. "I was at church. I was eight years old. A man stopped to give me a ride home from church." Cayla's voice took on more strength, tears flowed down her face. Still she spoke firmly. "He didn't take me home. He took me to the park. He assaulted me."

With that she collapsed into Denten's arms. A flood of emotion and years of anguish poured out as she gripped his shoulders, her fingers digging into his skin.

They stood holding one another, saying nothing.

"My God! I was there!" Denten confessed.

They both fell silent. Cayla looked up into his face, tears streaming down her face. "What do you mean?" she whispered, trying desperately to control her sobbing.

Denten stepped back. He ran his fingers through her hair, pushing it back over her ears. He spoke slowly, gazing into her eyes floating in tears. "On that Saturday morning, I was riding my bike. I was ten years old. I rode to the park. I heard cries of 'Help me, Help me.' I saw the black car and the man in the back seat with someone else. That someone else was you."

Cayla gasped. "My God!" The truth so long concealed sent a sudden flood of emotion flowing through her body. At the same time she began to feel a release, as if a door long ago locked had now opened, fresh air pouring in.

For several minutes they embraced, clinging to each other as they remembered that shared experience. Weak and emotionally depleted, they sat down on the bench. They talked freely now of the adversity they both had suffered from the dreadful incident. They talked about their refusing to tell their parents about what happened. They acknowledged each sharing the secret with a friend. Denten talked about his nightmares. She talked about her resistance to men and how a cold shiver ran through her body whenever one touched her.

Of course, they talked about the man responsible for their mutual agony. Denten mentioned the strange behavior of Reed Howard, of the note in the mail box and of his recent appearance in the dorm parking lot. He talked of his conclusion that Mr. Howard was the culprit. After all these years, Cayla confirmed it for him.

Finally, they talked about what they would do about the assault. Would Reed get away with the torture he imposed on two young people? They talked about the fear, the shame, the embarrassment for Cayla. They talked about their respective careers just underway. Through all this they agreed that someday justice would find Reed Howard paying for what he did. How it would happen, they did not know. They did know that sharing their experience removed an enormous weight from their shoulders.

Preparing to return to the house, they embraced. This time Cayla did so with less reluctance. It would take time for her to overcome her aversion to men touching her. However, at this moment she let Denten pull her closer. She also shared in a deep kiss.

As they separated, Cayla smiled up at Denten. Wiping tears from under her eyes, she recalled the conversation with Andrea to whom she had revealed her secret. Then she had made a promise. Tonight she made it again. This time she had an ally.

Chapter 20

"You people are the face of this company. You have been specially selected to work this program. I don't think I have to tell you how important this client is. We all need to do our best to ensure that they remain our client. Remember, smile. Never say no to a participant request. If you don't know an answer, say that you don't, but also say you will find out and let them know." Denten stood before a group of fourteen travel staff preparing to greet 400 arriving participants at Las Vegas' MGM Grand Hotel and Casino. Dressed in khakis and a long sleeve shirt with a button down collar, he assumed comfortably a leadership role for the travel staff that sat before him many of whom were about his age.

For two days Denten had been in Las Vegas offering assistance to the travel staff in their preparations at the sprawling casino. He did not always travel on site for contracted programs he helped negotiate. However, this was a critical telecommunications company, a long time client now being pursued by Travel Incorporated's major competition. What happened on this program could easily determine the future of Travel Incorporated's relationship with a valuable client.

For the past thirteen months, Denten had worked for Travel Incorporated, a small but efficient corporate planning company located in Mankato. Not a travel agency, it served several, mostly Minnesota companies by offering planning for both incentive and business programs. For example, if a company wished to offer its sales staff the chance to earn a trip to Hawaii or Las Vegas or Orlando or a number of other possible, attractive destinations, Travel Incorporated would sit down with officials from that company to plan in detail such a program. The travel staff would then precede the participants on site to ensure the proper implementation of the planned program and, of course, remain on site for the duration of the program. In addition to incentive and business travel, the company also offered training in employee and operational transition designed to assist companies in the process of change.

Founded twenty years ago by Henry Bennett, father of the current president, Ted Bennett, the company employed three account executives, three assistant account executives, twenty-five full and part time travel staff and ten internal staff whose responsibilities included accounting, marketing, program design, and routine office functions.

As an assistant account executive, Denten worked with Frank Getty, one of the three company account executives. In his mid forties and a fifteen year veteran in travel sales, Frank's trim body made him look even taller than his six foot three frame. Moderately handsome, articulate, and blessed with a disarming smile combined to make Frank a superb salesman. His careful attention to those with whom he related gave them an added feeling of importance. Frank's personality definitely gave him an advantage in the world of sales.

Though friendly and easy to talk to, Denten did not possess a forceful personality. He was more comfortable listening than talking. However, he did have a strong desire to succeed which enabled him to adapt rapidly to the incentive and business travel business. Denten's willingness to learn, a characteristic acquired from his early exposure to work on the farm, and Frank's patience, experience and sensitivity to others enabled the two to work together efficiently and amiably. One other quality which contributed to Denten's success as a travel account executive was his fascination with travel. Frequently, as he now had the opportunity to travel, during those long, tedious hours flying at 35,000 feet, he would reflect on the times he would stand in the farm yard watching jealously jets flying high in the sky over southern Minnesota.

However, actual travel assumed only a small part of Denten's responsibilities. His major role included seeking new clients as well as negotiating contracts with existing ones, always, at least until he gained experienced in the business, under the guidance of Frank Getty.

During Denten's first year with Travel Incorporated, he had been instrumental in securing two new clients as well as negotiating contracts with three other companies: two telecommunication companies and one with a large beer distribution company. Because his role in the contract with one of the telecommunication companies was critical, he was now on site in Las Vegas offering assistance where needed.

Since his graduation just over a year ago, Denten's life had changed. From a farm boy to an assistant, travel account executive made for a significant adjustment in his life style. Unlike the relative isolation of work on the farm, Denten now spent each day with others, either other members of the Travel Incorporated staff or with representatives of prospective or existing clients. The adjustment was not difficult for him. It did, however, take a little time for him to gain confidence and comfort in his new role.

One aspect of his life that did not change was the memory of that Saturday morning so many years ago. Sharing his secret with both Anna and Cayla had reduced the frequency with which he experienced those night time encounters with the dreadful memory. Revealing his secret to two people very dear to him definitely had relieved some of intensity of the memory. Nonetheless, it had not reduced the intensity of just what to do about Reed Howard. Cayla's confirming that the assailant was, indeed, Reed Howard had solved that mystery for Denten. At the same time it had produced another dilemma. What should they do about the truth of that fateful Saturday morning?

Since that highly emotional moment when Denten and Cayla discovered their shared secret, they had avoided discussing the incident or what they should do about exposing Reed Howard. For Cayla, the same concerns persisted. Who would believe her word against that of Reed Howard, a highly respected member of the community? Did she wish to drag the sordid details into the public? What would making the accusation against Howard do to her anticipated career in law? One of the more vital concerns of both Denten and Cayla was their parents. They still had no knowledge of the sexual assault. What effect would telling them now have after the passage of over fourteen years? Both sets of parents were not getting any younger. Discovering this now after so many years could have devastating effects for them.

Though they kept in frequent contact, Cayla in Chicago and Denten in Mankato or in some attractive, warm destination, they did not discuss the situation either in their emails or on their cell phones. It was simply not a subject one discussed at a distance. Both knew, however, that someday they would have to deal with the reality of what happened. After all they had promised themselves that they would see justice done.

Through the year, emails from Anna increased. More recent communication from her concentrated on them rather than just on her and her modeling. Also in recent emails she talked about her education, confessing an ambivalence about a major but leaning toward education or counseling of some type. Recent emails also contained hints that Anna faced disillusionment with the world of modeling. She even hinted that she had faced verbal abuse from Mr. Conti, the manager of the Florence office of the Alpha Modeling Agency.

Denten concluded his meeting with the travel staff who would now assume much of the responsibility for the success of the program at the MGM Grand. He would spend another day or so on site to serve in any way the staff needed him. After that he would return to Mankato to pursue a new client he had made initial contact with just before leaving for Las Vegas.

Walking the near half mile from the staff work room in the convention section of the expansive MGM, Denten entered his room to retrieve his briefing notes for this program. He had carelessly neglected to take them with him to the staff meeting. Upon entering, he noticed the blinking red light on hotel telephone. Probably another message from the hotel, he thought to himself. He picked up the phone, pressed the message button, and heard the familiar voice inform him that he had a message.

The message came from his mother. She had called earlier to inform him that Gilberto Deluca had suddenly passed away, a victim of a heart attack. Denten listened in shock to his mother's message, thinking of the time he had spent with Gilberto during their trip to Italy and the months that followed as Gilberto recovered from by pass surgery. Though he tried to think only of Gilberto and Alda, Denten could not avoid the image of Anna. He would make it home for the funeral.

Anna and Emma Moretti sat across the table from Alda Deluca. Pale, weary with puffy, red eyes, Alda struggled to grasp the reality of life without Gilberto. Most of her 84 years she had spent with him. Now she faced life alone.

Emma reached across the table to grasp Alda's frail hand. "We will be here for you as long as you need us." She promised.

Alda covered Emma's hand with her own. "Thank you so much." She whispered in a voice drained of emotion.

Gilberto's episode in Italy over two years ago served only as a hint of the future. The subsequent by pass surgery gave added assurance that Gilberto would enjoy many more years of good health. In a moment, days ago all that changed. All the expectations ended as Gilberto collapsed preparing to go to bed after a busy night in the restaurant. Alda's 911 call brought the rescue squad to the restaurant in minutes. Already it was too late.

With the help of the restaurant's nighttime hostess, Mary Chandler, friends and relatives were notified of Gilberto's death. An email reached the Morettis within hours. The Ballerys informed Denten in Las Vegas when they heard. Funeral services were scheduled for Monday, sufficient time for relatives like the Morettis to arrange to attend.

Anna and her mother never hesitated in their decision to attend the funeral, securing reservations for the very next day following receipt of the sad email. Anna's dad faced vital business obligations precluding his joining his wife and daughter.

Anna loved her distant uncle. For that reason alone she would attend his funeral. Also, she needed an escape from her rigorous routine. In addition, she had other reasons to travel again to America. Those reasons centered on Denton Ballery. Without a second thought, she agreed to accompany her mother to Minnesota.

During her long flight from Rome to Minneapolis, Anna reflected on the past two years and the changes they had produced in her young life. She smiled to herself remembering that late summer day and her first introduction to Nino Conti. Closing her eyes, she envisioned the first meeting with him in the Florence office of the Alpha Modeling Agency. Since then, the excitement had faded, but for just moments the initial excitement returned.

Since that initial meeting and the subsequent trip to the Los Angeles office of the modeling agency, much about her life had changed. At first she responded with pride to the encouragement she received from the Alpha Modeling officials. A career in modeling was most definitely within her grasp. Her natural beauty, her composure, and her charm would rapidly propel her onto the covers of major international magazines. At least this is what she was told. She was also told that all of this would not seriously interfere with her pursuit of a college degree.

Well into her first semester at the University of Florence, she discovered that not all she had heard was true. She desperately attempted to balance the academic demands of college with the mostly physical demands of modeling. Guilt often accompanied her communication with Denten. Many of her recent emails contained self-indulgent references to her personal achievements, none of them dealing with academics. She even had sent pictures of herself in a few of her emails. Her modeling schedule increasingly detracted from her study time, even her class attendance. Guilt even followed her into her classrooms.

Her growing disillusionment with her life, with modeling in particular, found her seeking help from her parents. Always, they had provided support for whatever Anna decided to do, confident that she would make intelligent choices. She did make good choices. Even as she confronted the turbulent preadolescent and adolescent years, Anna's parents treated her decisions with respect while she respected their advice. At this stage in her life she again needed their counsel.

Their discussions focused on just what Anna wanted from her life. Was modeling what she wanted? She had always dreamed of a college education. Did she still hold to that dream? Her mom and dad realized that her modeling was drawing her farther and farther away from the academic world. This she acknowledged. They also expressed concern for the rigid dietary requirements imposed by the modeling agency. Anna needed no one to guide her eating habits. Nonetheless, the agency tried. Denten's name came up in the discussions, Anna agreeing with her parents that she had not treated him respectfully.

In recent weeks this discussion occurred with greater frequency. Anna expressed more ambivalence each time about her future in modeling and her academic performance. Her parents suggested she sit down with Mr. Conti of the agency to discuss with him her concerns. She did.

That discussion, more than any other factor, convinced her that modeling wasn't her future. Etched permanently in her mind rested the image of Nino Conti, his greasy hair slicked back, his shirt left open to expose scraggily chest hair, and his ingratiating smile that revealed discolored teeth. He had agreed to take of his valuable time to meet with Anna. His response to her concerns about time, about college, about her future included a blunt reminder that modeling required a beautiful body and face, not a college degree. He reminded Anna that modeling was all about appearance, all about physical body, the more visible the better. "Yes," he said, "appearance is only skin deep. What's beneath," he affirmed, "was irrelevant."

Throughout the ordeal with Nino, Anna sat in mild shock, his words demeaning, insulting, and humiliating. She made no attempt to argue with him, the contempt she felt expressed clearly by her refusal to respond. At a pause in his diatribe, Anna moved back her chair, stood up, thanked him for his time, and walked out of the small conference room. Since that day her commitment to modeling had dwindled. Still her contractual obligation had prevented her from severing the relationship completely.

During the long flight Anna reached back into her memory to grasp the last time she and Denten were together. At that time she learned of the dreadful experience he guarded so closely for so many years. They had not discussed the emotional impact of that experience since they parted months ago. Still, the profound effect the experience had on Denten was evident in his struggle to talk about it. Her memory retained a vivid image of that struggle as they stood in each other's arms in the park where it all happened. Had Denten learned to cope with the power of his experience? As her anticipation of seeing Denten increased, her need to know was renewed. This time she hoped to have a greater chance to discuss it with him.

Denten paused in the entrance to the Deluca Restaurant, adjusting to the dimly lighted dining room. He stepped forward toward the bar area. In the distance Anna rose from her chair next to her mom. She moved slowly toward Denten, looking at him as if to memorize what she saw. They both stopped; eyes locked on each other.

Anna smiled that bewitching smile. "Hi, Denten." She spoke in a quiet voice.

"Anna." Denten answered.

Without another word, Anna rushed into Denten's open arms where for a few glorious moments they recaptured a part of their relationship.

"God, it's good to hold you again." Anna breathed into Denten's chest.

"It's been a long time." Denten answered quietly.

Hand and hand they walked to the table where Anna's mom and Alda sat watching the moving reunion. With tears in his eyes, Denten stood by Alda's side. She rose slowly from her chair, surrendering to Denten's arms.

"I'm so sorry. Gilberto was so special." Denten held Alda firmly.

"Thank you. You were special to him too." Alda leaned back, with her hand she brushed a tear from Denten's cheek. Her voice weakened by the trauma of Gilberto's passing, she said, "He never forgot all the time you spent with him after his surgery."

"I enjoyed it. Sorry, I couldn't be here sooner. I had to wait for a flight out of Las Vegas." Denten apologized.

"You are here now. That's all that matters." Alda reassured him. "Gilberto was so proud of your travel business." After a short pause for her to take a breath, she asked, "How are your parents?"

"They're fine. Thank you. They should be here any time. I talked with them on the way from Minneapolis. I stopped here first."

Gilberto's funeral filled the small catholic church not far from Deluca's Restaurant. A fixture in Riverside, the restaurant at one time or another probably served food to practically everyone in Riverside, some many times, some every day. Denten served as one of the pall bearers, placing him in one of the front rows of the sanctuary. The service included the opportunity for several people to speak about Gilberto, his generosity, his humor, and his good food. For an hour the people of Riverside shared the last chance to pay their respects to a dear neighbor and friend.

The service completed, the pall bearers followed the casket out the center aisle of the church. As he walked slowly, his hand upon the closed casket, Denten's eyes glimpsed the crowded sanctuary. For an instant, he caught his breath. His eyes focused on the face of Reed Howard seated half way back. Their eyes locked together only for seconds. In those seconds Denten detected an arrogant sneer on Reed's face. Denten felt only revulsion, Cayla's admission racing through his mind.

Chapter 21

Denten pulled into the parking lot next to the Deluca Restaurant. He parked at the far end near the door to the Deluca's private entrance to their living quarters. He shut off the car. He leaned back, closed his eyes, thinking about the situation he now faced. He enjoyed the interest of two very beautiful, dynamic women. Considering all the years when girls played virtually no role in his life, he smiled to think that now he was faced with a problem: two women. Visions of Cayla confessing her long held secret appeared in his mind. Visions followed of Anna listening to him confess his secret. Should he tell Anna about Cayla? Was strict honesty the next step in dealing with a potential problem?

He shook his head, opened the door, walked to the Deluca's private entrance. Yesterday's funeral offered little privacy for Denten and Anna. She and her mother would stay for at least two more days before returning to Italy. He had to return to Mankato the next day. An important client meeting required his attendance. For several weeks he had worked with a representative from a large insurance company who sought assistance with designing an agenda and destination for the company's annual meeting. Simply, Denten could not afford to miss the meeting.

Today he would spend the entire time with Anna. He reached for the door. It opened before he had a chance to knock.

"Good morning." Anna greeted him with her enchanting smile and a tender hug.

For an instant, Denten stared. He just could not get used to her captivating beauty and her intoxicating fragrance. 'How are you today?" He asked realizing how inane that likely sounded. For a fleeting moment he just didn't know what else to say.

"Come on in for a minute. Say hi to mom and Alda."

Denten walked into the small kitchen where sat Anna's mom and Alda sharing a late morning coffee. Alda had faced with courage the emotion of the previous day. She had already regained some of her color and energy.

"Thank you for everything." She got up to give Denten a gentle squeeze. "A big day planned?" She asked, her voice much stronger than yesterday.

"No, not really. Drive around maybe. A little lunch." Denten didn't admit that they simply wished to spend some time alone before they would have to return to their own private worlds, hundreds of miles apart.

Emma stood listening to Alda and Denten. She then approached him, also greeting him with a gentle hug. "Whatever you do, you two young people have a good time away from us oldies." As she stepped back, a smile spread across her face, a smile reminiscent of Anna's.

Anna and Denten drove out of the parking lot and headed toward his farm. They stopped to spend a little time with his parents before driving through surrounding countryside enjoying the simple beauty of an early summer day. They had no particular plan. They simply wished to spend time together. So much had happened since they last spent time together, they wanted to try to catch up with each other's life. Yes, they had shared emails over the past months. They could not convey the full meaning of the events which had taken place in their respective lives. An email could not convey the excitement of graduating from college and embarking on a new career. Likewise, emails could not possibly do justice to embarking on a course that would lead to a college degree or to entering the world of modeling.

As they aimlessly drove country roads bordered by fields flowing with young wheat and corn, they discussed their separate worlds. Anna explained her disappointment in modeling and the factors that had led to that disappointment. She hastened to apologize for those emails which only highlighted her modeling achievements. She reviewed only briefly the appalling meeting with Nino Conti. Even now his attitude repulsed her. She asked about Denten's new job and what it entailed. He took pride in the explanation.

Eventually the conversation came around to their fragile relationship. Anna reached over to touch Denten's arm. "What about us?" She asked, a troubled look shown in her face.

Denten turned to look at this wonderful woman who sat beside him. Following a deep breath, he confessed, "I don't know."

"Denten," Anna turned in her seat as much as her seat belt would allow. "I know I got wrapped up with this modeling thing. It seemed good at first. I kinda was distracted for a while."

"You certainly fit the role." This time Denten smiled and reached over to squeeze Anna's arm.

Anna's voice reflected her seriousness. "Denten, do you think we have a future together?"

Denten hesitated before answering. Ever since he found out that she would attend the funeral for Gilberto, he had debated whether to tell her about Cayla. At this point he was not sure himself anymore about his future with either Anna or Cayla. Deception had never been a Denten strategy. Always he had tried to deal with others openly and honestly, except, of course, for the dreadful episode in the park.

Now, he looked over at Anna again. "Anna, I need to level with you. I have been seeing another woman only casually, but I want you to know about it."

"Thank you for telling me. I really couldn't expect you sit home reading my emails." Anna stared straight ahead avoiding eye contact with Denten. "Can you tell me who she is?"

"Her name is Cayla Finch. She grew up here in Riverside. Attended a private school. I only met her by accident. At a local bar a couple years ago. Don't get the wrong idea. She's not that type. She's in law school at Northwestern University in Chicago."

"I'm impressed." Anna's response sounded sincere. "Are you serious about her?"

Again Denten paused to think about his answer. "She's a great girl with big plans. Honestly, I don't know where the relationship fits into those plans."

"Sounds familiar." Anna commented with a chuckle.

For a few minutes, the two drove in silence, each assessing the implications of the conversation.

"You hungry?" Denten's question broke the silence.

"Yeah, I think so." Anna agreed.

The topic of food reduced the tension clouding the space around them.

Denten drove to a small coffee-sandwich shop not far from Riverside High School from which he graduated. He explained to Anna that students frequently would avoid the school lunch in favor of a sandwich and soda at this small deli. Since summer brought vacation for the students, only a few customers sat scattered around the small dining area.

When they had ordered, Anna moved uneasily in her chair. With reluctance she asked about the nightmare Denten suffered so often. He found the subject much easier to talk about since he had shared it with Anna and with Cayla. He admitted that the dream had occurred less frequently and with less intensity. However, he still had to deal with it, a truth which had acquired a new reality since Cayla had confirmed the identity of her rapist. Denten did not share with Anna the full truth about the secret which now three people shared: Cayla, he, and Reed Howard.

The rest of the afternoon they spent enjoying each other's company. The conversation avoided a the delicate subjects of the morning. They did stop by a field where Denten's dad was cultivating corn. Oscar Ballery had adapted well to having one partially disabled arm. They had also stopped again to enable Anna to say good bye to Denten's mom. By the time they returned to the Deluca Restaurant, the sun had already set allowing darkness to settle over Riverside.

As he had that morning, Denten pulled into the parking lot next to the restaurant. Unlike the morning only a few places remained as people in the community came in for dinner. Near the back of the lot, Denten found a space. He parked, stopped the car, slumped in his seat, looked over at Anna and said, "Well, that was a day."

"It was." Anna agreed.

They both stepped out of the car, Denten walking around to Anna's side. They stood facing each other, lights from the parking lot casting long shadows upon the blacktop. Anna moved closer to Denten. Emotion rushed through Denten's body, images of those tender moments so long ago in Italy racing through his mind. Suddenly, they virtually leaped into each other's arms, months of separation feeding galloping emotions. Clinging to each other, their bodies pressed tightly together, they kissed long and with abandon. Frantic hands searched the contours of their bodies. Denten pressed her against the car. Her breasts pushed against his chest; his hand reached inside her top to squeeze lightly her hardened nipples. Anna's breath quickened, her lips showering Denten with kisses.

Car door slammed in the parking lot. The sound brought Denten and Anna back to the real world. They relaxed. Denten moved back a step still concentrating on Anna's face now gleaming in the moon light.

"Maybe I should go in." She whispered, shaking her head in obvious disappointment.

"You're probably right." Denten moved back letting his arms drop to his side.

"You leave tomorrow, don't you?" Anna asked.

"Yes, I have to." Denten answered quietly.

"I understand." Anna placed her hands behind Denten's head and focused her eyes on his. "I've enjoyed this time together." She paused before continuing. "I don't know what you call it, but I believe that what's supposed to be will someday happen. Let's let things work out naturally."

"I agree. Please keep in touch and have a safe flight home." Denten kissed her lips lightly this time, walked her to the private entrance door, and quietly bid her good night.

Back in his car, his mind whirled with the thought of Cayla and of Anna. Anna's comment about what was supposed to be would be, he wasn't sure about. He was sure that in the future a decision would have to be made about Anna and about Cayla.

In his small, efficiency apartment, Denten relaxed in front of the flat screen, HD TV, his one extravagance since embarking on his new career. He reflected on the last two days of intense discussions with representatives from a potential client. In his opinion, the discussions should give Travel Incorporated another client. He stretched in his reclining chair, smiled, and rested his head back on the chair. His cell phone rang. Jumping up and racing to his brief case he had dropped on the floor by the entrance door, he dug for the phone.

"Hello. This is Denten."

He heard only breathing then sobs. "Hello. Who is this?" He asked, perplexed by this mysterious call. Could it be another prank call he thought?

"Denten?" A frail voice asked then erupted into more sobs.

"Anna?" Denten moved quickly toward the window where he received better reception. "Anna? What's the matter? Where are you?" His voice revealing the panic that expanded with each passing second.

"Denten! We're in jail?" Anna announced struggling to control her emotions.

In shock, Denten exclaimed, "What? Where are you in jail?"

"The Hennepin County jail." She repeated firmly.

Denten caught his breath. He searched for words to express his consternation. "What in the hell happened?"

"I..It's.." She found difficult explaining what had happened. "It's a long story." Anna answered. "It's...It's for possession of marijuana." Her voice tapered off to a near whisper.

"Marijuana!" Denten shouted into the phone. " Where in God's name did that come from?"

"In our luggage." Anna admitted clearly, gaining control over her emotions.

"In your luggage!" Denten repeated. "How the hell did it get there?"

During the ensuing minutes, Anna explained their meeting with a Nicolas Watson at the Airport Hilton to pick up a package from him. The arrangement made by Nino Conti in Florence before she and her mother left for America and the funeral. The arrangements included the explanation that the package contained a special cosmetic make up with which the Florence office wished to experiment. Since Anna was in Minneapolis already, her picking up the package would facilitate its arrival in Italy.

In retrospect, Anna confessed to stupidity for accepting a package from a virtual stranger. Still Nino had arranged it. She had no specific reason to think that he trafficked in illegal drugs.

"Denten, I guess I have to hang up. This guy keeps giving me this sign." Anna paused. "Denten, we need your help."

"Of course. What can I do?"

Denten could hear Anna's deep breath. "A lawyer. Can you help?"

The request plunged Denten into thought. For a few seconds he said nothing. Cayla jumped into his mind. He would contact her for maybe some advice. Though she had attended law school for only a year, she still may have suggestions.

"Look, Anna, give me a bit of time. I'll see what I can do."

"Oh, God, thank you. We didn't know what to do."

"I'll get back to you as soon as I know something. Can you use your cell phone?"

"No!" Anna gave him the number where she could be reached at the jail.

Replacing the phone, Anna slumped in the hard chair next to her mother, who had said little since officials escorted them off the plane. They sat next to a small round, metal table in what presumably served as an interrogation room. Anna reached for her mother's hand squeezed it, let go then leaned forward resting her head on her hands spread on the top of the table. She let out a long breath. Her mother sat transfixed, an officer sat across the table.

"For now you will spend the night in a private cell." The officer balding and over weight pushed himself away from the table. "Not much can happen until you get a lawyer."

The cell was not the typical bunk bed with a hole in the corner that served as a toilet. Two single beds lined one side of the cell. A sink and toilet a privacy curtain concealed in one corner. No bars enclosed the cell. One window, high on the back wall, allowed the moon to shine in. One door with a small window provided entrance to the cell.

A middle aged woman with black hair streaked with gray brought them a small dinner of some kind of soup and chicken sandwich. Though only a meager meal, they had not eaten since earlier in the day. Any thing was appreciated. Anna and her mom ate in silence. Her mom suffered devastation and humiliation by the nightmare that had dragged them to jail. Emma ate only a few bites then lay back on the bed to wonder about tomorrow.

Anna's attempt to console her mother did little to allay her fear and humiliation. The reality of sitting in jail hundreds of miles from home crushed Anna too. She had contacted her dad to explain their delay. He, of course, had met the news with astonishment. She, by now, had abandoned the helplessness created by uncontrolled emotion. Now, she realized that patience, not panic would get them home quicker.

Anna lay back on her bed. She stared into the emptiness of the cell, a faint light coming through the one window. She thought about their day that had started with such excitement and anticipation. Saying good bye to Alda produced tears, hugs and promises to keep in touch.

Their late afternoon flight allowed them abundant time for the drive to Minneapolis, the stop at the Hilton, and the return of the rental car. Who would have thought the day would have ended for them in jail. Anna reflected on the package. She recalled the explicit directions for picking it up.

"Nicolas Watson will meet you in the main lobby. You can't miss him." Nino assured her. "He has a shaved head and a full red beard. Somewhere in his late 40's, I'd guess."

Lying on her small bed, she now realized how stupid she was. Why couldn't a cosmetic sample be shipped the normal way? She shook her head. Something that had happened a month ago which at the time carried no consequence now rushed into her mind. At the time Anna had complained to Nino about the rigors of her schedule. She hardly found time for a good night's sleep she voiced to him. Nino had grinned his lascivious grin and suggested he had something that would restore her energy. She refused his offer. She now speculated about what he had. Was it marijuana?

Eventually, Anna drifted off into a restless sleep, one interrupted far too soon by the same matronly woman who had last night brought them something to eat.

"Excuse me miss, but you have a phone call." She announced. "Follow me."

Anna sat up instantly, rubbed her eyes, stepped out of bed and followed the woman out the door. Emma called after Anna, who explained about the phone call. Her mother did not wish to stay alone in the cell. Anna assured her she would be right back. The woman guided her to the small interrogation room where she picked up the phone to hear Denten's voice.

"How ya doing?" He asked.

"Hanging in there." Anna uttered without conviction.

"How's your mom holding out?" Denten inquired.

"Crushed."

"I'm so sorry for both of you." Denten paused for a second. "Look, I think you have a lawyer."

"God! What a relief!" Denten could almost feel the jubilation over the phone.

"His name is Cole Ridgewood. Last night I contacted my friend who's going to Northwestern law school. Remember, I mentioned her."

"Yes, I remember."

"She did some checking and came up with this Mr. Ridgewood." Denten explained.

Anna sat by the phone speechless for a few seconds. "You'll never know how much that means to us, Denten."

"Glad I could help. Mr. Ridgewood should contact you at the jail later this morning. I plan to see you this afternoon." Denten's words eased slightly Anna's burden.

Later that morning Cole Ridgewood did meet with Anna and her mother. Young, handsome, with an engaging smile, and distinctive horn rimmed glasses, Mr. Ridgewood represented a large law firm with offices in Chicago and Minneapolis. Cayla's contacts at Northwestern University produced quick results.

Seated in the small, now called interrogation/conference room, Mr Ridgewood explained to Anna and her mom that possession of marijuana constituted a very serious charge any place but particularly in Minnesota. Directing his attention first to Anna and then to Emma, he continued, "Extenuating circumstances are on your side. No prior record and the small amount will definitely help your cause." He smiled, his words giving the mother and daughter some reason for hope that there was a way out of this mess.

"Now, we need to get you out of here. Bail has been set for $10,000."

Anna looked with alarm at her mom. Where would they get $10,000?

Again Cole smiled. "I know what you're thinking. Don't worry. I'll take care of that matter with a bail bondsman. Just don't plan to leave the country yet." He cautioned with a smile.

For over an hour Cole explained to Anna and her mother the complexities of Minnesota possession laws. They explained to him the events leading up to their apprehension aboard the plane. They also outlined specifically the roles of both Nino Conti and Nicolas Watson. Cole assured them that they would be thoroughly investigated.

By early afternoon Anna and her mom rested in a Best Western motel just minutes from the airport. They would have to remain in the Twin Cities until their meeting with a judge. Cole Ridgewood would, of course, accompany them during that meeting. Also by early afternoon Denten arrived to give support and encouragement to two frightened women.

Four days after Anna and her mom were unceremoniously escorted from their Minneapolis to Rome flight, they stood at the gate waiting to board the same international flight. Thanks to the rapid work of Cole Ridgewood they went before a judge who under the circumstances placed them on probation and allowed them to return home. He reminded them that the possibility existed that they many have to return. It all depended on the further investigation of both Watson and Conti. The judge displayed some compassion in his decision allowing them to leave the country. However, he lectured them on the dangers of taking packages from strangers.

Denten stayed in the Twin Cities until Anna and her mom boarded their flight to Rome. He accompanied them to their hearing before the judge. At the airport, they again had to say goodbye with a few tears, hugs and expressions of profound appreciation.

As Denten drove home to Mankato in the late afternoon, he delighted in knowing that the Morettis would soon enjoy the comforts of home, free from the ordeal they had faced, but fully aware that their case was not over. He, on the other hand, still had to face someday making the choice between two beautiful and talented women. He smiled as he gazed out at the natural beauty of the drive along the Minnesota River. His situation could have been much, much worse. He might not have met at all two women like Anna and Cayla.

Chapter 22

Reed Howard kneeled. He placed his hands on the tiny shoulders of Pamela Collins. He studied her vibrant blue eyes. His eyes took in her delicate nose and mouth, her colorful T-shirt, and her white shorts which covered diminutive hips and ass. A broad smile drew creases across his forehead and around his eyes.

"You know. You are the prettiest girl in the whole wide world." His words produced a giggle from Pamela, another quality that made her so alluring to him.

"I'll bet you're pretty all over, too." His hands slid down her arms and around her legs.

Pamela raised her petite eye brows, rolled her sparkling eyes, and shrugged her shoulders. "I guess, so." She answered in a sweet, seven year old voice.

Pamela Collins lived only three houses away from the Howard's. She and her parents had moved in when she was only a few months old. Her parents, Steve and Gloria Collins, owned a small clothing store in Riverside. In their late thirties, they had both worked in retail sales following college, most of the time in and around the Twin Cities. Married for nearly fifteen years, their lives had assumed a special excitement with the arrival of Pamela seven years ago.

Eight years of marriage had brought them no children. Pamela finally arrived after a grueling, often disappointing, series of fertility tests. Steve and Gloria had seriously considered adoption when they discovered Gloria's pregnancy. Pamela's arrival marked the beginning of a whole new phase in their lives. Starting a new business contributed to an excitement and challenge. To avoid the intense competition facing small businesses in the Twin Cities, the Collins searched for opportunities in smaller communities. Though neither possessed much familiarity with Riverside, they both had grown up not far from there. Their search ultimately ended in Riverside where they would open their own family, clothing store.

With Pamela came the demand for expanded living arrangements. Their small two bedroom apartment simply was not adequate, in their minds, for a family of three. The home they purchased suited them perfectly for now. Over forty years old, it contained three bedrooms along with abundant living area in a living room, family room and kitchen. It also was located in one of the oldest and more desirable parts of Riverside. Even in a town the size of Riverside, certain residential locations ranked highter than others.

One of the first people to welcome them to the neighborhood was Reed Howard. Reed had mastered the ability to project an image of trust and sincerity, skills he practiced almost daily in his position as president of Riverside's only bank. Besides, Steven and Gloria had secured a small business loan from Reed, enabling them to open their clothing store.

Over the years, Reed took note of Pamela as she grew into this pretty, charming, vivacious, young girl. With the capacity to play the avuncular role to perfection, he gradually gained her trust. He cultivated this trust by stopping to talk with her as she rode her trike on the sidewalk or played with dolls in the front yard. Neighborhood gatherings on July 4 or on Super Bowl Sunday also brought Reed in contact with Pamela.

His obsession with her grew. In recent years he had refrained from any physical contact with these special, young girls. Part of his reluctance resided in the presence of Denten Ballery and Cayla Finch. Seeing them together sent a cold chill through his body, a fear of exposure and the sacrifice of everything he had worked for. In place of the much preferred direct contact, over the years he had gained marginal satisfaction from his treasured collection of computer images depicting young girls in various degrees of undress and in various provocative positions.

His relationship with Pamela offered him some confidence that maybe she could satisfy his deepest desires. With utmost caution he pursued the relationship with Pamela. Often, he would comment about how pretty she was. He would increasingly risk touching her cheek, her arm, or squeezing her cute nose. Gradually, this contact expanded to references to body parts. Secrecy, of course, stood paramount in Reed's mind. He talked to Pamela about special gifts some people have, special gifts that special people share.

"It's like a special blanket or a special stuffed animal." He explained. "You don't share these with anyone but special friends."

He convinced her that touching showed love, but only between very special friends.

"I bet you're pretty all over." Reed repeated.

"I guess so. Mommy says so." Pamela giggled again.

Reed, kneeling before her, reached to pull down her small shorts. He moved his hand toward her tiny panties. An erection grew becoming more visible through his trousers. With one hand he struggled to open his zipper.

Pamela stiffened as Reed's hand inched its way inside her panties.

"Mommy said people have private parts." Pamela tried to move away from Reed's invading fingers.

Reed paused. "They certainly do. Good friends share their private parts. Why don't you touch mine?"

Pamela stood without moving, staring straight ahead. Reed slipped into his private sexual fantasy. His heart beat faster.

Pamela sneezed. The sneeze jerked Reed back to reality. He dared go no farther. He stood up and reached for Pamela's tiny, soft hand.

"Let's have that ice cream I promised."

He kneeled to face her again, a stern, serious look on his face. "Remember, we are special friends. Special friends have secrets. They don't tell anybody." Reed flicked his finger under Pamela's chin. "Do you understand?"

Pamela nodded.

Again Reed stood up. "Now, what kind of ice cream did you want?"

Chapter 23

Cayla slouched in one of the many uncomfortable seats in the lecture hall where she attended her class in criminal law. Two years of uninterrupted classes, term papers and hours of reading had taken their toll on Cayla. Though the professor spoke with clarity and command, Cayla couldn't concentrate at this time on the intricacies of criminal law. Always in the past she found academic work both challenging and rewarding. Through high school and college she rose above most others, maintaining a near perfect academic record. At Northwestern School of Law she discovered very early that all students brought with them academic success equal to hers.

Dreams of achieving the three year JD(Juris Doctor) degree dimmed as she found the demands just beyond her capacity to meet them. What had began as an adventure filled with excitement, a plunge into the world of a big time university had faded with the passage of time. The countless hours she devoted to reading previous criminal cases she couldn't begin to calculate. At times her mind faded into a blur as she stared at the words, comprehending none of them. Still she met the high academic standards of the university.

Her mind drifted as the professor talked on about the delicate divisions separating one criminal offense from another. For a time following the critical moment with Denten following her graduation party, she realized long periods of freedom from the shadow of her childhood assault and rape. Having told Denten offered a respite, a sort of cleansing that enabled her to go for weeks without any adverse influences from the tragedy of that Saturday morning. Recently, however, even the thought of telling Denten and the release it offered failed to allay her inner turmoil. She refused to call it depression. Nonetheless, she experienced periods of near despair. She often fell into a melancholy mood grasping for those times in the past when she was happy, when the burden of parts of her past was lifted by a focus on accomplishments or on beneficial relationships with others like Denten or Andrea.

Far too often recently her personal life collided with her academic life creating sadness and thoughts of simply giving up on the law degree. This deterioration in attitude she inadvertently communicated to Denten during the frequent contact they maintained mostly by cell phone. He worried about her. He encouraged her by reminding her of the marvelous opportunity she faced with a degree from such a highly respected university. She earned it, he reminded her. For a while this helped. Soon, however, unhappiness returned. She felt distraught about her life, the constant haunting memory of so long ago adding to her disappointment in the pursuit of a law degree.

The professor's reference to childhood assault crimes brought Cayla quickly back to reality. She sat up straight in the uncomfortable chair, training her eyes on the professor who wandered freely around the front of the lecture hall as he spoke with authority and without a note. What caught her attention instantly was the point that sexual abuse of a child, generally, carried with it no statute of limitations. This information reinforced what she learned very early in her law education. At about the same time, she also learned what she already knew, that childhood sexual assault could have lasting, debilitating effects on young victims. As Cayla listened intently to the words of the professor, her mind opened up to a rush of images, all related to the fateful Saturday morning. Was there no way she would ever rid her mind of those horrible images? Trying to cope with them was becoming more difficult all the time.

"Bringing the perpetrator to justice sometimes drastically diminishes the psychological damage these incidents cause."

Cayla took particular notice of that statement. She and Denten had discussed prosecution many times. Each time they had concluded that the timing wasn't right. As she listened to the professor, she asked herself, "When was the timing right?" She could not spend the rest of her life combating thoughts of her childhood tragedy. Maybe she should see a psychologist? She and Denten had discussed that too. However, Cayla rejected that option. "I'm not a psycho." She reminded Denten and at the same time, herself.

That evening, sitting in her small apartment which she shared with Colleen Chambers, another second year law student, Cayla tried desperately to focus on the assignment for the next day. Her cell phone interrupted that preparation. It was Denten.

She flipped open her phone. "Hi, Denten. How you doing?" Her voice reflected her melancholy mood.

"Hi, beautiful. You okay?" He had become more sensitive to her shifting moods over the past few months.

"Yah, I'm fine. Just into homework." Her voice hinted at a reluctance to talk right now.

"Look, I won't keep you long. I just wanted to tell you that I'm coming to your big city tomorrow."

With that news, Cayla's mood brightened. "That's great. How long can you stay?"

"Well, that depends on how fast I can smooth the feathers of one of my clients."

Cayla found some humor in that announcement. She chuckled, something she did far too rarely. "What happened?"

"Not to take up your time, but a small group is meeting at the Marriott there on Michigan Ave. Just some minor problems with one of those types who has no end to his demands." Denten explained.

"Is it a serious problem?" Cayla asked.

"No. I doubt it. Look, I'll let you go. I'll be there about mid morning. I'll contact you after I've dealt with the Marriott thing."

"You can stay here tomorrow night."

"That'll be great. Save the company some money."

After hanging up, Cayla returned to her homework. Talking with Denten always had a calming effect on her. She could hardly wait to see him.

In paging through her class notes, she noticed the phrase, "possession of marijuana." She remembered jotting down those words a few months ago as she listened to another professor discuss penalties for possession of controlled substances. She sat back in her chair, looking off at nothing in particular. Talking to Denten and seeing that phrase reminded her of Denten's desperate phone call seeking information about an attorney who could assist his friends from Italy. She vividly remembered the names of Anna and Emma Moretti. Her memory dragged her away briefly from her own emotional stress. She recalled the name of Cole Ridgewood, a young attorney associated with a legal firm with offices in Chicago and Minneapolis. The thought gave her a feeling of satisfaction.

Denten had mentioned Anna and the relationship they once had, but as far as Cayla knew no longer existed. At least that is what she believed. She had no reason not to believe it.

According to what Denten had told her some time ago, after several weeks of investigations, authorities uncovered compelling evidence that both Nino Conti and Nicolas Watson were involved in the international transportation of primarily marijuana. Evidence established that they had been involved for several years. Nicolas, the carrier from America to Italy, used an ingenious strategy to slide through airport security undetected. That strategy relied on the roll of fat around Nicolas' waist. He had, unbelievably, surgically created a pocket under the skin around his "tire." A small flap of skin allowed access to the pocket. Nino decided to try a different option for shipment, using Anna and her mother. It didn't work.

Cayla smiled as she recalled the sentencing: both Nino and Nicolas sentenced to two years in prison, probation for five years after that and a $10,000 fine, Anna and her mother one year probation and a $5000.00 fine. The court obviously recognized their vulnerability to exploitation. However, the judge reminded them of their responsibility for knowing the contents of their luggage.

Cayla closed her notebook. She got up from her chair, stretched, and walked to her bedroom to prepare for bed. Her conversation with Denten and what they had done together for Anna and her mother put her in a much better mood.

Into his second year as an assistant account executive, Denten had proven himself a convincing salesman. Not blessed with an extroverted personality, Denten, nonetheless, functioned very well when dealing with prospective clients. For much of his success he credited his partner, Frank Getty. Frank had seen in Denten a young man thirsty to learn about the travel business. That thirst combined with Denten's unassuming personality made for his success so far in dealing with clients. It was one of those clients who now required his immediate attention.

Ginger Harlow had called from Chicago to report that a Mr. Clare Sullivan, CEO of a large midwest insurance company and the executive in charge of a business meeting for fifty company officials, had registered a series of complaints regarding service and other petty grievances. Ginger served as the lead trip director for this program held at the downtown Marriott located on Michigan Avenue at the end of the Miracle Mile. Apparently, Mr. Sullivan expected prompt attention to his every need. According to Ginger, his complaints included the lack of diet Coke in his room, the fact that two chairs were missing in a morning meeting, and his sedan for shopping was three minutes late. Denten discussed the report with Frank. They agreed that Denten should travel to Chicago to pacify Mr. Sullivan, a perfect example of inordinate self-indulgence.

Upon his arrival at the O'Hare International Airport, Denten was met by a driver representing a transportation company in Chicago. They immediately headed for the downtown Marriott. After a brief contact with Ginger, Denten prepared to meet Mr. Sullivan to discuss his concerns. Denten had not previously met Mr. Sullivan. His contact with the company occurred with regional representatives in southern Minnesota. The actual company contact for Denten lived in the Twin Cities.

Slightly apprehensive, Denten proceeded to a small conference room near the Travel Incorporated work room. The door stood slightly open. He knocked, then cautiously opened the door wide enough to enter. Seated at a small table, Clare Sullivan was dressed in a perfectly tailored suit, a white shirt with French cuffs, and a bright red tie, perfectly knotted. A man in perhaps his late 50's, Sullivan had taken good care of his body. As he rose to shake Denten's hand, Denten could tell that under that suit coat was a body well proportioned and well exercised. His rimless glasses accentuated his penetrating, nearly clear eyes.

"I'm Denten Ballery." Denten moved confidently into the small room, reaching out to shake the extended hand of Clare Sullivan.

"Clare Sullivan."

Denten waited until Clare had taken a seat before he took one himself. They talked briefly about the traffic in Chicago along with the congestion on Michigan Avenue. However, the conversation quickly moved to the purpose of the meeting.

"I understand you have faced a couple problems." Denten stated.

Clare moved forward in his chair, placing his elbows on the table. "Yes. I've always valued efficiency and punctuality. Here I've met with very little of either."

"I'm sorry to hear that. Could you be more specific?"

"I know that to some this may sound petty, but I like diet Coke. I asked for it. I couldn't get any. I can't imagine why not."

"I can't either." Denten agreed.

"More important, facilities for two of our meetings have failed to meet expectations." Clare looked directly at Denten.

"I'm sorry for any inconvenience this has caused you. I will make sure that this won't happen again. Is there any thing you need right now?"

"No. I don't think so."

"Let me give you my card. If I can help in any way, don't hesitate to call. If you need immediate attention, talk with Ginger Harlow, our lead trip director. She has had several years of experience. She can get things done."

"I would have to agree with that. I did talk to her yesterday. Today you are here." Clare smiled.

Clare rose from his chair. Denten followed.

"I hope everything goes better from now on." Denten reached out his hand.

"I hope so too." Clare shook Denten's hand and walked out the door.

Denten entered the staff work room where eight of the ten member travel staff worked on a variety of tasks, many of them, admittedly, mindless tasks. He approached Ginger, in her late twenties, petite, with long reddish blond hair and a veteran in the travel business. Like other members of the travel staff, she wore a dark blue polo shirt with khaki slacks. The uniform did little for her figure. Of course, as other female members of the travel staff acknowledged, the job did not require a fashion statement.

"How did it go?" She asked.

Denten shook his head and rolled his eyes. "What we have to do to keep some people happy."

"Isn't that the truth." Ginger agreed.

After spending a few more minutes in the staff work room, Denten stepped out into the corridor to call Cayla.

Chapter 24

Cayla pushed herself away from where she had sat for an hour and a half, taking notes on constitution law, another of the requirements for the JD law degree. She stuffed her notebook and textbook into her backpack and headed for the exit. She stepped out to a startling view of Lake Michigan just across North Lake Shore Drive from the Thorne Auditorium where she met her constitution law class. She paused briefly breathing in the fresh air escaping from the cool waters of Lake Michigan. The weekend would offer a respite from a week of lectures and study.

The chance to spend time with Denten, if only for one night, helped appease the stress and tension she felt. His calm, considerate attention always helped her relax. He had resolved the minor complication at the Marriott leaving time for them to spend together in Cayla's apartment. For part of that time Colleen, her room mate, joined them, sharing their beer and pizza.

After Colleen retired to her bedroom to prepare for a Friday exam, Cayla and Denten talked quietly of the past few months. Mostly, however, they talked about Cayla and her discontent. He reassured her of his confidence that she would complete her law degree. She had only months remaining. Recently, she had expressed doubts that she could sustain the effort. They talked about Denten's increased responsibilities with Travel Incorporated.

Ultimately, the conversation drifted to "their secret." Each noted the strength the memory retained and its persistent effect on their lives. What should they do about pursuing legal action against Reed Howard? Cayla's subtle inquiries with two of her professors gave her comfort in knowing that child sexual assault carried with it dire consequences for the perpetrator. However, she gained no comfort in the dire consequences, so familiar to her, for the victim. As before, Denten and Cayla agreed that someday they would confront Reed Howard in court. So much work preceded that day.

Their conversation stretched to near midnight. Denten had to catch an early flight back to Minneapolis, and Cayla had an 8:30 a.m. class. Denten found a little comfort on the sofa in the apartment's living area. Neither considered any other arrangement.

At the conclusion of another mentally exhausting day, Cayla stepped from the Thorne Auditorium into the bright afternoon sunshine. The walk to her apartment, just over ten blocks from the Northwestern School of Law campus, gave her a chance for exercise following a day of sitting in classes. Today, though, she decided to walk the four or five blocks to Chicago's famous Miracle Mile.

On the way she met increasing crowds of people filling the sidewalk on a Friday afternoon. She headed for a small specialty coffee shop nearly hidden between a sprawling shoe store and a music store. Entering the coffee shop, she faced a line waiting to order as well as a line waiting to pick up an order. She placed hers finally and stepped into the other line. She waited patiently as the busy staff concentrated on creating tantalizing coffee drinks.

"Cayla. Cayla Finch!"

Hearing her name, she jerked around to determine who had called to her.

Casey Holt stood at the end of the ordering line, a smile lighting his face.

"Image seeing you here." He walked over to greet her with a gentle hug.

Cayla stiffened briefly as his hands grasped her shoulders. "What are you doing here? She asked. The image of their last time together in his car surfaced from deep in her memory.

"I live here. How about you?"

"In law school at Northwestern."

Casey's eyes widened. "Impressive." He paused to give his order. 'How long you been here?"

"Almost three years." Cayla retrieved her coffee and stepped over to a small, high table by the window.

"Let me get my order. Don't run off." Casey laughed.

Armed with his coffee, he joined Cayla at the table. Watching him approach, she reflected again on the last time they were together. She had made little progress in overcoming her aversion to a man's touch and the chill that traced through her body from that touch. That even included Denten though with him the barrier had weakened.

For much longer than Cayla expected, they talked about the years that had elapsed since they last shared a date. Casey worked in real estate and lived not too far from the loop. He had made Chicago his home. Finally, he suggested they meet for lunch some place, two refugees from southern Minnesota. Cayla preferred to bid him farewell; however, she also didn't wish to be rude. She suggested a small deli just across East Superior Street from the University Campus. They agreed to meet at 1:00 on Sunday afternoon when Cayla felt confident that she would not have to contend with any advances from Casey.

On Sunday afternoon, a beautiful early summer day, Cayla arrived at the deli to find Casey sitting at a corner table. He rose to greet her. He was dressed in a dark blue Polo shirt, tan trousers and dock shoes, attire appropriate for a successful real estate salesman. To Cayla, he had changed little since college days. Perhaps a bit heavier, he still obviously paid attention to his physical condition, his arms pushing at the sleeves of his Polo shirt. His dark brown hair touched the back of his collar.

Dressed conservatively in a pink top and white shorts, Cayla relaxed when Casey refrained from the greeting hug.

"Good to see you again." Casey grinned.

"Been a long time." Cayla joked.

"How does school go?"

"Fine." Cayla refused to get involved in a discussion of the rigors of law school.

Diverting attention away from school, she asked, "How's the real estate business?"

"Slow." Casey shook his head.

They ordered each a sandwich, a specialty of the deli. Conversation wavered as a lack of commonalty limited what they could talk about. Also Cayla just did not feel comfortable with Casey. As they completed their lunch, Cayla announced that she should return to her apartment. Her books awaited her. Casey offered to drive her to her apartment. She demurred since she lived only blocks from the deli and the campus. Nonetheless, he insisted.

He paid the check and guided her to his late model BMW parked in the deli parking lot.

"Real estate can't be too bad." Cayla quipped.

"In my business appearance counts." Casey admitted.

The ride to her apartment took just minutes. She wished to avoid any special goodbyes. Certainly, she did not wish for Casey to accompany her to the apartment. Colleen was spending the day by the lake. Dealing with a mildly aggressive man, as she remembered Casey, or dealing with any man in the confines of her apartment frightened her.

Casey pulled up to the curb, stopped and shut off the car. He turned toward Cayla, his arm resting on the back of her bucket seat. "Thank you for the lunch. It's good to see you again."

"Thank you." She echoed. She reached for the door handle, pushed open the door and prepared to step out.

"Maybe we could get together again?" Casey commented, his voice rising as in a question.

"Yes, maybe when our schedules permit." Cayla stepped out and missed the curb. She landed on the edge of the curb, twisting her ankle. Sharp pain shot through her leg. Slightly embarrassed, she still couldn't avoid a painful groan. She slipped to the ground, one leg on the street the other on the grass.

Casey tried to grab her before she fell out of the car, but she tumbled too quickly. He dashed out his side of the car, rushed around to where Cayla lay clutching her ankle.

"Are you okay?" Casey asked, louder than necessary.

Cayla breathed deeply. "My ankle." She looked down at her foot already visibly swelling. "I'm sorry. I'm such a klutz."

Casey kneeled down next to her. "Can you stand?"

"I don't know. I think it's just sprained."

"Here, let me help you up. Just hold on to me." Casey directed.

She grimaced as he helped pull her to a standing position, most of her weight on Casey's shoulder. She quickly realized that the ankle prevented her from walking unaided to the apartment. Casey realized the same thing. With his arm around her shoulder and her body resting against his, they managed to reach the first floor apartment.

They paused at the door as Cayla searched for the key in the pocket of her shorts. Entering the apartment, Casey guided her to the sofa, the same one on which Denten had slept just nights before. Casey helped her sit down.

"You need ice." He advised.

"In the frig." The impact of the fall made her slightly drowsy, the body's response to this minor trauma.

Casey placed the ice in a plastic bag, wrapped it in a towel and helped Cayla place it on her swollen ankle. In the process she lay back on the sofa, resting her leg on one of the sofa pillows. He rested on his knees along side the sofa. He looked at Cayla.

"You all right?"

"Yes. Thank you." She breathed deeply. Her eyes met his.

Apparently, taking that for some invitation, Casey moved over Cayla, placing his hands on each side of her head, oblivious to her ankle. She stiffened as a cold chill ran up her spine. She tried to push back from his advance, her heart beating fast. He kissed her hard on the mouth.

She shook her head. "No. No. Please don't." She pleaded.

Almost as if a challenge, her words induced in Casey even more aggressive advances.

"What the hell is with you!" He shouted. "Damed prick teaser!" His hand reached under her top, groping under her bra.

Cayla struggled. "Please, Oh please, stop!" She begged.

Deaf to her pleas, he snapped her bra latch. His hand surrounded her breast. She gasped for air, her arms flaying, her fingers scratching his face and pulling at his shirt. Still, his hand moved inside her shorts. She screamed.

As suddenly as it started, it stopped. Casey sat back on his knees and stared into Cayla's terrified eyes.

"God. I'm sorry." He whispered. "I don't know…I don't know." He shook his head.

Cayla quickly pulled down her top. She lay unmoving, looking vacantly at nothing. "Just go!" she commanded.

He stood up and looked down at Cayla. The ice pack rested on the floor. He picked it up and placed it on her ankle.

Cayla flinched. "Please, just go!" She repeated loudly.

Casey backed to the door, his eyes fixed on Cayla with each step. He turned before opening the door. He made one last look at Cayla, lying on the sofa, her shorts and top rumpled, her hair disheveled, and her eyes wide. He shook his head then walked out.

She tried to relax. Taking several deep breaths, she stared into the declining light of the apartment, the image vivid of Reed Howard on top of her. She closed her eyes. She erupted into uncontrolled sobs.

Cayla's hands covered her face. Tears leaked through her fingers. The shame and humiliation she, for years, had combated rushed over her. Her body stiffened with the thought of what had just happened. Why did it happen to her? Was it something she did to invite men to attack her? Guilt mixed with the shame and humiliation.

She tried to move on the sofa. Suddenly, pain shot through her leg. In the agony of what had just happened, she had forgotten about the sprained ankle. She rested back on a sofa pillow, her head beginning to throb with one of her headaches. She suffered them much more frequently in recent weeks. She needed a couple pain pills, prescription strength. Dr. Charles Phillips of Northwestern Hospital had prescribed stronger medication just weeks ago. Over the counter pain killers did little to relieve the pain of her headaches.

Slowly, Cayla attempted to sit up. She swung her legs onto the floor. Her ankle screamed in pain. She had, somehow, to reach the bathroom where she kept her medication. She rested in a sitting position. If only Colleen would come back. Cayla considered calling her, but her cell phone was not in reach either.

The pounding in her head exceeded the pain of her ankle. She just could not sit there. Reaching for a small footstool, she pulled it closer. Bracing herself on the footstool, she managed to stand. For seconds nausea swept through her body. She fought off dizziness. Ten feet away, the door to the bathroom stood open. She just had to make the ten feet; then she could use the door and the vanity for support.

With profound determination, she rested her damaged ankle by positioning her knee on the footstool. Carefully, she pushed the footstool ahead with her knee. This way she inched herself closer to the bathroom door. For the moment, her concentrated effort dominated all else.

At last, she reached the bathroom. She leaned on the vanity, resting her leg on the footstool. In the vanity cabinet, she grabbed the bottle of pain relievers. She twisted off the cap and reached for the paper cup on the edge of the sink. The cup filled with water, she swallowed two pills. The prescription restricted her to no more than four pills in twenty-four hours. She filled the cup again. She sipped more water.

She looked at herself in the mirror. What she saw shocked her. A sagging face with red, puffy eyes, hair hanging in strings and skin pale looked back at her. What she observed took her breath away. Her shoulders slumped. She breathed deeply and took another sip of water. She tipped two more pills into her hand. She quickly swallowed them. She paused. She looked at the mirror again. She studied the pill bottle, over half full. She dropped her head so that her chin rested on her chest. She reached for another cup and filled it with water. Again, she paused, staring down at the empty sink.

With resolve, she grabbed the pill bottle, emptied its contents into her hand. She threw several pills into her mouth, three of them falling into the sink. Ignoring those, she grabbed one of the cups and drank vigorously. Nearly gagging on the pill cluster, she reached for the other cup. She drank slowly. Then she did the same thing with the pills left in her hand.

She picked up the pill bottle and dropped it in the waste basket. She then stood unmoving, her leg still resting on the footstool. She waited, a smile widened her lips revealing those charming dimples. She thought about Denten as the pills worked to ease her tension and pain. A euphoria spread through her body. All her agony both physical and mental started to recede. She felt her body weaken. She gripped the edge of the vanity. The lights dimmed. She felt herself slipping. Darkness enveloped her. She collapsed on the bathroom floor, unmoving.

Chapter 25

Weary and distraught, Alice and Harvey Finch sat across the desk from Dr. Charles Phillips, head of emergency services at Northwestern University Hospital near Chicago's loop.

"Cayla suffered an acetaminophen overdose." Dr. Phillips explained. "Acetaminophen is common in many pain relievers. Just a short time ago she came to me to request something stronger than what she could get over the counter. We talked briefly about her need for pain relief. She didn't specifically identify a cause. She did mention her studies. Do you know why your daughter was taking pain relievers?"

Alice sat with her hands folded tightly in her lap. The last twenty fours hours she had hardly slept. Redness rimmed her eyes. Her face sagged. She searched for an answer to the doctor's question. "Not really." She finally found words to answer the question. "We know that she faced some tough classes here in law school." Alice wiped her eyes with a tissue. Harvey reached for her hand. He squeezed it gently. Alice glanced at her husband and then at Dr. Phillips. "She never had any trouble with academics before. Everything was always easy for her. Here wasn't that way."

Dr. Phillips placed his hands on top of his desk and leaned forward. "Are you aware of any problems with male companions?"

This time Harvey spoke up. "She hasn't dated much. Lately she has seen a young man from Riverside named Denten Ballery."

"Are you aware of any problems they've had?" Dr. Phillips asked.

"Definitely not." Alice responded firmly. "Denten is a wonderful young man. Cayla spoke fondly of him always."

"Maybe the overdose was accidental." The doctor continued. "What we do know is that without the quick action by her roommate, Colleen Chambers I believe is her name, Cayla's overdose could have been fatal." The doctor moved closer to his desk to emphasize the importance of his explanation. Looking first at Alice then at Harvey, he offered a brief outline of what happens with an acetaminophen overdose.

" Acetaminophen is processed in the liver. Too much acetaminophen overwhelms the liver forcing it into a secondary process which turns the acetaminophen into a very toxic substance that can severely damage the liver. Immediate action is essential to avoid tragic results."

Alice moved uncomfortably in her chair. "Did Cayla receive treatment soon enough?"

"We think so. Apparently, Colleen returned to the apartment shortly after Cayla fell unconscious in the bathroom. Generally, within two hours following the ingestion of an overdose, we need to induce vomiting and perform a stomach flushing to remove the acetaminophen from the system. We give activated charcoal which binds to the acetaminophen preventing any further absorption in the stomach." Dr. Phillips sat back in his chair. "Sorry for the lengthy explanation, but it's important that you recognize just what happened. Do you have any questions?"

"Will Cayla recover from this?" Harvey asked.

"I believe so. She's young and otherwise in good health. Physical recovery shouldn't take more than a few days. However, there are emotional issues that need attention. Those could take much longer."

Harvey and Alice discussed when Cayla could leave the hospital and what he recommended for recovery. He strongly recommended that she suspend her education and that she return home with them for as long as it takes for her life to stabilize. He also recommended that she see a psychologist who could offer assistance in resolving any emotional problems she might have.

They walked back to the intensive care unit where Cayla remained. Unconscious when she arrived at the emergency room, rapid responses by the staff in the emergency center rid her body of the offending acetaminophen. She regained consciousness in just a few hours. Still she remained in the intensive care unit for further observation. Her parents maintained a constant vigil both before and after their conversation with Dr. Phillips. During the hours they sat by Cayla's bed, they had no opportunity to talk with her. The treatment had exhausted her as did her body's battle with the toxins that were emitted before treatment. The Finches accepted the hospital's offer to stay in one of its family units where they could maintain close contact with their daughter.

On Tuesday afternoon Cayla, at last, responded to the voice of her mother, who asked if she could hear her. Cayla slowly opened her eyes to look into the face of her mom. She turned her head away from her mother and spoke in a voice weakened by the trauma she had faced over the past three days. "I'm sorry." Tears flooded her eyes.

Her mother touched Cayla's shoulder. She struggled to hold back her tears. "Honey, you don't have to be sorry. You're awake. That's what counts."

Harvey moved to the other side of the bed, took care not to bump the intravenous stand, and looked into his daughter's face wet with tears, her beautiful cheeks pale and sunken. "Cayla, we don't know what happened. We just want you to know that we love you and will be here for you as long as you need us." He never found easy dealing with emotion. Nonetheless, he did love his beautiful daughter. Seeing her so fragile and frail gave him strength to express his love.

Cayla managed a weak smile.

On Wednesday morning, the hospital staff moved Cayla to a regular room where she would stay for a couple more days or until the doctors felt they could discharge her. Early in the afternoon the Finches sat with Cayla engaging in limited conversation and avoiding any questions about what actually happened and why. As they passed the time, they also awaited Denten's arrival. Colleen had notified him of Cayla's hospitalization. In Hawaii on an important corporate program, Denten needed two days to make connections for his return. Frantic to get to Chicago, he had maintained contact with Colleen, who kept him informed as to Cayla's condition. Devastated to learn that she had possibly attempted suicide, he questioned Colleen about potential reasons. She knew of none. Reed Howard came to Denten's mind.

Denten stood before Northwestern Hospital's room 142, the door slightly ajar. His frantic journey taking him from Hawaii to Minneapolis to Chicago's Midway airport had added to the anxiety he faced after Colleen's phone call. He gently pushed the door open just far enough for him to step into the room. Instantly, Alice stood up from her chair and rushed toward Denten. He opened his arms. Alice welcomed his embrace.

"We're so glad you're here." Alice tried desperately to control her sobs. She rested against Denten's chest.

Harvey stood behind his wife. When Alice moved back out of Denten's embrace, Harvey offered his hand as he, too, expressed his relief in seeing Denten.

Over her dad's shoulder, Denten viewed Cayla, so fragile and pale under the pure white sheets of her bed. He stepped toward the bed where she lay, eyes closed, breathing steady. He moved closer to the bed, leaned over Cayla and kissed her lightly on her forehead. She stirred. Her eyes opened slowly. She turned to look at Denten, a tiny smile defined her lips, dry from the hours of agony and treatment over the last few days.

"How you doing?" Denten asked quietly.

Cayla slowly shook her head, tears gathering in those sparkling eyes now dulled by trauma. Choked with emotion, she tried to speak but words just would not come out. Her tears turned to sobs as she turned her head away from Denten. He leaned over her again. He gently placed his hand under her chin urging her to turn her head. Holding her head steady, he kissed her lightly on her lips. Her sobs weakened.

"I'm sorry." She whispered.

"No. No need to be sorry." Denten squeezed her arm. "What's important is how you feel."

Cayla again looked away. "I'm okay, I guess."

Denten moved self-consciously as he stood by her bed. "Can I get you anything?"

Cayla cautiously shook her head as if doing so caused pain.

A series of questions tumbled through Denten's mind, questions mainly about exactly what happened and why. Did Reed Howard have anything to do with what happened. Was the overdose accidental or deliberate? He just could not believe that Cayla would attempt to take her own life. She simply had too much to live for. She possessed a wonderful future. He felt so confused, so inadequate in seeking answers to the many questions the incident generated.

Denten turned to face her mom and dad. They reflected the same confusion and ambiguity he felt. He needed to spend time with Cayla alone. Her parents, he presumed, knew nothing about Reed Howard, who likely had no direct responsibility for what happened to Cayla. Nonetheless, Denten knew that the memory of Reed Howard still haunted her.

Sensing the need for Denten and Cayla to have private time together or simply wishing to take a break, Alice and Harvey suggested that they leave for a while.

After they left, Denten again turned to Cayla's bed where she lay wide awake, staring into the empty space above her. He debated in his mind just how to approach questioning her about what happened and about what produced her near tragic response. For several seconds he stood looking at the woman who had become so dear to him and who now faced a profound crisis in her life and in their relationship.

"Cayla," He spoke quietly but firmly. "Do you want to talk about what happened?"

She sighed and looked at Denten. Tears filled her eyes again. This time she made no attempt to stop the flow that would help to wash away the anguish of the past three days. He reached down to cradle her head in his hands.

"Let it all come out." He whispered.

For several minutes neither spoke a word. He stood motionless. Her hands spread over her face, tears seeping through her fingers. Finally, her tears gradually slowed. She took a deep breathe, turned to face Denten. "It happened again." She admitted in a voice barely audible.

"What happened?" Denten asked, shocked by the implications of what he just heard.

Cayla slowly, deliberately described what happened on Sunday afternoon. She included an admission that the overdose was no accident. Denten stood listening, each detail adding to the alarm her confession evoked.

"Do I bring this on somehow?" She asked as she completed her tragic story.

"Of course, not. You're an attractive woman. That's no reason to feel guilty." Denten offered. "Have you told your parents what you just told me?"

"No."

"Do you think you should?"

Cayla paused. She looked off again into the space above her. "If I did, they would want revenge. I'm not sure I want to get involved in that right now."

"Have you told them anything about the reason for the attempt?" Denten asked.

"Not yet. I just don't know what to do right now. I'm not a psycho case. I don't know. The world kinda collapsed. Too many things came together at the wrong time. I don't know." Cayla looked away, closed her eyes and took a deep breathe.

Denten stepped back from the bed. "Could I have a drink of your water?"

"Of course." A slight smile brightened Cayla's face.

He filled a plastic glass with ice water, took a long swallow, then offered to fill her glass. She shook her head. "What happens now?" He asked.

"I don't know exactly. Doctors suggest I spend some time at home, maybe seek some counseling."

"What do you think?" Denten moved closer to the bed.

"I suppose a little time away from law school would be good. It's been tough, but I'm so close now."

"I think you should take the doctor's advice. Spend a little time at home."

"You're probably right."

"Our secrets stay secrets." Denten suggested.

"You're probably right about that too."

Denten leaned down to kiss her firmly on the lips.

Chapter 26

Alice Finch eased open the door to Cayla's room. She peeked in to see if her daughter had awakened. As she stepped into the room, Cayla opened her eyes and raised up on one arm.

"Good morning, dear. How did you sleep?" Her mom reached down to push hair away from Cayla's forehead.

"Okay." Cayla lay back in her bed. Her hair spread out over the pillow. Her hair had lost its shine. Her eyes had lost the sparkle that lightened her face when she smiled. Her charming dimples vanished in her frail cheeks. For the past month Cayla had spent her time at home with her parents recovering from the devastating overdose. During that month, her parents had devoted themselves to her recovery. Her mom, in particular, was available at all times to respond to her daughter's needs. Sometimes determining those needs proved frustrating for her. Cayla talked little about what happened in her Chicago apartment, leaving her parents questioning just what caused the overdose. Even after a month they still did not know for sure if the overdose was accidental or intentional. They knew that the truth did make a difference in her recovery. Right now, though, they considered each day a success if Cayla showed fewer signs of depression and despair.

An only child, Cayla had enjoyed a pampered life. Her parents had not intended to limit their family to one child. However, before Cayla's third birthday, medical problems developed for Mrs. Finch which precluded her from having any more children. Alice and Harvey realized how easily they could spoil their lovely daughter with too much attention. Still, Cayla attracted attention with her charming dimples and her vivacious personality. In their minds, a beautiful child, Alice and Harvey Finch attended to Cayla's every need, but in their opinion not more so than any other parent. She responded to their attention with obedience and conscientious attention to her school work and her duties around the house. She simply was the perfect little girl, always happy, always smiling. During the summer of her eighth year saw a decline in some of that spirit and charm. The Finches noticed the change but said nothing to Cayla. They attributed the change to her approaching preadolescence. They frequently, in private, questioned Cayla's reluctance to date during her high school and college years. After all she was a beautiful young lady, an opinion shared by more than just her parents. Her outstanding academic performance and later her dedication to a goal of earning a law degree crowded out concerns about her social life.

With this background, to discover that this marvelous young woman who was their daughter would attempt suicide was almost incomprehensible to Alice and Harvey. Those first hours following the call from Colleen were among the most emotionally shattering they had experienced. Now they had dedicated themselves to helping their daughter cope with what it was that caused her emotional turmoil. Sadly, they had no idea what lay at the foundation of her private torment.

Only with Denten did Cayla discuss her secret. Only with her did he discuss his. She adamantly refused to give in and tell her parents. Always she talked about the guilt, the shame, the image, and the fear of being labeled as promiscuous. Furthermore, she feared her parents would rush to prosecute Reed Howard, action she, at this time, wished to avoid. When she would pursue that prosecution, as she in the past promised she would, she did not know. Her recent overdose reflected her confusion, apprehension, and ambiguity. Multiple forces combined at that moment, in Chicago, compelling her to give up on life.

Riverside did not offer a variety of medical services, particularly psychological ones. However, one of the clinics in town did have counseling service one day a week when a psychologist from the Mayo Clinic saw patients from the Riverside area. Cayla had met with the psychologist, a Dr. Cynthia Vincent, once a week for the past three weeks. Those sessions had accomplished little in easing the mental anguish Cayla suffered. As with her own parents, Cayla refused to divulge the secrets which haunted her, secrets which for over sixteen years had formed a barrier between her and the rest of the world.

Cayla finally made her way down to the kitchen. She had tried her best to make herself look presentable. Her face, pale and drawn, made her look much older than she was. She had not tended to her hair for several days. The flowing waves of the past hung in strings around her face. Those engaging dimples vanished in drooping cheeks.

"Can I make you something for breakfast?" Her mom tried desperately to accept that her daughter's appearance was only temporary. She needed to do whatever she could to help her during this critical period in her life.

Cayla looked around the kitchen, her forehead furrowed as if she faced a crucial decision. "Just toast, I guess." She slumped in a chair next to the kitchen table.

"Any special plans for today?" Her mom asked.

Cayla smirked. "Ya, for sure."

"Would you like to go shopping someplace?"

"Where?" Cayla stared down at the table in front of her.

"I don't know. Where would you like?"

Cayla took a deep breath. "Don't need anything."

Alice moved closer to the table. She touched Cayla on the cheek then titled her head so they looked at each other eye to eye. "Sweetheart, you can't just sit here in the house. You need to get out."

Cayla turned her head away from her mother's stare. "I don't feel like it. Look at me. I'm a mess." She slumped lower in her chair.

Alice closed her eyes momentarily, puzzled by her daughter's indifferent attitude so unlike her. "Look, honey, why don't we get cleaned up and go get our hair done?"

Cayla looked up at mom. That look of deep concentration crossed her face. "Maybe. Okay. That might be good."

That afternoon Cayla and her mom did go to the beauty shop. Not only did they have their hair done, they also had a manicure. They also stopped for lunch at the Deluca restaurant where they talked with Mrs. Deluca who had not seen Cayla for months. When Cayla and her mom returned home, some of that sparkle had returned to Cayla's eyes. Besides, she would see Denten in the evening.

Summer months saw a decrease in the time Denten had to spend on the road. Most of his time he devoted to dealing with clients in his office either in person or electronically. Consequently, he had a greater opportunity to meet with Cayla which he tried to do as often as his schedule would permit.

As he drove the familiar route from Mankato to Riverside, his thoughts drifted to the last few months, particularly the last month since the near tragedy in Chicago. His recent visits with Cayla gave him confidence that she was recovering from the trauma of the overdose. Though she had not admitted to her parents that the overdose was deliberate, she had made that admission to Denten. He, even more than her parents, had encouraged her to seek professional counseling. He also had seriously urged her to tell her parents the truth, the complete truth about the sexual abuse of years ago as well as about the more recent assault. As in the past, she had resisted for the same reasons they had discussed many times before. Denten did not insist on her revealing her secret, at least not while she struggled with fragile emotions.

On this beautiful summer, Friday night, he intended simply to persuade her to get out of the house. She had a difficult time in facing the world outside her home. Maybe they could take a short ride in the country side and later stop for a snack.

He pulled into Cayla's driveway, parked and shut off his car. Mr. Finch had already returned from work. His car sat parked in the garage. Denten approached the front door with just a hint of hesitation, not knowing exactly what to expect from Cayla. What mood would he find her in? Before he could knock, Mr. Finch opened the door.

"Good to see you, Denten." He reached out his hand to shake Denten's

"Thank you. Good to be here." Denten's eyes quickly scanned the living room for any sign of Cayla.

"The ladies are in the kitchen having a glass of wine."

Denten smiled. "That sounds good."

He followed Harvey into the kitchen where Cayla and her mom sat by the kitchen table. When he entered the room, Cayla got up, stepped directly to him and surrendered to his arms.

Denten moved her back at arms length. "You have a date? You look great."

Cayla blushed briefly. No one had said that to her for some time. "Mom and I went to the beauty shop."

Denten reached to touch Cayla's hair which hung in shallow waves almost to her shoulders. "If they sell beauty there, you got your share."

A smile spread across Cayla's face; even the dimples made a brief appearance.

"Could I get you something to drink, a beer, a wine, a coke?" Harvey asked.

"A beer would taste good."

Cayla led Benten to the table where they sat down together. Harvey brought a beer for Denten and one for himself. The four of them sat for a moment in silence.

"How was your week?" Alice broke the silence.

"Only mildly hectic. Things have slowed following our busy high season."

"Any travel coming up?" Harvey asked.

"No. Nothing major right now. This fall it's back to Hawaii for a couple important programs."

"Tough duty." Harvey chuckled.

"How's the machinery business?" Denten changed the subject.

"Not too bad. I saw your dad the other day."

Denten took a swallow of his beer. "Ya, he's getting along pretty well even without me."

"He talked of the coming harvest. Said you might give him a hand."

"Yes, I can use some time out of the office." Denten turned to Alice. "You have a busy week?"

She smiled, running her finger around the rim of her wine glass. "They're all busy, I guess. Today Cayla and I enjoyed a good day getting pretty and having lunch."

"I've noticed." Denten looked over at Cayla, squeezed her hand. Still, she said nothing, just smiled. Even the smile reflected well on her mood.

When they completed their drink, Denten took Cayla's hand, "Let's go for a ride. It's a great evening."

She rose from her chair, reached for his beer bottle, and placed her glass and his beer bottle next to the sink. "I'm ready."

Alice walked with them to the front door. Her smile and cheerful voice revealed her pleasure in seeing Cayla looking more like the Cayla of old. "You too have a good time, but get home early."

In the car Denten drove through town than out to his parents' farm. They stopped briefly to talk with them. They were just sitting down to dinner when Denten and Cayla arrived. They apologized for interfering with their dinner. Of course, the Ballerys would hear none of that. They talked briefly about Cayla's recovery, about Denten's job, and about the coming harvest. Wanting to spend more time enjoying the evening together, they bid Denten's parents good bye. Though they assumed as much, before leaving, Denten informed them that he would be likely spending the night there.

His mom laughed. "Thanks for telling us."

As Denten and Cayla walked to the door, Grace repeated what Cayla's mom had said. "Be home early."

Again in the car, Denten and Cayla rode in silence for a couple miles. He looked over at her as she focused on the road ahead. "You okay?"

"I guess so." She answered in a soft voice.

"Is there something wrong?"

Cayla held her focus on the windshield. "You know some things are wrong. But nothing new."

"You had a session with, what's her name again?

"Dr. Vincent." Cayla reminded him.

"How'd it go?"

"Okay."

"Not very exciting I take it."

Silence filled the car. They both concentrated on the road ahead.

Finally, Denten asked, "Have you said anything to this Dr. Vincent about Reed Howard?"

Cayla moved uncomfortably in her seat. She pulled on the seat belt. "No."

"Do you think you should?"

"I suppose so."

"Cayla, if you don't want to talk about it, I won't. We should, though."

"I suppose so." Her voice hesitant and just above a whisper.

"What about Casey? Said anything about him?" Denten asked.

"No." came the terse response.

Denten moved slightly in his seat. "Cayla, I know we've talked about this before. We've agreed to keep the truth to ourselves." He paused again refocusing his eyes on her. "I think we need to get the truth out to both our parents."

Cayla said nothing. She stared straight ahead.

"I think it's the only way we can go on. You can't go through life hiding this terrible truth."

Cayla breathed deeply. She pinched her eyes closed fighting the gathering tears. So many tears she had shed over two moments of disgrace. "I don't know, Denten. I don't know what to do."

Silence returned to the car. Both of them lost momentarily in their own thoughts.

Denten gripped the steering wheel. "I'm not sure I do either. But something has to change."

Cayla wiped her nose with a tissue. "What will they think?"

Puzzled by her comment, Denten asked, "What do you mean?"

She slowly shook her head. "When people find out what happened, what'll they think of me?"

"Oh, Cayla, Sweetheart, what happened to you wasn't your fault!"

"We know that. Will others believe that? Will they look at me as some kind of.." She paused reluctant to use the word. "slut"?

"Stop thinking that way. You've done nothing to cause what happened to you. You certainly can't help you're attractive."

"I wish I could believe that."

Denten pulled the car over onto a small access to a field. He stopped the car. Turning to Cayla, "We're not gonna park." He playfully reassured her. "Don't worry about that. I just want you to listen to me, okay?"

"Okay." Cayla turned to face him.

"I think you need to tell your parents what happened with Reed Howard and what happened with Casey. You can't.... We can't go on like this. Your parents will understand. It will give them some answers to what happened in Chicago."

"They'll want to get him right away. I know it." Cayla's spoke with conviction and control.

"No doubt." Denten paused. "Couldn't we get them to wait until you're ready? They'll do what's best for you."

Cayla looked down at her hands clasped in her lap. "Maybe, you're right. She looked out her side window at a bright moon that illuminated a wheat field nearly ready for harvest. "Such a beautiful evening."

The next day, Saturday, Denten agreed to join Cayla to explain to her parents what happened in Chicago and in the park so many years ago. Denten arrived just after lunch. Both Cayla's parents were at home. Her dad didn't often work on weekends this time of the year.

Again they welcomed Denten as he stepped through the front door. That he could spend more time with Cayla delighted them. She always seemed to benefit from his visits.

"You had a good time last night?" Mrs. Finch asked to spark conversation.

"Always with Cayla." Denten smiled.

The four of them sat in the living room, Denten and Cayla on the sofa, her parents on separate stuffed chairs facing them. Casual conversation failed to engage all four of them. Periods of silence made them restless. Finally, Cayla took the lead.

"Mom and Dad, we've something to tell you."

The comment caused a stir from both her parents. Pregnancy, marriage, breaking up, all floated through their minds. They both sat up straight, focusing on their daughter.

"I was raped." Cayla made the blunt confession.

Their mouths dropped and their eyes opened wide. Her parents sat in stunned shock. For several seconds they could find no words to respond to her confession.

"You were raped!" Alice echoed Cayla's admission.

Cayla's nodded her head.

"Now, in Chicago?" Her dad asked, hands gripping the arms of his chair.

"No. Years ago, right here in Riverside." Cayla's voice assumed a confidence and a control.

"When was that?" Her mom asked breathless.

Cayla breathed deeply. "Okay, just listen. Don't say anything until I finish." She took a deep breath. She looked directly at her mother and then at her dad.

In a voice quiet but firm, she began. "One summer Saturday when I was eight years old. Reed Howard offered to give me a ride home from church." Her voice gained authority as the details flowed from her mouth. "He gave me a ride home. But first he drove to the park where he assaulted and raped me."

Her parents sat with mouths open and eyes fixed on her. They said nothing. Her mom uttered a sound of alarm.

"In Chicago," Cayla continued. "Casey Holt, a guy I met in college, took me out for lunch on Sunday before the overdose. After the lunch he helped me up to the apartment after I had sprained my ankle getting out of his car. In the apartment, he sexually assaulted me. That's when I took the pills."

During her description of what happened, Denten sat quietly listening, observing both Cayla as well as her parents. When Cayla stopped, Denten described his haunting experience accidentally coming upon the rape during a morning bike ride.

For several seconds, Mr. and Mrs. Finch sat in stunned silence. Finally, Harvey asked, "Reed Howard at the bank?"

Cayla nodded her head.

"My God!" Alice declared.

"That bastard has gotten away with this for all these years?" Harvey spoke in anger. "You, honey, have carried this burden with you all these years!"

Alice got up from her chair and moved closer to her daughter. She kneeled down before her. "Why haven't you told us before?"

Cayla placed her hand on her mother's shoulder. "It's a long story. I guess it has to do with fear, guilt, shame, all kinds of things lumped together."

She turned her attention to Denten. "Did you tell your parents?"

"No. Not yet. I guess fear and guilt were a part of my decision too." He confessed. "I intend to tell them soon."

Harvey sat straighter in his chair. "Did either of you know this about each other when you met?"

"No." Both answered in unison.

Harvey shook his head, overwhelmed with the truth these two young people had shouldered all these years. "By God, that bastard is gonna pay!" Harvey announced.

At that point, Denten stood up and moved back a couple steps so he could address both Cayla's parents. "Yes, the bastard is gonna pay. Cayla and I have discussed this several times since we discovered the night of her graduation from St. Mary's that we shared this horrible secret." He moved closer to Cayla, reaching to grasp her hand. "We both hope that you will let us decide when the time is right to go after him. Right now is not the time." He looked down at Cayla. "Cayla has other things to take care of first.

Cayla stood up and moved into Denten's open arms. At that moment she felt an oppressive weight slip off her shoulders and a hideous memory dim just a little. Alice and Harvey walked over to embrace them. As the four of them embraced, Harvey assured them that they supported them in their wish to decide when to pursue Reed Howard. Alice agreed.

Cayla reached her arms around both her parents. "Thank you," she whispered. A tiny tear inched its way toward one of her dimples.

Chapter 27

The Ballerys and the Finches hurried through the small foyer of the Riverside High School auditorium. Scheduled for 8:00, they were already a few minutes late for an informational meeting to address strengthening the penalties particularly for sexual abuse of juveniles. As they sought seats in the back of the auditorium, they heard the words, "We must protect our young people against the sinister perversion of those who would take advantage of them."

Inconspicuously, they stepped around people already seated. Finally settled in their seats, they focused on the person standing behind the podium at the center of the auditorium stage. That person whose words they had just heard was Reed Howard.

In utter shock and disbelief, the Ballerys and the Finches looked at each other and then at the Reed Howard, who continued to emphasize the need for stricter laws against sexual abuse. They could hardly believe what they were seeing and hearing. Reed Howard campaigning for stricter abuse penalties?

During the past two months, the two families had spent time together joined by a common identity, parents of children who had suffered abuse by an adult. Cayla's confessing to her parents the horrible nightmare in the city park initiated a slow recovery from the trauma of the Chicago overdose. The confession began to heal the deep emotional wound she had suffered as an eight year old child, a wound that had not healed over the intervening sixteen years.

In addition, both Denten and Cayla sat with Denten's parents sharing their personal experiences. Astonished to hear what these two young people had carried with them all these years, they, as had the

Finches, immediately insisted on pursuing the prosecution of Reed Howard. Similar to the discussion Denten and Cayla had with her parents, they discussed with Denten's the reasons for a delay. Cayla simply did not wish, at this time, to confront the repercussions of her assault becoming public knowledge. The Ballerys understood.

The truth of the assault now known by both families served as a foundation for a unity that previously had not existed. Both families assumed a much more intense interest in sexual perversion of all kinds. The openness with which they now discussed the topic helped Cayla gradually accept the reality of what happened. The guilt she felt, the embarrassment, the shame that had haunted her for all those years gradually faded enough to give her a degree of freedom from the crushing memories of the assault.

The summer found the two families gathering frequently for Sunday afternoon lunches and Friday night barbecues. Though both families had made Riverside their homes for many years, the two families shared little until Denten and Cayla found each other. The social relationship of the two families offered perfect conditions for healing for both of them. Cayla gained confidence. She discussed candidly with parents the despair that had driven her to attempt to take her life. Denten talked freely, now, about the dreams that had shadowed his nights for so many years. Talking about their secret lives served as excellent therapy for both, especially Cayla, who, as the summer unfolded, grew more restless to return to Northwestern University and her law degree. Denten's career with Travel Incorporated took him away from Cayla for days at a time. Still, he found time to spend with her as travel slacked during the waning days of summer.

The informational meeting at the Riverside High School resulted from a campaign by State Representative Mark Linsted, who represented the southwestern part of the state, a part that included Riverside. A sexual predator had recently assaulted Representative Linsted's young daughter as she walked home from school. This tragic incident along with a recent increase in sexual offenses of other kinds motivated him to seek support for strengthening penalties for sexual assaults. He had scheduled a meeting at the high school auditorium, a meeting hosted by the local chamber of commerce. Reed Howard served as an officer in the chamber. Introducing Mr. Linsted was Reed's responsibility. As he did, the Ballerys and the Finches arrived to face hypocrisy in its rawest form.

Having made the introduction, Reed retreated to a chair behind and off to one side of the podium. While Mr. Linsted's told about his daughter and about other equally compelling stories of sexual abuse, Reed sat, with arms folded, listening with marked intensity, his body language reflecting the impact created by the representative's words.

Seated in the back of the auditorium, the Ballerys and the Finches found Reed Howard's presence and his words astonishing. With difficulty they listened to what Mr. Linsted had to say, distracted by Reed Howard sitting so visibly on the stage. His presence renewed the compulsion to expose him for the sinister, sexual deviate they considered him to be. If not for their interest in the topic Mr. Linsted came to address, they would have walked out about the time they realized the person they heard talking when they arrived was Reed Howard.

For over an hour they sat uncomfortably listening to Mr. Linsted and to several questions that came from the audience that nearly filled the auditorium to capacity. When the meeting concluded, they made their way to the foyer crowded with people moving slowly toward the exits. Some stood in small groups talking about what they had just heard. Others moved slowly, engaged in conversation with those walking with them.

Just outside the auditorium entrance, Harvey motioned for them to step out of the way. They stood off to the side.

Harvey looked briefly at each them. "Can you believe what we just saw?" He shook his head and pushed his hand into his pockets.

Silence hung over the four of them. Grace Ballery sighed. "I feel so helpless."

Her husband nodded. "Ya. I'm just so God damned mad! That bastard standing up there!"

"I agree completely." Harvey leaned back against the building. "God, to nail that bastard. Excuse my language. It's an outrage."

Alice Finch had said nothing, deeply influenced by Cayla's assault as only a mother can be. She looked down at the sidewalk then up to survey the three standing near her. "Nothing would please me more than to see justice. His audacity," She paused shaking her head. "His audacity…it's just awful. Prison is too good for him." Again she paused. The others waited for her to continue, sensing she had more to say. "So often I think of what Cayla and Denten went through. My, young people don't deserve that. But, I think, we have to respect what they said. Let them decide when the time is right to get that…." Her voice trailed off.

Preparing to leave, they bid each other good evening. As they did, Reed Howard approached. He walked slowly, staring malevolently at the small group. His eyes touched each of them, a sneer spreading across his face. Paralyzed with contempt, the four of them stared back, struggling with the need to strike back.

Chapter 28

Denten returned his lap top to its case and slipped it under the seat in front of him. He leaned back in his window seat, prepared for the six hours that stood between him and Maui. Of course, traveling to Hawaii represented the ultimate escape to paradise except when the purpose was business. In the time he had worked for Travel Incorporated, Denten had traveled to Hawaii five times. His clients accepted the idea that Hawaii more than any other destination offered the best inducement for their employees to strive to achieve the rewards of incentive programs. Denten now embarked on another, this time for a real estate company and this time in Maui.

The preceding weeks found Denten deeply involved in Cayla's struggle to recover from the near fatal overdose. He closed his eyes, letting his mind wander over recent events which had played instrumental roles in his life and the lives of so many others. His parents, Cayla's parents, of course, Cayla herself, and Anna, whose life evolved so far away, all were such a vital part of his life. He thought, too, of the countless nights he had awakened to the dreadful scene in the city park. How many nights had he awakened, his body damp with perspiration, his head throbbing, his mouth dry, to see the dark eyes targeting him from the back seat of the car?

Denten moved a bit closer to the window of his Delta flight non stopped to Maui. He stretched his legs as far as possible under the seat in front of him. He glanced out the window to see the puffy clouds beneath the plane that cruised at 36,000 feet. His mind drifted to the recent moments when he and Cayla sat with her parents to reveal her secret, their secret. Clear in his mind, too, was the moment when he and Cayla sat in the Ballery living room explaining, at last, to Denten's parents the events of that Saturday morning in the park. As with Cayla's parents, Denten's responded with alarm, disbelief, and finally compassion for what the two of them had faced all those years.

Since that time, the dreadful dream had nearly disappeared. Denten couldn't remember the last time the dream had awakened him. Certainly, part of the reason for the near death of the dream derived from his finally sharing it with others, first Anna, then Cayla and her parents and at last his parents. Sharing it with his parents should have happened years ago, he confessed to himself. Nonetheless, currently, he enjoyed near freedom from the dream.

A smile spread across his face as the vision of Cayla emerged vivid and real. Walking hand in hand, they had approached the security entrance in the Minneapolis/St. Paul airport. She held a boarding pass for her flight to Chicago. He recalled the scene.

"You look great." His eyes moved over Cayla from head to foot.

She smiled shyly, her dimples accentuating the charm of her smile. "Thanks. You don't look so bad yourself." She bumped him with her hip.

"You excited?" Denten asked.

"Yes." She took a deep breath.

"You okay about going back to school?" Denten looked into her eyes that had regained their sparkle.

She looked down at the floor then at Denten. "I think it's what I need. I don't know..." She paused. Then with confidence in her voice. "These last few weeks have taught me something about my expectations for myself. I think I can look at my future a bit more realistically."

Denten took her in his arms. She leaned against him. For a few moments they relaxed in the comfort of each other's arms.

"Remember. If you need to talk, please don't put it off. Call." He looked intently at her.

"I know. I promise."

He kissed her lightly on the lips. She joined the line which would take her through security. He waited with her until she placed her carry on luggage on the conveyor and stepped through the metal detector.

Denten again moved in his window seat as he saw in his mind Cayla approaching the security entrance and the innocent smile and the quick wave as she turned and disappeared in the crowd of travelers headed to their gates.

He recalled Cayla's summer struggle with the demons that had pushed her to the overdose. He thought of the hours they had spent together talking, sharing their love and reaching for answers to what had happened in Chicago and in the Riverside park. Confessing it all to their parents served as one of the answers. From the many hours they spent together, Cayla gradually gained more confidence and assurance that what had happened to her was not her fault. She had no shame to suffer. His support along with that of her parents paved the way for sufficient recovery to resume her education at Northwestern University.

Flight attendants interrupted his day dreaming. For a mere $3.00 he bought a stale sandwich. At least the can of soda came free.

Content with the meager sustenance offered by the sandwich and soda, Denten carefully adjusted his position in his window seat. Each subsequent boarding convinced him that the airlines reduced the space between rows. Not a particularly big person, he still found comfort elusive on extended flights.

Looking out the window, Denten could see that clouds had disappeared. Nothing but blue ocean below stretched for as far as he could see. At least, he concluded, his flight must be more than half way to Maui.

He reached under the seat in front of him for his lap top computer. Nothing at this moment carried any urgency. However, to pass the time while his flight raced on toward the middle of the Pacific Ocean, he decided to examine a few of the documents related to the program which he had negotiated several months ago. His computer stored arrival/departure manifests, activities lists, meal and lodging documentation, and a listing of the company executives. Company executives were most important for Denten. They made the decisions as to which company would receive the contract for their incentive and business meetings. Denten had spent weeks negotiating with a large midwest real estate company with headquarters in Chicago. Securing the contract stood as one of his greatest achievements in his short career. Consequently, he considered essential his attending the program at the Hyatt Regency Hotel just beyond Lahaina on the island of Maui.

He scrolled through the many documents stored for this program. He paused to look again at the list of executives scheduled to attend and when they would arrive. He checked quickly the golf schedule, perhaps the most important for many of the attendees who had worked diligently to qualify for this opportunity to spend time on one of Hawaii's most popular islands.

Continuing to scroll through the many documents, Denten chuckled to himself as he considered the hours needed to compile dozens of pages he had at his disposal. The electronic world intrigued him. Before putting the computer away, he took a casual look at the arrival manifest, curious to determine if he knew any winners of this trip. Listed alphabetically by flight, most of the attendees would arrive at Maui's Kahului airport in two days. A few would arrive at the Honolulu airport before taking an inner island flight to Maui.

He checked the flights from Minneapolis/St. Paul first. He found only a couple names that looked familiar. He tried next the flights from Chicago, the point of departure for most of the attendees. His eyes moved down the list of flights and the passengers on each one. On one flight he came across the name Casey Holt. He looked away from the computer screen. A strange sensation started in his neck and moved down his back.

"Could this be the Casey Holt he'd heard about?" Denten frowned as he contemplated Cayla's struggle that Sunday afternoon. He remembered that the Casey Cayla knew worked in real estate. A mixture of contempt, anger and curiosity gathered in his mind.

Denten leaned back in his seat, staring at the "fasten seat belt" sign above his row. Certainly, he could not mix personal and professional matters while on a program, particularly one as important as this one. Nonetheless, he definitely would investigate this Casey Holt, discretely, of course.

His personal life suddenly assumed priority over the impending program just a couple days away. Denten closed the computer and again returned it to its place under the seat in front of him. He pressed the small button that tilted his seat back. He adjusted the window shade to cut down on the glare. He closed his eyes.

Images of Cayla rushed to cloud those of the faceless Casey Holt, whom Denten had never even seen. Realizing that Cayla now stood ready to pursue her degree in law after having confronted and so far successfully overcome powerful feelings of guilt and inadequacy quieted some of that anger and contempt Denten earlier felt. Gradually, he drifted off into a shallow sleep. The image of Cayla blended with the image of Anna.

For the last several months contact with Anna had dwindled. Neither accused the other of neglect. They seemed to accept what neither would verbally admit; the possible ending of their relationship. The distance between them, the demands of her major in psychology and his career in the travel business combined to reduce the frequency of contact. A sign of this decrease was reflected in the emails which came only occasionally now and each time with an apology for that infrequency.

The attention to Anna awakened Denten. The recent challenges faced by Cayla had captured his attention for most of the summer. Not intentionally, but certainly in reality, he had thought little about Anna. A smile lightened his face at this moment as he thought about the first time he saw her on her uncle's wine and olive oil farm so long ago. Nostalgia produced a series of memories of Anna. The instant he first saw her would always stand as a remarkable moment. The time they spent together during his stay in Italy with the Delucas. The first time they kissed, Denten could almost feel her tender lips and smell the fragrance of her hair. Her trip to America and Riverside compliments of the modeling company. His confession to her in the Riverside park. The hours of communication by phone and email. The trauma of the collision with drug enforcement authorities at the Minneapolis/St. Paul airport. The tension of the hearing and the subsequent relief when released to return home. The conviction of Nicolas Watson and Nino Conti, who had yet to complete their sentence for drug trafficking. All of these memories rushed through Denten's mind prompting the thought of what might have been.

The images also prompted concentration on Anna's enchanting smile, the shiny flow of her black hair, her olive skin, her alluring figure, and her intelligent, charming personality. He chuckled to himself. How could anyone permit a girl with those qualities to escape? He shook his head as if to clear his mind. Just what had happened to erode their relationship? He suspected a host of forces played a part. Prime among them was distance between them. Cayla, of course, also came into his life. Mostly, though, both Denten and Anna realized that their lives moved in different directions. Unless they evinced a willingness to sacrifice portions of their goals, they acknowledged that the relationship would wither. A friendly relationship would survive but not a romantic one.

Denten recalled an email exchange which just months before had signified that they both accepted the end of any romantic relationship. He had stayed late in his Mankato office. After completion of communication with two clients, he decided to check his email. One of them came from Anna.

"How you doing? Traveling a lot?" Anna wrote.

Denten stared at the terse message, fighting a mild feeling of guilt. Then he typed, "Good to hear from you. Travel has slowed for summer." He sent the reply.

In just seconds, Anna responded. "Haven't heard from you for a while."

"Sorry. How's school?"

"Same old drag." Came the reply. "How about your business?"

"Same old drag." Denten typed."Just kidding. Summer usually slow."

"Any trips to Italy planned?"

"I'm afraid not. Would like one though."

"Would you, really?" Anna's response hinted at a mild criticism.

"Of course. Who wouldn't want to go where the best wine in the world is?"

A longer delay produced from Anna. "Is that the only reason you'd come?"

Denten bit his lip, not a good thing to have said he reminded himself. "You don't really think that, do you?"

Another delay followed. Then Anna wrote, "Denten, I don't know what to think."

Denten could feel a growing tension in the communication. "You don't know what to think about what?"

"About us." Came a quick reply.

Denten moved in his seat, seeking a little more comfort. He closed his eyes again, reflecting on that exchange and how difficult it proved to discuss their relationship or more specifically the decline of their relationship by email. They did acknowledge the obvious problem of distance. In addition, Denten had admitted his evolving relationship with Cayla, whose intervention assisted Anna and her mother during their encounter with authorities at the Minneapolis/St. Paul airport nearly two years ago. In the end they agreed to preserve their friendship. The exchange ended with both of them feeling a sense of loss but also with fond memories of a friendship that under different circumstances could have flourished into something more.

The announcement from the captain that the flight had started its descent into Maui's Kahului Airport rescued Denten from his lengthy venture into the immediate past. Upon landing, Denten gathered his luggage and caught a taxi for the twenty minute ride to the Hyatt Regency Hotel.

In the taxi Denten concentrated on the impressive scenery along the route to the hotel. Following closely the coast line, the road circled around small hills while passing beaches flocked with young surfers. Through Lahaina and just beyond sat the marvelous property occupied by the Hyatt Regency Hotel. Arriving at the hotel, he paid his taxi fare, directed the bellmen to his luggage, then proceeded to check in at the registration desk. Not until he settled into his spacious room did he again think about Casey Holt.

Denten's thoughts focused on mixing personal with professional business. Did he really need to meet Casey Holt? What difference would confronting him make? Certainly, Denten did not wish to create a scene while on this program. This company was a very valuable client to Travel Incorporated. However, Denten could not dismiss the need he felt to meet someone who would viciously assault an innocent girl, a girl like Cayla. He would have to consider just what he would do. Arrival day was yet two days away.

During those two days preceding arrival day, the travel staff faced a few minor problems in room assignments as well as with the welcome ceremonies. Denten assisted where he could, resolving conflicts with the transportation from the airport of executive hosts whom he strived to please at nearly all costs. Still not convinced that he wished to pursue a meeting with Casey Holt, he, nonetheless, talked with Ginger Harlow, a familiar travel staff leader with whom Denten had worked several times. Ginger would serve as the lead at the hospitality desk where all participants would check in upon arrival to register and to receive welcome packets with information about the program and a schedule of activities.

"Ginger, would you do me a favor?" Denten stood in front of the hospitality desk as staff sorted through the dozens of welcome packets.

"Sure, Mr. Ballery, what can I do for you?" In Denten's opinion, people like Ginger generally determined whether a program would evolve successfully or not.

"Look," Denten hesitated momentarily, shifting from one foot to the other. "I'd like to meet a Casey Holt, one of the participants. Could you tell me when he arrives? I think it's tomorrow afternoon. He comes from Chicago."

Ginger reached for her briefing notes and the master arrival manifest. "Okay, let's see. Casey Holt. Yes, there he is. He arrives in Maui about 2:30 tomorrow afternoon."

"Great. Could you call me on my cell phone when he arrives?"

"Absolutely." Ginger gave Denten her classic customer service smile.

"Thank you. I won't bother you any more today."

"Oh, you're no bother. Any time."

The next day, arrival day, the travel staff had completed all preparations and sat ready to receive participants as they arrived following their endless flights from the mainland. Denten moved around checking with various travel staff members in a search of any questions or special concerns. This was a very important client for Denten and for the company.

By early afternoon, he escaped to his room to check on emails and to begin work on a meeting in a few days with another client. Still doubtful about confronting Casey Holt, Denten attempted to focus attention on his next meeting with prospective clients. About 3:30 his cell phone rang.

He rushed to the dresser where he had placed the phone. Noting the caller, he answered,"Yes, Ginger."

"Mr. Ballery."

"Speaking."

"I hope I'm not intruding." Ginger said in an apologetic voice.

"Of course not."

"A Mr. Holt from Chicago checked in at the desk about fifteen minutes ago. You wanted to know when he arrived."

"Thank you. Yes, I did. Did you happen to get a room number?"

"No. He hadn't checked into the hotel yet. Sorry."

"That's fine. I'll just call the operator. Thank you."

"You're welcome." Ginger answered, again, in her best customer service voice.

"Could you connect me with the room of Mr. Casey Holt?" Denten spoke with the hotel operator.

Two days had passed since Ginger informed Denten of Casey's arrival. Denten debated just what he should do. At last he had decided that until he actually confronted Casey Holt, the thought would shadow him forever. He waited until the program's activities had commenced before attempting to contact Mr. Holt. He picked a time during the day when a lull in scheduled events would likely find participants in their rooms.

Denten stood near the desk in his room, the hotel phone pressed against his ear. He waited as the phone rang and rang. After several rings, he almost decided to hang up when a voice sounding heavy from sleep answered.

"Hello."

Denten breathed deeply. "May I speak with Mr. Holt, please?"

"This is Casey."

"Mr. Holt," Denten spoke carefully almost as if rehearsed. "My name is Denten Ballery. I'm the account executive for this program. I would like to meet you to discuss a matter of some importance to both of us."

Denten heard no response.

Then in a voice with added strength, Casey asked, "Denten.. What is the last name?"

"Ballery. I work for Corporate Travel, the company that arranged this program."

"Oh, yes. What do you wish to discuss?" Casey sounded skeptical.

"I would rather not discuss it on the phone. Could I meet you someplace or could I come to your room?"

More silence. "Well, ah. Okay, I guess. Come to the room. I'm here for another half hour or so."

Denten moved restlessly by his desk. "That's good. I'll be there in a minute."

Denten hung up the phone and took a deep breath. He checked himself in the bathroom mirror before making sure he had his room key then headed to room 513 and a meeting with Mr. Casey Holt.

Denten stood looking at the number 513 before he knocked on the door. He again breathed deeply, not quite sure just what he would encounter. A brief knock brought Casey to the door instantly. He opened the door and stepped back. Dressed casually in a wrinkled golf shirt and khaki trousers, Casey was bigger than Denten expected. The longer hair and the robust build conflicted with what he envisioned Casey to look like.

"Mr. Ballery?"

"Yes, I'm Denten Ballery. Mr. Holt?" Denten extended his hand toward Casey's.

"Come on in." Casey directed. "Forgive the messy room."

Denten stood just inside the entry to the typical hotel room with two double beds, an entertainment center, a desk, night stands and two chairs. The room extended to a small deck overlooking the beach five floors below and the blue Pacific beyond.

Casey looked around his room for a convenient place for both of them to sit. "Why don't we step out on the deck."

"That's fine." Denten followed Casey through the patio door and onto the small deck furnished with a round table and three chairs.

Casey leaned against the deck railing motioning for Denten to have one of the chairs. Denten, instead, elected to stand.

"Now," Casey asked. "What would you like to discuss?"

Denten looked down at the floor of the deck then up at Casey. "Do you know a Cayla Finch?"

The question slammed into Casey. He stood straight, his body rigid, a sensation rushed through his stomach. He averted Denten's steady gaze. "Ya, from college. Why ask?"

Denten stood facing Casey, his resolve giving him confidence to pursue the questions. "When was the last time you saw her?"

Casey turned his back to Denten and gripped the narrow wrought iron railing. "What are you after?" He demanded, abandoning any sense of hospitality.

Denten shifted slightly on his feet, stepped to grab the back of one of the chairs. "Mr. Holt, the last time you saw Cayla, you viciously and brutally assaulted her."

Casey whorled around. With hands on his hips, he yelled, "I don't know what you're talking about!"

Denten gripped the chair back. "Like hell you don't! The last time you saw her was on a Sunday afternoon. You assaulted her in her apartment."

Casey stood rigid, staring at Denten. "I don't think it's any of your fucking business what I did then or what I did anytime!"

"It's my fucking business because after what you did, she attempted to kill herself!" Denten fought to control his temper.

Casey's mouth dropped open. He stood in shock, unmoving.

"Do you feel a little guilty for what you did?"

Casey stood speechless.

"Her roommate found her before the overdose killed her. She spent all summer trying to get control of her life."

Casey turned again to look out over the ocean. In a quiet voice, he asked, "What do you want from me?" Shaking his head, "I had no idea."

"And you never bothered to find out either, did you?"

"I…I." Casey's voice trailed off.

"Right now I only wanted to meet the guy who almost destroyed Cayla. What happens next I don't know." Denten pushed the small chair out of his way, stepped back into the room and out the door. He stopped in the hallway, leaned against the wall. A shiver rushed through his body. He reached into his pocket for a tissue. He wiped perspiration from his forehead and around his neck. His breath came in short pants. For several minutes he leaned against the wall struggling to gain control of his emotions.

Back in his room, Denten grabbed a can of beer from the small snack bar and stretched out on the sofa chair. He closed his eyes, thinking about the scene with Casey. Had he done the right thing? What would Casey do knowing he faced potential prosecution? Denten took a long swallow of beer then reached for his cell phone on the night stand. Not thinking about the time difference between

Hawaii and Chicago, he dialed Cayla's number. He reached only her voice mail. At the tone, he said, "Sweetheart, I miss you, and I love you."

The next day Mr. Casey Holt checked out of the Hyatt Regency Hotel.

Chapter 29

Reed Howard slumped in his office chair. Bank business always increased in late summer and early fall. Farmers needed money for harvest. Office hours for Reed had demanded too much of his time. However, the work in the office diverted his attention from a swelling concern for his exposure as a pedophile. Naturally, he did not think of himself in those terms. He merely relented when faced with powerful urges which had dominated his life from the time he first discovered the wonder of a young girl's body. So far he had avoided prosecution. In the past he never seriously considered his capture. His reputation in the community, his position of leadership in more than one organization had helped conceal the truth about his private, sexual appetite. That Denten Ballery or Cayla Finch would, after all these years, come forward to accuse him of sexual assault seemed to Reed unlikely. Pamela Collins, the neighbor who had satisfied his sexual needs, had moved away with her family. Just where they moved, Reed did not know. He did feel secure that he faced no repercussions from the brief thrill she had given him.

A week had passed since the meeting at the high school featuring Representative Linsted, who headed a campaign to increase the penalty for sexual abuse in general and abuse of juveniles in particular. Reed's part in that meeting further shielded his proclivity for young, tender bodies. Disturbing, however, was the presence at the meeting of both Denten's and Cayla's parents. Their presence likely confirmed that Denten and Cayla had discussed with their parents that Saturday in the park. This realization bothered Reed. All week he had contemplated what he would or even should do.

In the past, intimidation had shielded him from exposure. Reed twirled around in his chair to look out the large window that formed much of one wall in his office. His mind drifted to the time months ago when he placed in Denten's mailbox the note stating, "I Know Who You Are." He remembered with a smile the time in Mankato that he encountered Denten in the apartment parking lot. His efforts against Cayla had succeeded in quieting her. At least they had played a part in quieting her. Her parents, as well as Denten's however, might prove more formidable in their willingness to pursue him.

Reed turned back to his computer where on the screen he looked at the records of Alice and Harvey Finch. Staring at the provisions of a home equity loan secured over a year ago, he considered how they would respond to the kind of intimidation he used successfully with Cayla. Reed gazed at the computer screen. The Finches had secured a home equity loan for over $25,000 for purposes unspecified. Probably for Cayla's college expenses. Their loan required a $850.00 a month payment. As he scanned the payment record, he imagined the consequences of casually deleting payments made over the last six months. He looked away from the computer to stare off into the emptiness of the far corner of the office. Of course, any manipulation of the records would come at great risk. Bank examiners missed little unscrupulous, fraudulent activity. Still it would be the bank's word against the Finch's.

Next he brought up the records of Oscar and Grace Ballery. Bank customers for decades, the Ballerys sought frequent loans much like most of the area farmers. The recent Ballery loan amounted to $10,000, secured in the preceding spring, likely for seed. Provisions of the loan allowed Oscar to pay it off within one year. The arrangement required no monthly payments unless he wished to make them. Staring at the computer screen, Reed again considered making the lack of a monthly payment justification for legal action against the Ballerys.

Reed suddenly sat back in his chair. Perspiration glistened on his forehead and above his upper lip. He banged his hands against the chair's arms. What in the hell was he thinking? Manipulating bank records? Never in all his years as president of the bank had he entertained such stupidity. He breathed deeply. He reminded himself of just who he was. He didn't need to succumb to fear of reprisal. He didn't have to jeopardize his bank. He just had to use his head. He smiled as he shut done the computer. He stood up and walked to the large window over looking Riverside's main street. Positioning his hands on the window sill, he leaned forward. If he needed a defense against the potential attacks of the Finches and the Ballerys, he had one, his own story of what happened that fateful Saturday morning. Why hadn't he thought of that before? It would be his word against that of Denten and Cayla.

Reed stared unseeing out the window. In his mind his own version of what happened on that Saturday morning slowly emerged. Vividly, the image of the park evolved in his mind. He saw his car as he drove into the park, empty on this Saturday morning. Already, he had an answer for his presence there on a Saturday morning. He searched out a location for a family picnic. His mind generated more clear images. A bicycle leaned against one of the picnic tables. Clothes hung over one of the benches near the table. Most important to this fictional creation was what he saw beyond the bench. In the morning grass, two young kids, one boy and one girl, lay entwined, completely naked, fondling each other. In his mental image, Reed slowed his car but never stopped. The two kids apparently never saw him. Their busy hands never paused.

Reed turned from the window. He stood for a moment contemplating the scene he had just created. Much different, he admitted, from the truth, it would definitely serve him well if he ever faced prosecution. Why hadn't he thought of that before instead of stumbling around with crude attempts at intimidation? He breathed deeply again, sat in his chair and reached for his private collection of precious CD's. Grabbing the phone, he called to remind his secretary that he did not wish to be disturbed for the next half hour. Inserting the CD into his computer, he waited while the image of a young girl dressed only in panties emerged on the screen. Reed leaned back in his chair, a smile spreading across his face.

Since the meeting at the high school, the Finches and the Ballerys had gotten together to discuss the absurdity of Reed Howard standing at the podium voicing the need for harsher penalties for sexual predators.

Sitting around the Ballery kitchen table, the four of them just finished dinner.

"Wonderful meal, Grace." Harvey Finch pushed his chair back from the table.

"Thank you."

"You out did yourself, dear." Oscar patted his wife's hand.

Grace smiled as she moved away from the table to begin cleaning up the dishes.

"Why don't you let us do that?" Harvey volunteered.

"Yes. I think we can handle it." Oscar joined in. "You and Alice relax in the living room. It won't take us long."

"Harvey," Alice cautioned. "Don't you break anything." She smiled then briefly explained the recent bad luck her husband had dropping dishes onto the kitchen floor.

"Yes, dear. I'll be careful." As he answered, he feigned dropping three plates he carried to the sink. "Oops. Almost." He laughed when Alice stopped in momentary shock, waiting for the plates to crash in pieces on the floor.

In minutes the two men had cleaned the table, rinsed the dishes and stacked the dish washer. They paraded proudly into the living room. Making a bold entry, they paused to stand in front of the ladies.

"We did it without a scratch." Harvey proudly announced.

"Oh, come on and sit down you show off." Alice patted the place next to her on the sofa.

Casual conversation about weather and about harvest eventually turned again to Denten and Cayla, who found school therapeutic. The Finches expressed relief in hearing from her almost daily with reports that all went well.

"I just can't believe yet that this Howard guy would lead the local campaign for stricter penalties." Harvey shook his head as he, with some reluctance, waded into the subject of exposing Howard for what he was. "I know we have talked about this a lot. But, I…I can't get it out of my mind."

"I can't either." Oscar agreed.

Silence settled over the four of them as they faced reluctance to discuss this issue again.

"Have you heard anything from Denten?" Alice asked.

"We talked to him about the meeting. He about choked when we told him about Howard's role." Grace crossed her legs and leaned back in a large stuffed chair.

"Did he say anything about going after Reed Howard?" Harvey asked.

"No, not directly." Oscar took over from his wife. "He did say that he and Cayla had talked a lot about when. No decisions, though."

Alice moved closer to the edge of the sofa. "Cayla has said about the same. I think time is coming for an answer to when."

"That's good news." Grace offered. She too sat up straighter. She looked first at Alice and then at Harvey. "Let me ask you something." She paused. "What do you think about exposing this guy for the creep that he is?"

"If I had my way," Alice quickly responded. "I would have turned him in a long time ago."

"What about you, Harvey?" Grace asked.

Harvey nodded his head. "I agree with my wife." He paused. Then said facetiously, "For a change."

"I can't believe the kids have kept this secret for so many years. It's tough enough being a kid without that shit hanging over your head. Excuse the language." Oscar apologized.

Silence drifted over the living room. Recently, they had addressed this topic so many times. They felt shackled by the commitment they made to both Denten and Cayla that permitted only them to make the decision about the right time to indict Reed Howard.

Alice resumed the discussion. "Cayla has talked a little about legal stuff. She apparently has asked some questions of her professors. I have nothing specific. I just think that soon something will happen."

Almost in unison, Grace, Oscar and Harvey all voiced, "God, I hope so!"

"Sweetheart, something bothering you?" Vivian Howard sat across from her husband while she paged through the local paper. Reed sat on a sofa chair looking at the TV but probably not actually watching it.

He jerked his head to look at his wife of almost thirty years. "Ah, what'd you say?"

She shook her head then repeated. "Something bothering you?"

Reed glanced at this wife. "Sorry. Of…of course not. Just a bit tired."

"Maybe you need a vacation." Vivian folded the paper and placed it on her lap. "When was the last time?"

Reed sat, obviously distracted. "What?"

"When was our last vacation?"

"I don't remember. Maybe a couple years ago."

Vivian stood up, placed the paper on the small table next to her chair, and walked across the room to stand by her husband. A one time petite figure had rounded over the years yielding a plumpness to her five foot three inch frame. She was a dedicated wife who for years stood in the shadow of her husband, whose outgoing, dominate personality contrasted with her unassuming acquiescence. The combination had served them well over the years.

She placed her hand on her husband's shoulder, squeezed gently. "Let's do something, go somewhere."

Reed looked up at his wife and smiled. "You're probably right. Let's think about it."

At this time Reed had other things to think about. Over the last few days, his moment of revelation in creating his own version of the park scene had diluted his recent feeling of increasing vulnerability. Nonetheless, that both Denten's and Cayla's parents now, very likely, knew of his encounter with Cayla bothered him. Seeing the Ballerys and the Finches at the recent child abuse meeting confirmed what he suspected.

Over the years his position in the community, his family, long time members of the community, and his position as president of the local bank, he believed, always shielded him from any suspicion. He resented having to confront possible exposure. Thinking of the Ballerys and Finches huddled outside the high school auditorium following the meeting deepened his resentment. He resented the people who conspired to deprive him of what he found most gratifying, fondling the delicate bodies of innocent, young girls. Reed considered it his destiny to enjoy the pleasures of fondling tender, young bodies. A shiver traced through his body as he thought about that pleasure. Now these people threatened to deprive him of this pleasure. At the same time they would destroy all he had worked for and accomplished for his family and for the community. Until a few days ago, he had struggled with what he considered an assault on his freedom. Now he had the means of combating the assault.

Reed patted his wife's hand. "I have couple banking things to do." He stood up and walked toward his sanctuary, his den.

"Don't spend too much time there tonight. You need your rest." His wife cautioned.

Reed walked down the short hall. He turned his head, "I won't."

In his private world he sat down at his desk. He awakened his computer. He began typing. *"It has come to my attention that maybe your daughter has fashioned a twisted story about an event years ago in the Riverside Park. With this letter I wish to clarify what happened that Saturday morning. Yes, I drove to the park that morning to search out a place for a planned family picnic. When I arrived at the park, I came upon a scene which included two young people, a boy and a girl, lying in the grass, naked, engaged in what looked like mutual fondling. It was none of my business. I drove on. However, I now believe that your daughter was one of the young people I saw that morning. Whatever else she has told you about that morning is a lie. Any action based on that lie could have dire consequences for you and for you daughter. I tell you this since recent events suggest to me that your daughter has told you lies about what actually happened."*

Reed reread what he had just written, leaned back, and rubbed his eyes. He stared off into vacancy of the ceiling. A feeling of satisfaction, of contentment swept over him. He sat up straight in his chair. Read his letter again. He printed two copies, the second one revised to apply to Denten. He signed both. He then unlocked his file cabinet, reached in and withdrew a CD. Settling comfortably in his chair, he inserted the CD and waited anxiously for the delicious images it contained.

The next day he mailed the two letters, one to Alice and Harvey Finch and one to Oscar and Grace Ballery.

Chapter 30

Alice Finch completed her house cleaning. She poured another cup of coffee and sat down for a brief rest at the kitchen table. Her rest was interrupted by the mail man stuffing mail into the box attached to the house. Not expecting any significant mail, Alice did not race to the mail box. Instead she perused the morning paper while she savored her third cup of coffee. She noted with interest an article about Reed Howard and his leadership in the campaign to strengthen the penalties for sexual abuse. Just reading his name sent a wave of nausea through her body. How anyone could so completely deceive a community astonished Alice. She shook her head in disbelief. She looked up from the article and once again quietly committed herself to see justice done for her daughter, for Denten, and for Reed Howard.

She folded the paper, got up to place her coffee cup in the sink. She remembered the mail had arrived. She opened the front door, reached into the mail box, and grasped a hand full of mail. As usual, most of the mail included advertising flyers and more requests for contributions to one charity or another. Almost lost in the collection of useless mail was a plain white envelope with no return address. Addressed to Alice and Harvey Finch, typed in large bold print. Alice looked at the simple envelope, turning it over in an attempt to determine just where it came from. The post mark revealed it had been mailed right there in Riverside. Strange, Alice thought.

Sifting through the mail, she quickly discarded most of it. Bills for electricity and for a credit card she carefully separated from the rest of the mail. She looked at the plain white envelope. She would never know its purpose until she opened it. Back in the kitchen she placed the "junk" mail in the recycling bin just outside the door leading to the garage. She ran her finger under the flap of the envelope to discover a single, half sheet of paper with no identifying information. A short message printed in large bold type covered most of the half sheet. Alice ran her eyes over the sheet until she saw the name Reed Howard at the bottom.

"My God!" She exclaimed.

She sat down at the kitchen table, grasping the half sheet in her hand. She took a deep breath and read.

"It has come to my attention that maybe your daughter has fashioned a twisted story about an event years ago in Riverside Park." Slowly, she read the description written in the letter. Two sentences near the end caught her attention. **"Whatever else she has told you about that morning is a lie. Any action based on that lie could have dire consequences for you and for your daughter."**

Alice laid the letter on the table. She slumped in her chair. What she had just read made absolutely no sense. Would Cayla have fabricated this story about Reed Howard? Images of Cayla struggling to survive the overdose rushed through her mind. Confusion clouded her thinking. Could Cayla have deceived her parents? Alice shook her head. "No! No!" She repeated out loud. Her daughter would never do such a thing. But then…she picked up the letter again to reread the short message.

For a few minutes she sat in the kitchen, stunned by the letter, fighting to control an emerging outrage over its implications. Harvey was at his office at the farm machinery warehouse. Should she call him or wait until he came home later? In her mind she debated what she should do. She had to speak to someone or she would explode in anger and frustration. She stood up and stepped to the phone mounted on the kitchen wall. She called Harvey.

"What! You're kidding!" was Harvey's immediate response once he calmed Alice sufficiently to understand what had disturbed her.

Alice read the letter to her husband. That produced a terse response. "Bull shit!" He exclaimed.

"What should we do?" Alice asked her husband.

"Look, honey, don't do anything. When I get home, we'll talk about it. Outrageous! That's what it is."

"I can't deal with this anymore." Alice pleaded with her husband.

"I know, honey. Just try to relax. I'll come home as soon as I finish with this customer. At most an hour."

"All right, I'll see you then." Alice slowly hung up the phone, turned to drop the letter on the table. She retrieved her coffee cup, refilled it, and walked into the living room where she slumped into a sofa chair.

In just over an hour Harvey parked in the garage. When he entered the house, he faced a distraught wife whom he eagerly embraced. "You okay?"

Tears flooded Alice's eyes. "I'm so sick of this stuff. The lies, the pretense." She buried her head in Harvey's chest.

"Let's go in the living room. Where is the letter?" Harvey asked.

"It's right there on the table."

Harvey picked it up. He read it quickly. "The sonofabitch is getting desperate. He can feel the noose tightening."

Harvey poured himself a cup of coffee and followed his wife into the living room. They sat opposite each other, she on the sofa, he in the large sofa chair.

"No, I think, he does sense some increasing vulnerability." Harvey sipped his coffee.

"Maybe, but why? What has happened to do that?" Alice asked.

"I don't know for sure, but he must know that we know. He hints at something at the end of the letter when he talks about 'recent events'."

"What could they be?" Alice set her coffee cup down on the coffee table.

"About the only thing I can think of is that meeting we attended with the Ballerys on sexual abuse."

"So what? We have an interest in that." Alice spoke firmly.

"Yes, we do. But I guess it might suggested to Reed that our interest is based on real experience."

They both sat quietly for a few moments. Harvey sat forward in his chair, placing his coffee cup on the coffee table. "You know," He paused, the veins in his neck enlarged and throbbing. " His story makes no sense."

"I agree." Alice offered. "Wouldn't someone not as close to it as we are maybe believe it?"

"I suppose." Harvey ran his hands through his hair. Would both Cayla and Denten face nightmares and a fear of a man's touch if what they did was only a bit of petting? My God, experiences like that could only lead to sweet dreams, as far as I'm concerned."

That comment elicited a chuckle from Alice.

"Would Denten wake up night after night for years dripping with sweat just because he had fondled our daughter when he was ten years old? Would Cayla try to avoid boys all those years simply because she let Denten touch her?

"I suppose you're right." Alice concurred.

Harvey sat back in the sofa chair. His memory working. "Do you remember Denten telling us about the letter he received a few years ago, a letter saying something like 'I know who you are'"? Wasn't Cayla threatened by Howard on the road someplace?"

"Ya, I think I remember that."

"If he had nothing to hide, why would he have done these crazy things just to intimidate?"

Alice considered what her husband had just shared with her. "That makes sense to me."

At that moment the phone rang. Harvey reached over to take the call on the phone positioned on an end table. Caller ID disclosed the caller.

"Good afternoon, Oscar."

"Good afternoon to you, too, Harvey."

"Have you read your mail yet today?" Oscar asked.

"Have we."

"Then you know why I've called." Oscar admitted.

"Yes, I certainly know."

"What do you think?" Oscar asked.

"I think it's all bull shit!" Harvey exclaimed.

"I agree. The nerve of this hypocrite. Mr. community savior." Oscar's voice dripped with anger and resentment. "What do you think we should do?"

"Well, eventually, see this bastard in court. Still we need to discuss this with the kids."

"You're right. We need to do that." Oscar agreed.

"Besides, we don't want to rush into anything without firm legal guidance. I think Cayla has done some thinking about that already."

"Should we call them to explain this latest development?" Oscar asked.

"I don't think so. I would rather discuss it face to face rather than on the phone or even email." Harveyexpressed his thoughts firmly.

"Ya, you're probably right." Oscar paused before asking, "Should we ask them to come home now?"

"I don't think so. Thanksgiving break is only a few weeks away. I think it can wait until then."

"Maybe by then the kids will decide about legal action against our great community leader." Oscar affirmed.

"I hope so."

"I won't take any more of your time. Just quickly, how is Alice?"

"After she recovered from the initial shock, she's fine. Just fed up."

"Sounds like home." Oscar bid his good bye and hung up.

Though Alice had listened to the entire conversation, she inquired about Oscar's reaction to Harvey's suggestions. Of course, she had heard only one side of the conversation. Harvey sat down next to his wife on the sofa. He placed his arm around her shoulder and kissed her gently on the cheek.

"Sweetheart, we'll get this worked out. Oscar agrees that we wait until we can talk to the kids face to face. I know we have used patience over the years. We just need to use a bit more."

Chapter 31

Denten jumped out of the cab. He stretched then reached in the window to place a twenty dollar bill in the outstretched hand. The money evoked a quiet, "Thank you." With his brief case resting on his shoulder, his light coat over his arm, he stood before the two story building housing Cayla's apartment.

He almost skipped up the front steps and through the front door which opened into a small entrance with two mail boxes and two other doors. His gentle tap on one brought a quick response. In seconds, he stood facing a radiant Cayla. He dropped his briefcase and coat. Unlike the past, even during the early days of her relationship with Denten, she displayed no reluctance to submit to his arms. For several tender moments they stood in the doorway, saying nothing, just enjoying each other's touch. The embrace ended with a long, welcome kiss.

They stepped into her apartment and closed the door. Denten stood looking at Cayla. "You look great."

She smiled. "Thank you. You don't look too bad yourself."

"Well, sitting at meetings all day hasn't done too much damage." Denten stepped to the sofa where he set down his briefcase and coat.

Cayla joined him on the sofa. She leaned into his shoulder as he grasped hers. Silence captured them. Cayla then looked up at Denten. "How was your day?"

"Long." He rested his head on the sofa back. "Inspection trips always drag on. So many questions and too many vague answers."

"Can't the people involved make any decisions?" Cayla had heard this story before. Denten frequently faced indecision and ambiguity from clients. Part of the job, he admitted.

"Eventually, yes. It just takes time. Today involved picking out locations for various functions at one of these sprawling, Michigan Avenue hotels. Never easy." He kissed the top of her head. "It's over now. I'm here, away from all that stuff. How was your day?"

Cayla sat up straighter. She paused before responding, as if she needed to select words carefully. "Denten, my day was wonderful. I got up happy. I went to class happy. You make me happy. Can't do much better than that."

Denten smiled as he squeezed her shoulder. "God, you don't know how great it is to hear you say that."

"Nobody knows that more than I do."

They snuggled briefly.

"I talked with my advisor this afternoon."

"About your program?" Denten voice revealed his interest in her comment.

"Yes, partly. He said all was in order for a spring graduation." Cayla's voice cracked as she tried to control the emotion she felt.

Denten turned in the sofa to face her. He placed his hands on her shoulders. Looking directly into her beautiful eyes, he expressed his delight. "That's fabulous, sweetheart. God, I'm so proud of you."

"You're part of it, Denten. I don't know how things would have turned out without you."

"I only did what anyone would do for someone as beautiful as you."

Cayla smiled along with Denten.

Another pause as they sat looking into each other's eyes. At last Cayla spoke again.

"I can't believe all that has happened these last few years. So much of it to either you or to me." Her voice took on a nostalgic tone. "Can you believe how fast time has gone since that day we sat in the Riverside Bar sharing a beer? So much has changed since then."

Denten shook his head in agreement. He had not told Cayla of his meeting with Casey Holt in Hawaii. He questioned the wisdom of even bringing up the subject of Casey Holt. Still, he didn't believe in hiding the truth.

"You know, Cayla, I've not said anything before, but a few weeks ago I ran into that Casey Holt during a program in Maui."

Cayla, displaying little alarm, moved to the edge of the sofa. "What was he doing there?"

"He was part of an incentive program sponsored by the real estate company he works for. I knew he worked in real estate so kind of watched for his name to come up on the many documents we deal with on these trips."

"You met with him?" Cayla asked.

"Yes, in his room. Our desk people informed me when he checked in. I contacted him a couple days after his arrival."

"That must have been an interesting meeting." Cayla grinned as she studied Denten's face.

"A bit hostile at first. Learning what happened to you shocked him. The next day he checked out of the hotel."

Cayla stood up from the sofa. She turned to face Denten who remained seated. "Now it makes a little more sense."

Denten's forehead furrowed, perplexed by her casual response. "What makes sense?" He asked.

Cayla walked to the small desk across the room. She reached into the center drawer and withdrew an envelope. She again turned toward Denten. "Four-five weeks ago, maybe longer, I don't know exactly, I received this letter of apology from Casey. I was curious as to what motivated him to send it after so long. Now I think I know."

Denten stood up and moved toward Cayla. Again they embraced. "I guess we're even. You didn't tell me about the letter either."

"I guess so." She responded with a chuckle, which revealed so much about her present emotional status and her attitude.

Cayla fell into Denten's arms as they celebrated together her impressive progress in gaining control of her life. Their bodies pressed hard together. Hands, both his and hers, ranged over fabric, searching for something more intimate and warm. During all the months of their evolving relationship, they had deliberately avoided that ultimate intimacy. Respectful of Cayla's anxiety over a man's touch, Denten had approached their loving-making cautiously, never insisting but also never completely ignoring that part of their relationship. It had produced a fine line for Denten to follow.

As they stood in the center of the living room floor, engaging in mutual groping, all that went before dimmed in the mind of each. All that mattered was the moment, a time filled with happiness, with honesty, with love. Cayla offered little resistance to Denten's searching hands as he unbuttoned her blouse and reached for her tender breast. With the rhythm of breathing increasing for both of them, Denten eased Cayla back to the sofa. For an instant that time months ago flashed through Cayla's mind. The power of her recovery, of her love for Denten suppressed those thoughts. She believed that her time had arrived to overcome the fears that festered in her memory.

She submitted to Denten's careful, tender touch and to the removing of her slacks. She helped him unbuckle his belt, waiting with growing anticipation for what only months ago would have plunged her into an emotional panic. Denten carefully positioned her on the sofa. He leaned down kissing her passionately on the lips. Her arms tightened around his neck. She now could wait no longer. She grasped his butt and pulled hard. Denten's entry sent sensations of pleasure throughout her body. Never did she imagine the ultimate pleasure that she experienced despite the minor initial discomfort of a first time.

Physically and emotionally spent, they lay in each other's arms, savoring the glory of their first time. Their breathing gradually slowed. Their bodies relaxed. They kissed.

"I love you." Cayla whispered.

"I love you too." Denten carefully moved himself off her and stood up. "Sweetheart, that was wonderful."

Cayla closed her eyes, smiled broadly, her dimples saying more than words.

Later that evening, they shared a light dinner after which they prepared for their short trip back to Minnesota the next morning. Since Denten was in Chicago already and Cayla intended to spend

Thanksgiving with her parents in Riverside, they decided to combine their flights. Luckily, Cayla secured a seat on Denten's flight, though they did not have seats together.

With dinner completed and bags basically packed, they sat down to watch the late news. The evening had included no references to Reed Howard, an issue that some day they would have to confront. Cayla reached for Denten's hand as they sat together on the sofa.

"Honey, I mentioned earlier I talked with my advisor. We did talk about graduation." She paused, locking her eyes on Denten. "We also talked about that subject that still haunts us."

"I know. You're right. It does haunt us. What did he say?" Denten asked.

"He said we should not wait too much longer. He didn't think the statute of limitations was a problem. He'd have to check for me since states differ. For our own piece of mind, he urged us to pursue the case. What do you think?"

"Lately, I have thought about it more than I would like. You're right. We've got to get on with it. I know our parents would agree with that." Denten affirmed.

"That's for sure." Cayla agreed.

"When we're both home now, we need to maybe make some decisions." He suggested. "By the way, did your advisor say anything about a legal firm we should contact?"

"Yes, he did. Remember that young attorney who helped your friends from Italian out of that airport mess? His name is Cole Ridgewood. My advisor didn't necessarily suggest him, but he did suggest the firm that he works for. They have a branch in Minneapolis."

"Good work. When do you think we should contact them?"

Cayla stood up to emphasize her decision. "As soon as possible." She walked to the sink. "Do you want a drink?"

"Please."

Grabbing ice from the frig, Cayla filled two glasses and walked toward Denten still sitting on the sofa. "By the way, what ever happened to the girl and her mother from Italy?"

Obviously, that was not a subject demanding much attention from either one of them. Denten reached out to accept his glass of water. "Thank you."

Denten had said little about them except to tell Cayla of the fate of the two scoundrels who had attempted to use Anna and her mother as couriers for their drugs. He now felt little reluctance explaining to Cayla the email exchange he had with Anna some months before. That exchange ended the romantic part of their relationship.

He looked directly at Cayla. "We're still friends, I guess. I have not heard from her in months. I think she graduates about the time you do."

"Thank you for telling me. We should probably get to bed. We have a big day tomorrow and maybe the next. Not just because it's Thanksgiving either."

"You know, sweetheart, we just agree on everything." He stood up and held out his hand in an offer to assist her in getting up. They embraced. "Now that you're off my bed, I can get some sleep."

Flying Southwest Airlines brought them into the Humphrey Terminal where Denten's parents waited to pick them up. The one hour flight hardly gave them time to get settled in the plane before the captain announced the beginning of their descent into the Minneapolis/St. Paul airport.

The Ballerys greeted them just outside the baggage claim area. While Denten and his dad walked across the street to the huge parking ramp to retrieve the car, Grace and Cayla waited just inside the terminal. The temperature on this November day, despite the bright sunny, reminded people that they were in Minnesota.

During the ride back to Riverside, the conversation ranged over a variety of subjects.

References to the harvest, Cayla's classes, Denten's meetings, Cayla's parents all made the short drive pass much faster. By choice neither Oscar nor Grace mentioned anything about the letters they and the Finches had received from Reed Howard. That revelation would have to wait until they all assembled the next day, Thanksgiving Day.

The aroma of roasted turkey and all the trimmings drifted through the Finch household. The Finches and the Ballerys had essentially drawn straws to determine who would host the Thanksgiving dinner. Certainly, without question they would discuss Reed Howard. They just needed to decide where they would do it. The Finches, according to Harvey, won. Since Cayla's battle with depression during the summer, the absurdity of Reed Howard leading the campaign for harsher penalties for sexual predators, and the shocking letter of a few weeks ago, the Finches and the Ballerys had spent an abundance of time together, much of it devoted to Reed Howard and just when he would have to answer to charges they expected some day they would level against him.

Though both families wished to respect the tradition of Thanksgiving, they still determined that the issue of Reed Howard had gone on long enough. Consequently, they intended to reserve a part of Thanksgiving Day to a discussion of what the families should do and when they should do it.

By 4:00 all had eaten much more than necessary, savoring the turkey, the stuffing, the gravy, the creamed peas, the mashed potatoes and the apple pie. With dishes rinsed and stacked in the dish washer, everyone gathered in the Finch living room, waists exerting greater pressure on waist lines. Denten joined his parents on the sofa. Cayla sat on the window bench between her parents, who occupied large stuffed sofa chairs.

"Mom, the dinner was wonderful." Cayla reached over to pat her mother's hand.

A chorus of similar comments followed.

"I don't think I'm gonna eat for a few days." Oscar Ballery voiced the opinion of most of them.

"You have to have more pie and ice cream later." Alice kidded.

"I think I'll take a rain check on that." Oscar laughed.

Conversation centered on Cayla's progress and on Denten's busy schedule even at this time of year. Denten inquired about events in Riverside since he only occasionally had time to spend at home. Gradually, the conversation turned to Reed Howard. Harvey explained the meeting they had attended when Reed served as local coordinator of the push for stricter penalties for sex offenders. For Denten and Cayla, again hearing of the meeting evoked disbelief.

"The guy is crazy!" Denten declared. "Does he really think he can continue to fool people?"

"I don't know what he thinks. I do know that he must feel he has some protective shell around him." Harvey shared.

The conversation lagged momentarily as all of them reflected on the arrogance and insolence of the town's most notable citizen. At last Harvey moved up to sit on the edge of his chair. He took a deep breath then described the recent letters accusing Denten and Cayla of fabricating the sexual assault claims against Reed. He got up from the chair and stepped to the desk stationed at the end of the living room. From the center drawer he extracted the letter.

He turned to face the group. "A few weeks ago we received this letter and so did your parents, Denten. We have not said anything about the letter. We wanted to share it with you in person." He read the letter.

Denten and Cayla stared at each other in total disbelief. For a few seconds they said nothing. Then Denten laughed, the absurdity of the claim so shocking he found it almost humorous. Cayla simply shook her head.

Denten stood up and reached for the letter. May I read it?"

Harvey handed it to him. "Of course."

Having completed the reading of the short letter, Denten shook his head and asked, "What do you think of the accusation?" After all, he assumed, something like that could have happened, not to them but still a possibility.

"Of course, it's nonsense." Harvey affirmed.

"Dad?" Denten asked.

"Not for a minute did we believe a word of it."

Harvey again sat down in his chair. "Look, Denten and Cayla." He made eye contact with each one. "This letter is obviously a product of a desperate man. Just consider for a moment his take on what happened. Would both of you suffer trauma all those years if all you did is play with each other's bodies? Cayla, would you have had this fear of men if that's all you did in the park? Denten, would you wake up at night in a cold sweat over fondling a cute young girl? It seems that would give you some good dreams." Harvey smiled.

"It's a bold lie, but now it becomes his word against ours." Denten suggested.

"Son, it was that way anyway. It's just a different lie now." Oscar reminded his son.

For the first time Cayla spoke. "I don't care what the letter says. I know what happened that morning. It was not pretty." She looked down at her hands folded in her lap. Her voice cracked as she swallowed. She forced back the tears that threatened to weaken her resolve. "I know what happened!" She repeated. "I've stood in the way of exposing this creep. I'm done with waiting."

The attention of all concentrated on Cayla. She sat straight and confident. "I have discussed the case more than once with professors at Northwestern. Just the other day the last time. They have recommended a legal firm in Minneapolis, the same one that helped the people from Italy a couple years ago. Denten and I have discussed this and decided that we should wait no longer. This was before this stupid letter. The letter only confirms the decision we have made. Monday I will contact the recommended legal firm. They will take it from there." Cayla stopped and looked at the people sitting around her, the most important people in her life. Now, mom, can I have that piece of pie and ice cream?"

Silence settled over the group as it absorbed the definitive commitment just offered by Cayla. Then they applauded, each getting up, walking over to her, and giving her a reassuring hug.

She stood up, turned to the window, and pretended to shout to the city, "Mr. Howard, we will see you in court. Have a happy Thanksgiving."

Chapter 32

In the classic elegance of the Drake Hotel's Cape Cod Room, Denten and Cayla looked at each other from opposite sides of a small table positioned in a quiet, discrete corner of the restaurant. Situated at one end of Chicago's famous Miracle Mile, the Drake Hotel enjoyed for decades the reputation as one of Chicago's most celebrated hotels. It was in this special environment that Denten and Cayla chose to celebrate the first anniversary of the guilty verdict handed down in the case of Finch, et al, vs Howard.

Dressed in what Denten termed delicate conservatism, Cayla studied the elegance of the classic restaurant. Her black evening dress emphasized her charm, her natural beauty, and her sparkling eyes. Her fascinating dimples enhanced her captivating smile.

"This place is gorgeous." Cayla announced.

"Something you have in common with it." Denten responded with a smile. He reached across the table to squeeze her hand. "I don't think I've ever been so happy as I am right now." He looked deeply into Cayla's eyes reflecting specks of light from the lamp that hung above them.

She said nothing for several seconds. She only met Denten's eyes across the table. She took a deep breath, holding back a surge of emotion. "Denten, we've in so many ways been blessed. At times I wondered about that. We had a few bad moments. But look at us. Look at this place. Look at our lives." She shook her head and reached for Denten's hand with both of hers.

"A little persistence can make a difference." He added.

"A lot of love can make a bigger difference." Cayla spoke with a confidence grown out of her education and her experience working with poor, disadvantaged victims of society's far too often indifference.

Since graduation from Northwestern University with her law degree, Cayla had worked with Chicago's human services department where she faced, on a daily basis, the victims of grinding poverty and neglect. Ironically, she specialized in sexual abuse cases and in just over a year of employment she had already played an important role in the prosecution of three pedophiles. The many years since her own devastating encounter with Reed Howard, her struggle for years with fear and lack of self-confidence, and her desperate attempt to end it all with an overdose had combined to challenge her to take control of her life. With help of her family, of Denten, and so many others, she had emerged a strong, confident, loving person who had control of her life and who now dedicated herself to helping others.

Denten rejoiced in her success as well as in his own. He recently had received word from Ted Bennett, president of Travel Incorporated, that he would advance to the position of account executive. His work along with that of other company staff had created new clients which made possible the promotion. Though Denten's office remained in Mankato, his travels took him across the country, frequently to Chicago where Cayla retained the same apartment she lived in during her time at Northwestern University. Many times they discussed her moving to some other apartment considering the history of the one she lived in. However, she decided that reality was reality. She would cope with it, not fall victim to it.

On this night Denten and Cayla looked ahead, not back, as they contemplated their future. Sipping a glass of wine, they talked of the two weeks since they last were together. They talked of their work. They talked of the distance that at times separated them. They talked of the excitement of meeting following extended periods of absence. They did not talk about Reed Howard.

Nonetheless, tonight they celebrated the first anniversary of his guilty verdict. One year ago today, the jury, following sixteen hours of deliberation, brought forth a verdict of guilty on two counts of criminal sexual abuse. The second verdict related to a Pamela Collins, the former neighbor who with her family had moved away. They joined in the suit against Reed Howard shortly after the Finches filed theirs.

When Finches filed their suit, Howard was out of town on vacation. Only with reluctance did he return. Throughout the investigation and trial he consistently claimed his innocence. He did so with belligerence and defiance, clinging vehemently to his story about two kids fondling in the park.

News of the accusations against Howard disrupted life in the small community of Riverside. With alarm, residents of the community listened to and read about the charges against one of the community leaders. Considering the intensity and diversity of opinion in the community, Howard's legal team successfully filed for a change of venue. The trial took place in Minneapolis at the Hennepin County Court House. At the trial that dragged on for two months, both Denten and Cayla testified for hours, consistent in their stories and reliving, at times, the slicing emotional trauma they both endured for years. In the end, their courage, their determination, and their patience had secured justice. Reed Howard would spend the rest of his life in prison.

Denten and Cayla delayed ordering their dinner. Instead they ordered another glass of wine.

"Here's to us, sweetheart." Denten offered up his glass as Cayla did the same, the glasses touching in the middle of the table.

They sipped their wine. They set the glasses back on the table. The emotion of the moment precluded words. Denten stared down at his glass, grasping the stem and turning the glass nervously. Cayla watched him. She smiled.

"You nervous or something?" She asked playfully.

"No." Denten answered much too quickly. "Just thinking."

"About what?" Cayla took another small sip of wine.

Denten reached into the inner breast pocket of his suit coat. He withdrew a small ring case, opened it, and presented it to Cayla. "About this."

Cayla reached for the small ring case. Her eyes opened wide. That enchanting smile spread across her face. Flecks of light danced in her eyes. With a remarkable grace considering the emotion of the moment, she asked, "Does this mean you want to marry me?"

Denten stood up from his chair. He moved around to kneel before Cayla. He covered her hands in his. "My sweetheart, will you marry me?" His voiced trailed off as he gazed into her eyes.

She gazed back into his. "Of course, I will. I've been waiting for you to ask." Cayla stood up to face Denten. They embraced, a tender kiss produced discrete applause from dining customers at nearby tables.